To Live Again

To Live Again

by

Robert Silverberg

PULPLESS.COM, INC.
775 East Blithedale Ave., Suite 508
Mill Valley, CA 94941, USA.
Voice & Fax: (500) 367-7353
Home Page: http://www.pulpless.com/
Business inquiries to info@pulpless.com
Editorial inquiries & submissions to
editors@pulpless.com

TM

PULPLESS.COM, INC.

First Pulpless.Com™, Inc. Edition May, 1999.
Library of Congress Catalog Card Number: 98-83272
ISBN: 1-58445-018-5

Book and Cover designed by CaliPer, Inc.
Cover Illustration by Billy Tackett, Arcadia Studious
© 1999 by Billy Tackett

For Damon and Kate Knight

Table of Contents

There is therefore but one comfort left, that though it be in the power of the weakest arm to take away life, it is not in the strongest to deprive us of death: God would not exempt himself from that; the misery of immortality in the flesh he undertook not, that was in it immortal.

Sir Thomas Browne: *Religio Medici*

Chapter 1

The lamasery rose steeply from the top of the bluff on the Marin County side of the Golden Gate. Feeling a faint cramp in his left calf, John Roditis got out of the car near the toll plaza and, stretching and kicking, looked across the water at the gleaming yellow building, windowless, sleek, ineffably holy as a fountainhead of good karma. It was an extraordinarily warm day. San Francisco had been gripped by an unaccustomed heat wave throughout the four days of Roditis' visit. Hot weather in the psychological sense did not trouble Roditis; he thrived on it, in fact. But when heat came to him not as a function of metaphor but as a blazing golden eye staring from above, he longed to switch on the air conditioner.

There was no way for him to change the outdoor environment to that degree. At least, not yet. Given enough minds in one skull, though, who was to say what limits a man might have?

Roditis gestured at the lamasery. "I hope it's cooler in there, eh?"

"It will be," Charles Noyes said. "The guru is cool."

Roditis scowled at his associate's pun. "Still infested with the antique slang?"

"Not me. It's—Kravchenko." As he spoke the name of the persona who shared his body, Noyes' grin turned to a grimace, and he clung to the polished railing just before him. His long body sagged. His elbows trembled and beat against his ribs. "Damn him! Damn him!" Noyes grunted.

"Have him erased," Roditis suggested.

"You know I can't!"

"When an unruly persona threatens the integrity of the host, he ought to be expelled," said Roditis crisply. "If Kozak made trouble for me I'd throw him out in a minute, and he knows it. Or Walsh. Either of them. I can't afford to have a troublemaker in my head. Can you?"

"Stop it, John."

"I'm just talking common sense."

"Kravchenko doesn't like it. He's giving me a hard time."

Noyes' arm came up from the railing in a fitful jerk.

"He's fighting me. He's trying to speak."

"You won't be satisfied," said Roditis, "until he goes dybbuk on you. Throws you out of your own body."

"I'd kill him and me both first!"

Roditis scowled. "You're becoming an unstable bastard, you realize it? If I weren't so fond of you I'd let you go. Come on: into the car. Mustn't keep the cool guru waiting, or he'll get hot under the toga. Or whatever he wears."

Roditis, chuckling, opened the car door and pulled Noyes away from the railing. There was momentary confusion as Noyes struggled to regain full control of his limbs. Then Roditis thrust his companion into the car, got in beside him, and slammed the door.

"Finish the route as programed," Roditis said to the car.

The generator thrummed and the car backed out of the plaza area, swung around, and headed for the tollbooths. The actuarial sign over the row of booths announced the day's vehicle toll: 83¢. As the car passed through a booth, a brief data interchange took place between the bridge computer and the car, and Roditis' central bank account was automatically billed for that amount. Onward sped the car over the elderly bridge and toward the yellow shaft of the lamasery just beyond.

Within the cool depths of the car, Roditis flecked perspiration from his corrugated brow and regarded the other man uneasily.

He was growing more and more worried about Noyes, who perhaps was becoming a risky liability. It would be a pity to have to let Noyes go, after a relationship that had lasted so long and worked so well.

They had met in college, nineteen years before. Their roles had been reversed then: Noyes was the campus leader, tall and dashing, appropriately Anglo-Saxon, with the fair hair and blue eyes of the highest caste, and seven generations of respectable money behind him, while Roditis, the immigrant shoemaker's son who looked the part, was short, thick-bodied, dark, a scholarship student, a nobody.

But Noyes had a gift for dissipating his many assets, Roditis a gift for capitalizing on what little he had. It was an attraction of opposites, instant, permanent. Now Roditis controlled an empire, and Noyes was a cog in that vast wheel. Poor Noyes. He hadn't been able to handle his own wealth, couldn't deal with a fine wife, was even making a mess of his persona transplant. Roditis hated to patronize anyone, but he couldn't help a certain feeling of smugness as he contemplated his own position vis-à-vis Noyes. Sad. Sad.

The car purred to a halt in the gravelly parking oval adjoining the lamasery. The men got out. It seemed to be at least ten degrees hotter on this side of the bridge. Reflected heat from the lamasery's polished sides, Roditis wondered? He looked up, and felt Anton Kozak within him responding affirmatively to the chaste elegance of the architecture. Roditis had become infinitely more aware of esthetic matters since taking on Kozak's persona. It had seemed odd to some that a businessman like Roditis would choose a sonic sculptor for his second transplant, but Roditis knew what he was going toward. He was assembling a portfolio of personae as another man might assemble a portfolio of common stocks-for diversity, and for ultimate high profit.

"Feeling better?" Roditis asked.

"Much," said Noyes.

"Kravchenko is pushed way down?"

"I think so. He's had his exercise for the day."

"If there's more trouble while we're here, ask the guru to help you. He'll run a few simple exorcisms, I'm sure."

Looking pale, Noyes said, "It won't be necessary, John," and they approached the building.

Sensors scanned them. They were expected; the tall Gothic doorway peeled open, admitting them. Within, all was dark, cool, reflective. Roditis caught glimpses of saffron-robed monks scuttling to and fro in the rear arcades. A great deal of money had gone into the building of this lamasery; some of the best families had contributed to the fund. They said that the late Paul Kaufmann had donated over a million dollars fissionable. it was funny to imagine a rich Jew contributing that much money to a Buddhist monastery's construction fund; but, Roditis reminded himself, Kaufmann had not been a terribly orthodox Jew, any more than these monks were terribly orthodox Buddhists. And what had a million dollars more or less mattered to Paul Kaufmann? The crafty old banker had had his motives. Roditis saw a kindred spirit in Kaufmann. He himself had reached wealth too late to aid in this place's construction fund, but now he was here to make amends for that and for what he thought were much the same motives.

Two shaven-headed monks emerged from inner rooms. They made appropriate pseudo-Buddhist gestures, tracing mandalas in the air, touching cardinal points of their bodies, murmuring gentle welcoming mantras. Roditis, unsmiling, flicked a glance at Noyes. The tall man seemed as awed as though he stood at the threshold of God's throneroom. Once upon a time, Roditis would have envied Noyes his ability to don such a goddam sincere expression of respect, as contrasted to Roditis' own look of impassive, poker-faced piety. But now Roditis was not at all sure whether Noyes was faking anything. In these latter troubled years, old Chuck might well have turned into a believer. Stranger things had happened.

"The guru will be with you shortly," said one of the monks. "Will you remove your worldly coverings and join us in prayer?"

He indicated a room where they might change. Within, Roditis stripped away his sweat-stained clothing and gratefully shucked his shoes. His body, at thirty-seven, was tight-muscled and solid, a compact bullet of flesh still traveling unswervingly on its designed trajectory. Noyes, who was no older, still gave the illusion of lanky grace, but it was only an illusion. Beneath his clothes the tall man was thickening at the paunch, going flabby at thigh and rump. Such weakness of the flesh struck Roditis as a symptom of the decay of the will. He judged men harshly in this respect.

Arrayed now in loose, billowing robe and soft sandals, Roditis said, "It's certainly more comfortable this way. If men were saner they'd dress like this all the time."

"It wouldn't be practicable."

"No," Roditis agreed. "It leads to undue relaxation. A slackening of striving. Are we supposed to wait here for them to come back and get us?"

"I suppose," said Noyes.

The room was bare of furniture, but for the two saddle-backed benches on which they had left their worldly clothes. The walls were of some dark, highly reflective stone, slabs of black marble, perhaps, or possibly onyx. If onyx could be had in such quantities, Roditis thought. There was an inscription in inlaid letters of gold leaf on each wall. The one facing Roditis said:

> If so far you have been deaf to the teaching, listen to it now! An overpowering craving will come over you for the sense-experiences which you remember having had in the past, and which through your lack of sense organs you cannot now have. Your desire for rebirth becomes more and more urgent; it becomes a real torment to you. This desire now racks you; you do not, however, experience it for what it is, but feel it as a deep thirst which parches you as you wander along, harassed, among deserts of burning sands. Whenever you try to take

some rest, monstrous forms rise up before you. Some have animal heads on human bodies, others are gigantic birds with huge wings and claws. Their howlings and their whips drive you on, and then a hurricane carries you along, with those demonic beings in hot pursuit. Greatly anxious, you will look for a safe place of refuge.

They read it in silence. Roditis said, "That's a lot of gold to waste on such nonsense. Recognize it?"

"The *Bardo Thödol*, of course."

"Yes. The good old Book of the Dead, eh? A hot line of revelation straight from the Himalayas?"

Noyes pointed to the inscription on the rear wall. "What do you make of that one?"

Roditis turned, narrowing his-eyes. It read:

He who lacketh discrimination, whose mind is unsteady and whose heart is impure, never reacheth the goal, but is born again. But he who hath discrimination, whose mind is steady and whose heart is pure, reacheth the goal, and having reached it is born no more.

A muscle twitched in Roditis' cheek. He said bleakly, "It's pure nirvana-propaganda. Subversion. I thought they didn't try to push that concept in the Western world."

"They can't help allowing a little of the orthodox theory to survive," Noyes said, sounding apologetic.

"Why not? We've adapted all that Oriental foolishness to our own purposes. And our own purposes don't include nirvana at all. To be swallowed up in the cosmic all? To be born no more? That's not our object at all. To live again, that's what we want. Again and again and again. So why do they put that up?"

"They pose as the heirs to Eastern mysticism," said Noyes. "Catering to Western pragmatism. In theory, rebirth is undesirable, freedom from the wheel of existence is the highest goal. Yes?"

"Yes. In theory. Not for me."

A monk entered. "The guru now will see you," he murmured.

Roditis shuffled forward through clouds of incense, his sandals sliding on the smooth stone floor. Over the arch of the door he found another slogan in letters of gold:

It is appointed unto man once to die.

Yes, he thought. Once to die: I'll grant that. But many times to be reborn. He felt the warm presence within him of Anton Kozak and Elio Walsh, who lived again because he had chosen their personae from the soul bank. Had they hungered for nirvana's sweet oblivion? Of course not! They had bided their time in cold storage, and now they walked the world again, passengers in a busy, well-stocked, active mind. Roditis would leave nirvana to real Buddhists. He preferred the Westernized version of the creed.

The guru looked like a salesman of motel appliances who had seen the light. Not even his shaven skull and saffron robes could conceal the blunt, earthily American features, the jutting jaw, the prominent lips, the glossy, somewhat hyperthyroid blue eyes, the domed vault of the forehead. He was squat of physique, even shorter and stockier than Roditis, and was perhaps sixty years old, though it was difficult to be certain of that. The only creases in the holy man's face were those of its youthful geography made deeper: the deep valleys alongside the strong nose. His skull, newly mown, was pink and smooth. It had a curious occipital bulge.

Taking Roditis' hand with his left, Noyes' with his right, the guru offered a blessing and a wish for many lives for them both. Roditis was reassured. He had no interest in being fobbed off to nirvana while reincarnations were available.

"To my study?" the guru suggested.

Hideous Tibetan scrolls defaced the walls. Roditis eyed them with displeasure; within him, Anton Kozak surged with delight, but Elia Walsh, the bluff old philistine, voiced distaste even stronger than Roditis'. There was a desk, and on it a very secular-looking telephone with vision and data-transmitting attachments. Beside the telephone lay a book expensively bound in full morocco. The guru, smiling as he noticed Roditis' interest in the volume, handed it to him.

"A priceless first edition," said the holy man. "Evans-Wentz, the original translation of the *Bardo*, 1927. You won't find many of these about."

Roditis caressed the book. Its cool binding held a sensual appeal for him. Opening it with care, as though he expected pages to spring free of their own will, he eyed the familiar text with its lengthy burden of prefaces, its endless table of contents. He turned to the first section, the *Chikhai Bardo*. "HEREIN LIETH THE SETTING-FACE-TO-FACE TO THE REALITY IN THE INTERMEDIATE STATE: THE GREAT DELIVERANCE BY HEARING WHILE ON THE AFTER-DEATH PLANE, FROM THE PROFOUND DOCTRINE OF THE EMANCIPATING OF THE CONSCIOUSNESS BY MEDITATION UPON THE PEACEFUL AND WRATHFUL DEITIES."

Nonsense, Roditis knew, and Elio Walsh echoed the sharp judgment while Kozak registered mild annoyance. On a different level of his mind Roditis admitted that it was useful nonsense, in its way. How mumbo-jumbo from the icy plateaus of the yak country could be a guide to American man was a complex matter, but so it had befallen, and Roditis, comforted by his multiple personality, was flexible enough to accept and reject in the same moment.

"It's a beautiful volume," he said.

"A gift from Paul Kaufmann," the guru replied. "One of his many kindnesses to our establishment. His loss is truly a great one."

"Luckily, only temporary," Roditis pointed out. "It can't be long before a transplant of his persona will be awarded."

"Quite soon, now, I understand."

"Oh?" Roditis lurched tensely forward. "What do you know about that?"

The guru looked startled at Roditis' eagerness. "Why, nothing official. But he has been dead several months now. The family period of mourning is over. Surely they have processed the applicants for Kaufmann's persona by now, and a decision soon will come. So I assume. I have not been told anything."

Relaxing, Roditis saw Noyes' quick glower of disapproval. He knew he had acted in bad form, blurting like that. Too damned bad. Noyes had nicer manners; but Noyes wasn't hungry for Paul Kaufmann's persona. Sometimes there was a strategic advantage to a seemingly accidental tipping of your hand. Let the guru know what he wanted. It couldn't hurt.

Roditis said, "Kaufmann was a great man and a great banker. I don't know which aspect of him I admire more."

"For us his greatnesses were combined. He favored us with many donations and sometimes with his presence at our rites. Shall we pray?"

A couple of sandaled monks had slipped into the room. Roditis heard the soft chanting of the great mantra: *"Om mani padme hum."* Beside him Noyes' voice took it up. Roditis, too, unselfconsciously began to repeat the catch-phrase. They said it was the essence of all happiness, prosperity, and knowledge, and the great means of liberation. *Om.* The liberation they talked about was one Roditis did not seek: nirvana, oblivion. *Mani.* No one sought that, really, except possibly in places like India, where rebirth meant yet another breaking on the wheel of karma. *Padme. Hum. Om.* Who wanted liberation from existence? First a man wanted nourishment, and then strength, and then power, and then long life. And then rebirth so he could savor the cycle once more. *Om mani padme hum.* Roditis participated in the chant but not in any wish that the chant be fulfilled, and he suspected that of those about him only Noyes might seriously feel otherwise. *Om.*

The religious interlude was over.

It was time to talk business.

His voice tougher, less ethereal now, the guru said, "I'm glad you took the trouble to visit us, Mr. Roditis. Some men a whole lot less important than you can't be bothered to pay a personal call even on their own philanthropies."

Roditis shrugged. "I've been curious about this place for a long time. And since I had to be in San Francisco anyway—"

"Was it a successful trip?"

"Very. We closed the contracts for the entire Telegraph Hill redevelopment. Five years from now there'll be a hundred-story tower on top of that hill, the biggest thing that's been put up anywhere since '96. It'll be the Pacific headquarters of Roditis Securities."

"I look forward to blessing the site," said the guru.

"Naturally. Naturally."

"In our humble way we have our own building program here, Mr. Roditis. Would you care to view our grounds?"

They stepped through an irising gate of burnished beryllium steel and entered a broad spade-shaped garden several hundred yards deep. The rear was planted in blue flowers, delphinium, lupine, convolvulus, several others of varying heights, surmounted by a massive wistaria whose tentacles reached in all directions. Cascades of flowers dangled from the many limbs of the wistaria. Closer by were humbler flowers, and it dawned slowly on Roditis that the entire garden was laid out in the shape of some vast mandala, circles within circles, an esoteric significance of the highest degree of solemn phoniness. The thought came from Kozak; Roditis himself had not perceived the pattern. Beyond the garden lay rocky, uncleared land sloping down the hillside.

"There is to be our refectory," said the guru. "Here, the library. On the far side, overlooking the bridge, we anticipate building a guidance center for the uninformed.

"And just here to our left we will establish a soul bank."

"Your own soul bank?"

"For storing the personae of the chapter members. Obviously we can't allow our own people's personae to be thrown into the general bank. We must remain in control of each incarnation. So we propose to establish a complete Scheffing-process installation here and carry out every stage of rebirth."

"That'll cost you a fortune!" Roditis said.

"Exactly."

Noyes said, "When do you expect to build it?"

"Within the next several years. It depends on our receipt of funds, of course. We have the basic equipment for a pilot plant now. We've already had a fine contribution from the estate of Paul Kaufmann. And I understand his young nephew Mark is planning to match it."

"Mark. Yes." Roditis sucked his belly in sharply at the painful mention of his enemy. "He would. A very generous man, Mark Kaufmann."

"A generous family," said the guru.

"Quite. Quite. They all recognize the obligation of the wealthy to repay the society that has treated them so well. As do I," Roditis said a moment later. "As do I."

Noyes looked pained. Roditis kicked pebbles at his ankle. A rich man does not need to be subtle, he told himself, except where subtlety pays.

They received the full tour. They were handed rare Tibetan manuscripts, prayer wheels, and associated sacred artifacts. They visited the young lamas in their chambers. They received samples of the lamasery's publications, its painstaking theological substructure for the modern materialistic cult of rebirth. Noyes fidgeted, but Roditis calmly followed the guru about, asking questions, nodding in frequent response, showing utter concentration and complete patience. The shadows lengthened. Twilight was creeping across the continent. The guru made no request for a contribution; Roditis offered none. At the end, they were back in the guru's own chamber for farewells.

"May you attain your heart's desire," said the guru, "whatever it may be. I'm right to assume that a man of your station has some unfulfilled desires, even now?"

Roditis laughed. "Many."

"I have no doubt that some of them will be gratified shortly."

"That's kind of you," said Roditis. "I'm grateful for your sparing us so much of your time today. The visit was fascinating."

"Our pleasure," said the guru.

A youthful lama with a bony face took them to the room where they had left their clothing. They dressed and departed from the lamasery in silence. Noyes seemed to have a powerful headache. Probably good old Jim Kravchenko was hammering on the inside of Noyes' skull again.

They got into the car.

"In the morning," said Roditis, "transfer a million dollars fissionable to their account."

"That much?"

"Kaufmann gave them a million and then some, didn't he? Can I afford to do less?"

"You're not Kaufmann," Noyes pointed out.

"Not yet," said Roditis.

Chapter 2

Risa Kaufmann was sixteen years old: old enough for her first persona transplant. She had come of age, so far as the Scheffing process was concerned, three months earlier, in January. But that had been the time of old Paul's death, and it was bad taste for her to bring up the matter of the transplant just then. Now things were quieter. The black armbands had gone into the drawer; the rabbis had stopped bothering them; family life had reverted to normal. Talk of transplants was very much in the air. Everybody in the family was worried about who was going to get old Paul. They didn't speak about it much in front of her, because they still assumed she was a child, but she knew what was up. Her father was sizzling with fear that John Roditis would get Paul. That would be a funny one, Risa thought It would serve everybody right for being so rude to the little Greek. But of course Risa knew that her father would fight like a demon to keep Paul Kaufmann's persona from finding its way into Roditis' mind.

She giggled at the thought. Touching a shoulder stud, she caused her gown to drop away, and, naked, she stepped out on the terrace of the apartment.

A thousand feet below, traffic madly swirled and bustled. But up here on the ninety-fifth floor everything was serene. The April air was cool, fresh, pure. The slanting sunlight of midmorning glanced across her body. She stretched, extended her arms, sucked breath deep. The view down to the Street did not dizzy her even when she leaned far out. She wondered how some passerby would react if he stared up and saw the face and bare breasts of Risa Kaufmann hovering over the edge of a terrace. But no one ever did look up, and anyway they couldn't see anything from down there. Nor was there any other building in the area tall enough so that she was visible from it. She could stand out here nude as much as she liked, in perfect privacy. She half hoped someone would see her, though. A passing copter pilot, cruising low, doing a loop-the-loop as he spied the slinky naked girl on the balcony.

Risa laughed. This building belonged to the Paul Kaufmann estate. Once they got the will straightened out, title would pass to her father, Paul's nephew and chief heir. And one day, Risa thought, this building will be mine.

She let her unbound hair stream free in the morning breeze.

She was a tall girl, close to six feet tall, with a slim, agile body, dark hair, dark, sparkling eyes, and what she liked to think of as a Semitic nose. It pleased her to pretend she was a Yemenite Jew, a lively daughter of the desert, a descendant in a straight line from the stock of Abraham and Sarah. Certainly she looked like some Bedouin princess; but the sad genetic truth was that the Kaufmann line could be traced back to twentieth-century London, to nineteenth-century Stuttgart, to eighteenth-century Kiev, and then became lost in nameless Russian peasantry. She clung to her tribal fantasy anyway. She began to touch her toes, rapidly, not bending her knees. Hup. Hup. Hup. She could do it a hundred times, if she had to. Her small breasts bobbled and jiggled as she moved down, up, down, up. Risa was profoundly glad she hadn't sprouted a pair of meaty udders, even though bosoms were becoming fashionable again lately. She went in a good deal for nudity in her costume, and small girlish breasts were more pleasing to the eye, she thought than full heavy ones. Of course, she might get bigger later on, but she didn't think so. She hadn't grown much, in height or bust or anything else, since she had turned fourteen. Hup. Hup. She lay down on the terrace, cool tile against her back and buttocks, and lashed her heels through the air.

It might be interesting, she thought, to find out what it was like to be bosomy. To know what it is to carry all that meat below your clavicles. Risa made a mental note to request some top-heavy breasty wench when she applied for her first persona transplant. By checking through the memories she inherited, she'd get a notion of what voluptuousness was like without the bother of gaining all that nasty weight.

When will I get the transplant, though?

That was the frustrating part. At sixteen she was medically old enough for the Scheffing process, but not legally competent to apply for it. She needed her father's consent. It had been simpler last year when Risa decided it was time for her to part with her virginity; she merely took the next rocket to Cannes, picked out a likely stud, and surrendered. But they'd throw her out of the soul bank, Kaufmann or not, if she walked in without the proper consent form.

She looked over her shoulder and saw figures moving on the far side of the sliding glass door between the living room and the terrace. Risa got to her feet. Her father was coming toward her. His girl friend, the Italian bitch, Elena Volterra, was with him. Smiling, Risa lounged against the wall of the terrace and waited for them to come out to her.

Her father was wearing some sort of sprayon business suit, very chic, very shiny. His long black hair was slicked down across his skull in a style that highlighted the savage cragginess of his features, the hard thrust of the cheekbones, the vulpine chin, the corvine nose. Somehow he managed to be handsome, Mark did, despite the collection of outcroppings and bladed planes that was his face. Risa was desperately in love with him, and they both knew it of course. And hid the fact, as they must. His eyes barely flickered over his daughter's angular nakedness.

"Looking to visit the hospital?" he asked. "April's too early in the season for sunbathing in this latitude."

"It's warm enough out here, Mark," she said sullenly.

"Put something on."

"Why should I if I'm not cold?"

"All right," Mark said. "Don't. But I don't have to talk to you, either. Not while you're bare."

"How bourgeois of you. Mark. Since when have you enforced the nudity taboo?"

"This has nothing to do with taboos, Risa. Simply with your health. Now and then I have to take some sort of interest in your physical welfare, don't I? And—"

"Very well," Risa said. "We'll talk inside."

Defiantly naked, she sauntered past them, through the glass door, and slung herself down in the abstract webfoam cradle near the great screen-window, wrapping her hands about an upraised knee. Her eyes passed from her father to Elena, who was clearly annoyed by the interchange. Good. Let her stew. Elena had the sort of body Risa had been thinking about a short while back. Fleshy. Indeed. Full hips, solid thighs, high, bulky breasts. And always dressed to display her assets. Risa didn't envy her father's mistress her figure. Usually Elena kept herself cosseted with stays and braces so that the flesh made its intended effect; but it was easy for Risa to summon the memory of that beach party last year when they had all been swimming naked, and poor Elena had jiggled and bounced so dreadfully. A body like that was designed for the nakedness of the bed, or the semibareness of formal dress, but not for casual outdoor nudity. Risa asked herself if, should Elena die tomorrow, she would request her persona on a transplant. She doubted it. It would be a pleasantly spiteful thing to do to Elena, but Risa didn't think she cared to have the woman in her mind, even as a temporary.

Mark and Elena came in from the terrace. Risa chuckled. She had won that round by a dozen points. Her father had come up here with Elena because he knew it annoyed her to see the two of them together, but he had found her nude, which annoyed him because it awakened the nasty Electra thing in him and humiliated him before Elena, so he had made a fuss about her catching pneumonia in the cold outdoors. Whereupon she had come obediently inside, but remained nude, compounding the effect of rebellion and provocation. Mark was smiling too; he knew that he'd been beaten by an expert, and he couldn't help being proud of her.

His apartment was a floor below hers. She had left a message for him, asking that he come up and see her when he came home for lunch.

She said, "I wanted this to be a private conference, Mark."

"You can talk in front of Elena. She's practically a member of the family."

"That's odd. I didn't see her at Uncle Paul's funeral."

Mark winced. Risa chalked up another cluster of points. She was really sharp this morning. Elena was fuming!

Huskily, Elena said, "If this is a family conference and I'm intruding—"

"I'd just like to talk to my father a little while," Risa said. "If it's all right with the two of you. I hate to come between you, but—"

Mark shrugged a dismissal. Elena snorted in a way that made the pounds of flesh above her neckline ripple and dance. Wigwagging her hips, she stalked from the apartment.

"Now will you put something on?" Mark asked.

"Does my body make you that uncomfortable, Mark?"

"Risa, it's been a difficult morning, and—"

"Yes. Yes, all right" She knew when it was time to cash in her winnings. She picked up a robe, wrapped it about herself, and politely offered her father a tray of drinks. He chose one capsule and pressed it to his arm. Risa did not hesitate to select a golden liqueur herself, administering it expertly and shivering a little as the ultrasonic spray drove the delicious fluid into her bloodstream. She eyed her father carefully. He was tense, wary; this Roditis thing had him worried, no doubt. Or perhaps it was merely the complexity of unraveling Uncle Paul's will that keyed him up.

She said, "I think you know what I want to ask you about?"

"Summer vacation on Mars?"

"No."

"You need money?"

"Of course not."

"Then—"

"You know."

He scowled. "Your transplant?"

"My transplant," Risa agreed. "I'm well past sixteen. Uncle Paul's funeral is out of the way. I'd like to sign up. Can I have your consent?"

"What's your hurry, Risa? You've got a whole lifetime to add new personae."

"I'd like to begin. How old were you when you got your first?"

"Twenty," Mark told her. "And it was a mistake. I had to have it erased. We were incompatible. Can you imagine it, Risa, despite all the testing and matching I took on the persona of an ardent anti-Semite? And of course he woke up and found himself in a circumcised body and nearly went berserk."

"How did you pick him?"

"He was a man I had admired. An architect, one of the great builders. I wanted his planning skills. But I had to take his lunacy with his greatness, don't you see, and after three months of sheer hell for both of us I had him erased. It was several years before I dared apply for another transplant."

"That must have been unfortunate for you," Risa said. "But it's getting off the subject. I'm old enough for a transplant. It's unreasonable of you to deny your consent. It isn't as if we can't afford it, or as if I'm unstable, or anything like that. You just don't want to let me, and I can't understand why."

"Because you're so young! Look, Risa, sixteen is also the minimum legal age for getting mated, but if you came to me and said you wanted to—"

"But I haven't. A transplant isn't a marriage."

"It's far more intimate than a marriage," Mark said. "Believe me. You won't merely be sharing a bed. You'll be sharing your brain, Risa, and you can't comprehend how intimate that is."

"I want to comprehend it," she said. "That's the whole point. I'm hungry for it, Mark. It's time I found out, time I shared my life a little, time I began to experience. And there you stand like Moses saying no."

"I honestly think you're too young."

Her eyes flashed. "I'll translate that for you, dearest. You want me to stay too young, because that way you stay young too. So long as I remain a little girl in your estimation, your whole time scheme stays fixed. If I'm eight years old, you're thirty-two, and you'd like to be thirty-two. But I'm past sixteen, Mark. And you won't see forty again. I can't make you accept the second, but I wish you'd stop denying the first."

"All your cruelty is exposed today, Risa."

"I feel like going naked today. Physically and emotionally. I won't hide anything." Languidly Risa selected a second drink for herself; then, as an afterthought, she offered her father the tray. As she pressed the capsule's snout to her pale skin she said, "Will you sign my consent form or won't you?"

"Let's put it off till July, shall we? The market's so unsettled these days—"

"The market is always unsettled, and in any event it has nothing to do with my getting a transplant. Today is April 11. Unless you give in, I'm going to bear an illegitimate child on or about next January 11."

Mark gasped. "You're pregnant?"

"No. But I will be, three hours from now, unless you sign the form. If I can't experience a transplant, I'll experience a pregnancy. And a scandal."

"You devil!"

She was afraid she might have pushed her father too far. This was a raw threat, after all, and Mark didn't usually respond kindly to threats. But she had calculated all this quite nicely, figuring in a factor of his appreciation for her inherited ruthlessness. She saw a smile clawing at the edges of his mouth and knew she had won. Mark was silent a long moment. She waited, graciously allowing him to come to terms with his defeat.

At length he said, "Where's the form?"

"By an odd coincidence—"

She handed it to him. He scanned the printed sheet without reading it and brusquely scrawled his signature at the bottom. "Don't have any babies just yet, Risa."

"I never intended to. Unless you called my bluff, of course. Then I would have had to go through with it. I'd much rather have a transplant. Honestly."

"Get it, then. How did I raise such a witch?"

"It's all in the genes, darling. I was bred for this." She put the precious paper away, and they stood up. She went to him. Her arms slid round his neck; she pressed her smooth cheek to his. He was no more than an inch taller than she was. He embraced her, tensely, and she brushed her lips against his and felt him tremble with what she knew was suppressed desire. She released him. Softly she whispered her thanks.

He went out.

Risa laughed and clapped her hands. Her robe went whirling to the floor and she capered naked on the thick wine-red carpet. Pivoting, she came face to face with the portrait of Paul Kaufmann that hung over the mantel. Portraits of Uncle Paul were standard items of furniture in any home inhabited by a Kaufmann; Risa had not objected to adding him to her décor, because, naturally, she had loved the grand old fox nearly as deeply as she loved his nephew, her father. The portrait was a solido, done a couple of years back on the occasion of Paul's seventieth birthday. His long, well-fleshed face looked down out of a rich, flowing background of green and bronze; Risa peered at the hooded gray eyes, the thin lips, the close-cropped hair rising to the widow's peak, the lengthy nose with its blunted tip. It was a Kaufmann face, a face of power.

She winked at Uncle Paul.

It seemed to her that Uncle Paul winked back.

Mark Kaufmann took the dropshaft one floor to his own apartment, emerged in the private vestibule, put his thumb to the doorseal, and entered. From the vestibule, the apartment spread out along three radial paths. To his left were the rooms in which he had installed his business equipment; to his right were his living quarters; straight ahead, directly below his daughter's smaller apartment, lay the spacious living room, dining room, and library in which he entertained. Kaufmann spent much of his time in his Manhattan apartment, though he had many homes elsewhere, at least one on each of the seven continents and several offplanet. At each, he could summon a facsimile of the comforts he enjoyed here. But these twelve rooms on East 118th Street comprised the center of his organization, and often he did not leave the building for days at a time.

He walked briskly into the library. Elena stood by the fireplace, beneath the brooding, malevolent portrait of the late Uncle Paul. She looked displeased.

"I'm sorry," Kaufmann told her. "Risa was simply in a bitchy mood, and she took it out on you."

"Why does she hate me so much?"

"Because you're not her mother, I suppose."

"Don't be a fool, Mark. She'd hate me even more if I *were* her mother. She hates me because I've come between herself and you, that's all."

"Don't say that, Elena."

"It's true, though. That child is monstrous!"

Kaufmann sighed. "No. She isn't a child, as she's just finished explaining to me in great detail. And she's not even monstrous. She's just an apt pupil of the family business techniques. In a way, I'm terribly pleased with her."

Elena regarded him coldly. "What a terrible tragedy for you

that she's your own daughter, isn't it? She'd make a wonderful wife for you in a few years, when she's ripe. Or a mistress. But incest is not one of the family business techniques."

"Elena—"

"I have a suggestion," Elena purred. "Have Risa killed and transplant her persona to me. That way you can enjoy both of us in one body, quite lawfully, gaining the benefit of my physical advantages joined to the sharp personality you seem to find so endearing in her."

Kaufmann closed his eyes a moment. He often wondered how it had happened that he had surrounded himself with women who had such well-developed gifts of cruelty. Steadier for his pause, he ignored Elena's thrust and said simply, "Will you excuse me? I have some calls to make."

"Where do we eat lunch? You talked yesterday about Florida House for clams and squid."

"We'll eat here," said Kaufmann. "Have Florida House send over whatever you'd like to have. I won't be able to go out until later. Business."

"*Business*! Another ten millions to make before nightfall!"

"Excuse me," he said.

He left Elena arrayed like a fashionable piece of sculpture in the library and made his way to his office. He touched the doorseal, full palm here, not merely thumb. The thick tawny oaken door, inset with twining filaments of security devices, yielded to him, an obedient wife that would surrender only to the right caress. Within, Kaufmann consulted the stock ticker the way an uneasy medieval might have searched for answers in the sortes of Virgil, or perhaps in a random stab into the Talmud. The market was off six points; the utilities averages were up, finance steady, interworld transport a little shaky. Kaufmann's fingers tapped the console as he executed two swift trades for ritualistic purposes. He closed out at 94 a thousand shares of Metropolitan Power purchased that morning at 89¾, and an instant later accepted a realized loss of half a point on a lot of eight hundred Königin Mines. The net effect on his central credit balance was inconsequential, but Kaufmann had learned the therapeutic value of making small trades in times of stress from his uncle, long ago.

Next he switched on the neutron flux scanner with which he monitored Risa's apartment. There was little of the voyeur in his psychological makeup; he merely regarded it as good sense to keep an eye on his increasingly more unruly daughter. Especially when, as today, she had blackmailed him into giving his consent to a transplant by the elegantly simple method of threatening to get pregnant. Now that she had voiced the notion, he knew he had to guard against it. He was well aware of Risa's sexual adventures of the past year, and had no objections to them, but a pregnancy was beyond the scope of the acceptable.

He watched her for a few moments.

She was naked again, rushing about the apartment, getting ready to go out. No doubt to make the preliminary arrangements for her transplant. Kaufmann allowed himself the pleasure of admiring her coltish grace, her long-limbed sleekness. Then he switched the scanner over to record and let it run; it would monitor her apartment so long as he wished.

Swinging around to his desk, he activated the telephone.

"I want my daughter traced wherever she goes today," he said. "I expect her to visit the soul bank, and don't interfere with that but tell me where she goes afterwards. Especially if she goes to any of her friends. Male friends. No, no interceptions; just surveillance."

He suspected he was being overcautious. Nevertheless, he would have her watched, at least today. If necessary, he'd order surreptitious external contraceptive measures as an extra precaution. Risa could sleep around all she liked, but he had no intention of allowing her to get more than a few days into any premarital pregnancies just yet.

Kaufmann said to the telephone, "Get me Francesco Santoliquido."

It took more than a minute. Even Mark Kaufmann had to be patient about getting a call through to Santoliquido, who was not merely an important man, as chief administrator of the soul bank, but also a very busy one. Whole light-years of secretarial barricades had to be penetrated before Santoliquido could discover who was calling and was able to free himself long enough to respond.

Then the amiable face blossomed on the screen. Santoliquido was about fifty, ruddy of skin, white-haired, with a large, commanding oval face. He was a man of considerable wealth who had entered the bureaucracy out of a sense of mission.

"Yes, Mark?"

"Frank, I wanted you to know that my daughter will soon be on her way down to your bank to pick out a persona."

"You broke down, then!"

"Let's say Risa broke me down."

Santoliquido shook with pleasant laughter. "Well, she's a strong-willed girl. Strong enough to handle a transplant I'd say. What shall I give her? A Mother Superior? A lady banker?"

"On the contrary," said Kaufmann. "Someone softly feminine, to balance all the aggression in her. Someone who died young, quite sadly, after a life of suffering for love. Preferably a girl of an opposite physical type, too, less athletic, less masculine of build. You follow?"

"Certainly. And what if Risa isn't interested in a person of those specifications?"

"I think she will be, Frank. But if she isn't, give her what she wants, I suppose. I'll leave the final decisions up to the two of you."

"You'll have to," said Santoliquido. His eyes regarded Kaufmann with some amusement. "You know, Mark, you were supposed to come to the bank yourself this month. You haven't been recorded in nearly a year."

"I've been so damned busy. Paul's death, and everything—"

"Yes, I know. But you shouldn't neglect the semiannual recording. A man of your stature—you owe it to the world, to the
future inheritors of your persona, to keep yourself up to date, to
etch all the new experiences into the record—"

"All right. You sound like a recruiter."

"I am, Mark. We've been expecting you for weeks."

"What if I come tomorrow, then? I wouldn't want to be there
today. If I ran into Risa, she'd think her horrible old father was
spying on her."

"True. Tomorrow, then," Santoliquido said. "Is there anything
else, Mark?"

"Just one thing." Kaufmann hesitated. "The question of Paul's
persona."

"No decision's been taken yet. None. We've had dozens of applicants."

"Roditis among them?"

"I couldn't say."

"You *could* say. Maybe you *won't* say, but that's a different thing.
I know Roditis is hungry to add Paul to his collection of transplants. I'd merely like to emphasize that such a transplant would
be distasteful and offensive not only to the immediate Kaufmann
family, but to—"

Santoliquido's ringed hand swept across the screen. "I'm aware
of your feelings," he said gently. "However, family wishes cannot be binding upon us. The decisions of the soul bank are made
strictly on an impersonal basis, taking into account the stability
of the recipient and the merit of his application, and you know
very well that we regard it as desirable to go outside the genetic
group whenever possible."

"Meaning that you favor giving Paul to Roditis?"

"I said nothing of the kind." Santoliquido's geniality began to
ebb. "We're still weighing all applicants."

"I wish I could take Uncle Paul myself, and keep him out of the skull of that—that fishmonger!"

"What about the consanguinity laws?" Santoliquido asked. "Not to mention your uncle's own will? He'll have to go outside the family, Mark. And I suspect we won't be giving him to any Schiffs or Warburgs or Lehmans or Loebs, either. Can we drop the subject, now?"

"I suppose?"

Santoliquido smiled again. "I'll see you tomorrow. And then, Saturday, your party, Dominica."

"Yes. Dominica on Saturday"

The screen went dark. Kaufmann felt cross; he had played his hand poorly, making that frontal attack on Santoliquido just now. Risa had upset him, clearly, shaking his tactical faculties. Or was it Roditis? *Roditis. Roditis.* For ten years, now, Kaufmann had watched that grasping little man accumulate first wealth, then power, and then some measure of social prestige. Now the audacious upstart wished to thrust himself deep into the core of a fine old family, making up for his own lack of ancestry by seizing the available persona of the late Paul Kaufmann. Mark scowled. He was less of a snob than he had a right to he, considering who and what he was, but nevertheless the thought of Roditis lying down on a pallet in the soul bank and emerging with Uncle Paul was intolerable to him. He had to be blocked.

Kaufmann's own three personae stirred and squirmed. Ordinarily they were mild, passive, guiding him without making their presence known, but the tensions of this hideous morning were seeping into their place of repose. He put his hands to his forehead. I'm sorry, friends, he told the three captive souls beneath his scalp. We'll all relax on Saturday. I'm genuinely sorry about this.

Damn Roditis!

Kaufmann turned back to the ticker. The market was rallying, but now the utilities were weak. He scanned the tape, made a quick velocity projection of Pacific Coast Power, and went five thousand shares short at 43. Moments later it came across the tape on high volume at 45½. Not my day, Kaufmann thought, and covered his sale for a rapid loss. Not my day at all.

Chapter 3

Charles Noyes awoke slowly, reluctantly, fighting the return to the waking world. He lay alone in a bed that was just barely long enough for his lanky body. His arms twitched; his eyelids fluttered. Morning was here. Time to rise, time to toil. He fought it.

—Come on, you cowardly bastard, said James Kravchenko within his mind. Wake up!

Noyes moaned. He jammed his eyelids together. "Let me alone."

—Up, up, up! Greet the morning's glow.

"You aren't supposed to talk to me, Kravchenko. You're just supposed to be there."

—Look, I didn't ask to be pushed into your brain. Anytime you'd like to let me out, you know where to go.

"You don't mean that. You're only bluffing. You want to stay right where you are, Kravchenko. Until you can take me over entirely, and run me like a puppet"

Kravchenko did not reply. Several minutes passed, and the persona remained silent. Once again Noyes considered getting out of bed, but waited, convinced that Kravchenko would nag him again, and willing to arise only when nagged. But in the continued silence he knew the onus was on him to get their shared body up. He pushed back the covers and disconnected the night monitor.

Beside his bed lay the deadly flask of carniphage. Noyes eyed it tenderly. His first thought upon arising, like his last at night, was of suicide. No. Duicide. When he went he would take Kravchenko with him. He picked up the flask and cradled it in his hand, stroking it with affection.

Within the fragile container lay a lethal quantity of beta-13 viral DNA, a replicative molecule whose action it was to persuade the cells of the body to release autolytic enzymes, certain acid hydrolases, from the lysosomes or "suicide bags" within themselves. Moments after ingestion, the carniphage created such a cascading wave of autolysis that the body literally fell apart; cell death was general and consecutive, and as each cell in turn succumbed to the flow of fatality, the carniphage devoured it. It was a swift but unusually agonizing way to die, since the body turned to slime from the digestive tract outward, and as much as eight or ten minutes might pass before the nerve centers were no longer able to register the pain of dissolution. But the splendor of the poison lay in its total irreversibility. There was no known antidote, nor even a conceivable one; neither could a stomach pump or any sort of similar device halt the process once it had begun to affect even a few cells. Let that cascade of destruction begin, and the victim was irrevocably doomed. Noyes sometimes thought of it as the Humpty Dumpty effect

He set the carniphage down.

—Go on, gulp it, why don't you!

"Very funny, Kravchenko."

—I mean it. Do you think you frighten me, waving that suicide juice around? I'll get a new body soon enough, once you're gone. Maybe you'll be right in there with me, when I'm transplanted the second time.

Noyes reached for the flask.

—Just put it to your lips and go crunch. It's easy.

"No, damn you! I'll do it when I want to. Not to amuse you!"

It seemed to him that he heard Kravchenko's ghostly laughter. Putting the flask aside again, Noyes shed his nightclothes and began his morning rituals.

Religious observance. He reached for the *Bardo*. Untold generations of Episcopalian ancestors whirred like turbines in their New England tombs as the last and least scion of the Noyeses opened the barbarous Tibetan holy book. He turned, as usual, to the *Bardo* of the dying, the early section, before the demons appear, when nirvana is still within reach. In a low voice he read:

> O nobly-born, listen. Now thou art experiencing the Radiance of the Clear Light of Pure Reality. Recognize it. O nobly-born, thy present intellect, in real nature void, not formed into anything as regards characteristics or color, naturally void, is the very Reality, the All-Good. Thine own intellect, which is now voidness, yet not to be regarded as the voidness of nothingness, but as being the intellect itself, unobstructed, shining, thrilling, and blissful, is the very consciousness, the All-good Buddha.

Cleanliness. He stood in the vibrator field for a minute.
Nutrition. He programed an austere breakfast.
Bodily hygiene. Grunting a bit, he performed the eleven stretchings and the seven bendings.

He ate. He dressed. The time was ten in the morning. He had returned with Roditis from San Francisco the night before, and he was still living on Pacific Standard Time, which made his awakening even more difficult than it normally was. Activating the screen, Noyes saw that the outer world looked cheerful and sunny, and the sunlight was the yielding light of April, not the harsh winter light that had engulfed this part of the world so long. He lived in a small apartment in the Wallingford district of Greater Hartford, Connecticut, close enough both to Manhattan and to his ancestral Boston. He tried to keep away from Massachusetts, but old compulsions drew him there periodically. One, at least, was external: at Roditis' insistence, the two of them attended their Harvard class reunion each year. That was painful.

Any window into the past was a source of pain. Anything that reminded him of a time when he had been young, with prospects before him: a legal career, a fruitful marriage, a fine home, the joys of tradition. He had flunked out of law school. Flunked out of marriage, too. Today he was a wealthy man, but only because Roditis had picked him up from the junkheap and stuffed money in his pockets, as the price of his soul. Noyes' credit balance was high, but he spent little and lived in a kind of genteel poverty, not out of miserliness but merely because he refused to believe that the largesse Roditis had showered upon him was real.

"Charles! Charles, are you up yet?"

—His master's voice, said Kravchenko slyly.

"I'm here, John," Noyes called into the other room, while sending a subliminal shout of fury at his persona. "I'm coming!"

One entire wall of the sitting room bore a viewscreen that was hooked into Roditis' master communications circuit. No matter where Roditis was, at any station along the territory of his far-flung empire, he could activate that circuit and introduce himself, life-size, three dimensions, into Noyes' apartment. Noyes presented himself before the screen and confronted the blocky figure of his friend and employer. The furniture surrounding Roditis was that of his office in Jersey City: stock tickers, computer banks, data filters, the huge green eye of an analysis machine. Roditis looked wide awake. He said, "Feeling better?"

"Passable, John."

"You were in lousy shape when we got back last night I was worried about you."

"A night's sleep, that's all I needed."

"The acknowledgment on the lamasery gift just came in. Want to see what the guru's got to say?"

"I suppose."

Roditis gestured. His image shattered and vanished, and for a moment a cloudy blueness filled the screen; then came the sharp snap of a message flake being thrust into a holder, followed by the appearance in Noyes' sitting room of the holy man from San Francisco. Noyes had the illusion that he smelled incense. The guru, all smiles, poured forth a honeyed stream of praise and gratitude for Roditis' generous gift. Noyes sat through it impatiently, wondering why Roditis was bothering to inflict these few minutes of fatuity on him. Of course the guru was going to sound grateful, after having been handed a million dollars; of course he was going to say that Roditis was blessed among men in wisdom, and worthy of many rebirths. Noyes had the uneasy suspicion that Roditis genuinely *believed* what the guru was saying— that he felt it was praise earned through merit, not merely bought for cash. It was something like a sonic sculptor who bribed the *Times* critic to give him a rave, then called up all his friends and proudly read them the glowing review. Not a day passed on which Noyes failed to rediscover the core of naïveté that lay within John Roditis' energetic, shrewd, ruthless spirit.

The guru reached his peroration and vanished from the screen. Roditis returned, beaming.

"What did you think *of that?*"

"Fine, John. Wonderful."

"He really sounded happy about the gift"

"I'm sure he was. It was very handsome."

"Yes," said Roditis. "I'll give him some more, by and by. I'll make them name a whole damn wing of that place after me. The John Roditis Soul Bank for Departed Lamas, or something. Onward and upward, yes? *Om mani padme hum*, fella."

Noyes said nothing. Kravchenko seemed to chuckle; Noyes felt it as a tickling in his frontal lobes.

Then, as though experiencing some inner shifting of gears, Roditis lost his look of jovial self-satisfaction, and a glimmer of strain showed through his carefully abstract expression. He said, "Mark Kaufmann is giving a party Saturday at his Dominica estate."

"He's coming out of mourning, then?"

"Yes. This is the first social thing he's done since old Paul was gathered to repose. It's going to be a big, noisy, expensive affair."

"Are you invited?" Noyes asked.

Roditis looked scornful. "Me? The filthy little *nouveau riche* with delusions of grandeur? No, of course I'm not invited! It's mainly going to be a party for various Kaufmanns and their Jewish banking relatives."

"John, you know you shouldn't use that phrase."

"Why? Does it make me seem a bigot? You know I've got nothing against Jews. Can I help it if the Kaufmanns are related to the other big Jewish bankers?"

"When you say it, somehow, it comes out like a sneer," Noyes dared to tell him.

"Well, I don't mean it as a sneer. You don't sneer at a social and cultural elite. What you hear in my voice isn't anti-Semitism, Charles, it's simple envy without any neurotic irrational manifestations attached. There'll be a mess of Lehmans and Loebs at that party. There won't be any John Roditis. Frank Santoliquido is going to be there, too."

"*He's* not Jewish."

Roditis looked annoyed. "No, dolt, he isn't! But he's important, and he's socially well-placed besides, and Mark Kaufmann is trying to buy his support in this business of the old man's persona. Santoliquido and his girl friend are flying down on Mark's own jet; that's how tight things are getting. And you can bet that Mark is going to spend the whole day letting Santo know how important it is to keep Uncle Paul out of my clutches. That's got to be counteracted somehow. Which is why you're going to go to the party, too."

"Me? But I'm not invited!"

"Get yourself invited."

"Impossible, John. Kaufmann knows I'm connected to your organization, and if you're on the dead list, you can bet that I—"

"You're also connected to the Loebs, aren't you?"

"Well, my sister married a Loeb, yes."

"Damn right, she did. Won't she be at the party?"

"I suppose she's been invited, at any rate."

"I know she has. I've got the complete guest list right here. Mr. and Mrs. David Loeb. That's your sister, right?"

"Right."

"Fine. Now, what happens if she phones Kaufmann and says she's in the air over Cuba, say, and she'll be landing in five minutes, and she's happened to bring her kid brother Charlie along for the party? Is Kaufmann going to say no, send the scoundrel home?"

"He'll be furious, John."

"Let him be furious, then. He'll have to maintain decorum, though. It's not the sort of formal party where one extra guest throws the whole thing out of balance, and he can't very well refuse you permission to attend with your sister. You'll be admitted. The worst that'll happen is you'll get a few sour stares from Kaufmann. But socially you'll be among your equals, and everybody else will be glad to see you, and there'll be no hard feelings."

Noyes' fingers began to tremble. Kravchenko scrabbled derisively against the walls of his cranium. Carefully, Noyes reached to his left, out of the range of the sensors relaying his image to Roditis, and scooped a drink capsule from a tray. He activated the capsule and let the fluid flow into his arm. That was better. But not good enough. He felt sick. The idea of muscling his way into a party like this, parlaying his own tattered status and his sister's connections by marriage into Roditis' advantage, chilled and saddened him.

He said, "Assuming I succeed in crashing the party, John, what's the purpose of my going there?"

"Mainly to get next to Santoliquido and work on him."

"About the Paul Kaufmann persona?"

"What else? You can be subtle. You can be indirect. He's going to make up his mind about the transplant any day now. I want it so bad I can taste it, Charles. Do you realize what I could do with Paul Kaufmann inside my head? The doors that would open for me, the plans I could bring off? And it's all up to Santo. He'll be down there, relaxed, out in the sunshine, drinking too much.

And you can work on him. Use the old charm. That's what I pay you for, the old Episcopalian Anglo-Saxon charm. Turn it on!"

"All right," Noyes muttered.

"And even if you don't get anywhere immediately with him, perhaps you can find a plan of action. Some vulnerable spot in his makeup. Some opening wedge that we can get leverage on."

Appalled, Noyes said, "Are you thinking of blackmailing Santoliquido into approving your request?"

"Now, did I say that? What a terribly crude suggestion, Charles! I expect more finesse from you." Roditis laughed heavily. "Call your sister. Get everything set up. Oh— Charles? How's Jimmy-boy?"

"Kravchenko? I think he's asleep."

"I'm sure he'll appreciate going to the party too. He'll see many of his old friends there. Call your sister, Charles."

The screen darkened.

Noyes looked at the floor. He knelt and dug his fingers into the carpet, trying to steady himself. His head seemed to be splitting into segments.

—Call your sister, Charles. Didn't you hear the man?

"I won't!"

—You'd better. You don't dare defy him.

"It's filthiness! To crash a party so he can use me to suck up to Santoliquido—"

—He wants the old Kaufmann persona, doesn't he? It's his ticket to social respectability. Your job is to help him get what he wants.

"Not at the cost of my integrity."

—You got rid of that a long time ago. Come on, Chuck. He's right: I want to go to that party. At least three of my wives ought to be there. I'd love to see how they're aging.

"I'll kill myself first!"

—If you had the guts, I suppose you would. Pick up the phone. Call your sister.

Noyes heard mocking laughter in his skull.

He returned to the bedroom and eyed the carniphage flask. But, as ever, it was only a dramatic gesture, fooling neither himself nor the demonic persona he harbored. Defeat dragged at his muscles. He seized the phone and jabbed out the numbers. Moments later, his sister's privacy code appeared on the little gray screen. She's taking her morning bath, Noyes thought. He said, "It's me, Gloria, just Charlie. Your wombmate."

The screen cleared, and the face and shoulders of Gloria Loeb appeared. She wore some sort of flimsy wrap, and her cheeks and forehead were glossy with whatever mystic preparation she favored to keep her complexion eternally young. She was three years older than Noyes, and looked at least a dozen years younger. They had never liked one another. Her marriage to David Loeb had been a stunning social event sixteen years ago, a grandiose blowout, as was appropriate for the union of old New England aristocracy with old Jewish aristocracy. That was the fashionable sort of marriage these days, rapidly creating a tribe of Anglo-Saxon Hebrews whose formidable bloodlines linked them securely to Plantagenets on one hand, Solomon and David on the other, an unbeatable combination. Noyes had become very drunk at his sister's wedding; in a way, his decline and fall had begun that evening, a few weeks after he had turned twenty-one.

She said coolly, "How good to hear from you again, Charles. You look well."

"That's a polite lie. I look terrible, and you can feel free to let me know about it."

Her lips quirked impatiently. "Is something the matter? Are you all right?"

Noyes took a deep breath and said, "I need a tiny favor, Gloria."

Chapter 4

The building housing the soul bank rose in stunning tiers from a broad plaza three superblocks in area. The site had been chosen with an eye toward deliberate ostentation, at Manhattan's southern tip in an area thick with historic associations. Here, Peter Minuit had haggled with Indian braves and bought a world for a handful of beads; here, Pegleg Stuyvesant had tromped in choleric efficiency; Washington had walked these streets, as had J. P. Morgan, Jay Gould, Thomas Edison, Bet-a-Million Gates, Joseph P. Kennedy, Paul Kaufmann, and Helmut Scheffing, along with others. Few traces of that history remained. A block of eighteenth-century buildings had been preserved as a sort of museum; the seventeenth-century New York was gone, as was the nineteenth, and all that survived of the twentieth in this neighborhood were a few scruffy, faded curtain-wall skyscrapers put up by the big banks during the boom of the midcentury, shortly before the panic. Serene, isolated, set apart from its neighbors by thousands of priceless square feet of pink noctilucent tile, rose the glowing shaft of the Scheffing Institute tower: eighty stories, then a setback and forty stories more, and a twenty-story cap tipped with black granite. The tower was easily visible from Brooklyn, from Queens, from Staten Island, from New Jersey, and especially from Jubilisle, the floating pleasure dome in New York harbor. One looked up from the sins and gaming tables of Jubilisle to see the reassuring bulk of the Scheffing Institute at the edge of land, offering the promise of rebirth beyond rebirth, and it was comforting. The architects had taken all that into account when planning the building.

To the Scheffing Institute that Friday morning came Mark Kaufmann to renew his lease on life. His small hopter landed as programed on the flight deck at the tower's first setback, and

waiting guards hustled him inside to see Santoliquido. The morning was cool; he had chosen a thick-fibered tunic that sparkled
with dark brown and red highlights.

Francesco Santoliquido's office was deep, high, consciously
impressive. In one corner stood a sonic sculpture, the work of
Anton Kozak: a beautiful piece, all flowing lines and delicate
rhythms, emitting a gentle white hiss that swiftly infiltrated itself into one's consciousness and became rooted there.
Kaufmann's pleasure in the lovely work was marred by his awareness that Anton Kozak, who had died nine years ago, had returned to the corporate form as one of the implanted personae
of John Roditis.

Santoliquido's desk split obediently and the administrator came
through the sections to greet Kaufmann. He was a bulky man,
heavier than the fashion prescribed, but he carried himself well.
His thick fingers glittered with the rings that betrayed
Santoliquido's innocent predisposition toward vanity. At his throat
hung a cluster of small beady-eyed crustaceans, violet and green
and azure, within a crystal container: products of the mutagenetic
art, elaborate little baroques that moved through their prison in
an unending stately dance. Santoliquido's shirt was green, his
epaulets vermilion. In the blaze of color his white, slicked-back
hair took on a compelling vividness.

The two men touched hands. Santoliquido returned to his desk,
extended a tray of drinks, took part with Kaufmann in the moment of pleasure. Shafts of sunlight danced across the room. The
window, a vaulted arch, was wholly transparent. From where he
stood Kaufmann enjoyed a superb view of the harbor, and peering down into gay Jubilisle from this height was like staring into
a prismatic image from some unimaginable protonic
subuniverse.

"Well," said Santoliquido, "we had the pleasure of your lovely
daughter's company here yesterday. She seems hard to please,
though. We unrolled our best carpets for her, but there was no

deal."

"Not yet. She'll be back."

"Yes, certainly. Next Tuesday. She's choosing among three interesting alternatives."

"I'd like to scan them," said Kaufmann.

"That would be a little irregular."

"I know."

Santoliquido smiled elegantly. Kaufmann had always had a good working relationship with this man; they had participated in several joint ventures, most notably a power scheme in the Antarctic, and always Santoliquido had come out of them with his considerable fortunes considerably enhanced. Reciprocal favors were not impossible.

The pitch of the Kozak piece altered perceptively, growing more definite, more passionate. Once Kaufmann had had several Kozaks. After Roditis had received the sculptor's persona, Kaufmann had found occasions to bestow the works on delighted friends.

Kaufmann said, "Nothing new on Uncle Paul since Wednesday?"

"Nothing new.

"I'd like to see him, too."

"Really?'

"You'll satisfy my curiosity, won't you?" Kaufmann leaned forward at the waist and fingered an amber rubbing stone on Santoliquido's desk. "There's a therapeutic reason. I find it hard to believe that the old man's really dead. You know, he rose above the whole family like such a colossus—

"So that when you see him taped and carded, you'll finally accept that he's gone?"

"Yes."

"It's not the first time I've heard something like that Mark." Santoliquido clasped his hands over his belly and laughed. "Paul was quite the titan, wasn't he? I'll admit I ran his persona off myself, after the funeral, just to get some feel for the man. And I was awed. Let me tell you, Mark, I don't awe easily, but I was awed."

"Toying with the idea of taking him on yourself?"

Santoliquido looked displeased, and even the crustaceans at his throat rapidly changed hues, as if somehow attuned to the flavor of his thoughts. "I have no desire whatever to have that terrible old man mixing in my nervous system," said Santoliquido firmly. "And in any event, considering the demand for his per-sona, it would be a grave breach of trust if I were to appropriate him for my own use. Yes?"

"Of course. Of course."

The look of affability returned. "Anyone who wants your uncle's persona is welcome to it, so far as I care personally. What a pow-erhouse! He'd overwhelm nine out of ten who took him on."

"Just as he overwhelmed us all in life," said Kaufmann. "He reduced my father to a hollow shell, an errand-boy. Me he had a harder time with, but he gave me twenty years of hell before he'd recognize me as a worthy heir. And the others! Of course, we all loved him. He was simply too dynamic to hate. But when he died, Frank, I felt as though a hand had been removed from my throat."

"I can understand that."

"One more thing. None of us could accept the news, when he had the stroke. I mean, he was still a young man, hardly past seventy. We assumed he'd be around at least fifty more years. But his own vitality must have burned him out."

"He'll be back among us all soon enough," said Santoliquido.

"As a persona, yes. That's not quite the same as having Uncle Paul striding through the rooms booming out orders."

"Time will tell about that. It'll take a strong man to hold him down, Mark."

"You're expecting Paul to take over his host?"

"I'm not expecting anything, officially. I'm merely a bureaucrat, and it's not my business to expect. Come. I'll take you to see your uncle."

"And Risa's three possible personae," Kaufmann reminded him.

"Those too," said Santoliquido.

Kaufmann followed him from the office into a private dropshaft that moved so serenely he was unaware of motion; even the tug of gravity was absent. Here in this monstrous house of death and rebirth Kaufmann always felt ill at ease and badly orientated. He had no real notion of the contents of the infinity of offices on these hundred forty floors, nor did he even know how deep into bedrock the structure extended, what possible maze of stories lay out of sight. Within this too conspicuous edifice were filed the personae of the notable dead, some eighty million of them that had died since the introduction of the Scheffing process as a commercial fact. Yet the storage even of eighty million personae, Kaufmann knew, could be accomplished in modest space. There were many rooms in this building where persona recordings were made, and other rooms in which the transplants took place, but a great deal of the building's volume was unaccountable to him.

He did not know where in the tower Santoliquido had taken him now, whether toward the soaring summit or deep into the bowels. He merely followed, through silent passageways agleam with living light.

The Scheffing Institute was a quasipublic corporation, closely regulated by the Government, its administrators chosen by Congress, its board of directors containing a specified quota of Government appointees. Its schedule of fees and services was subject to Federal supervision. In effect, the Institute was a public utility of death and rebirth. No common stock was available for purchase; its frequently issued debt securities were offered only to municipal and institutional investors; its profits, which were great, went primarily into renewed research, once amortization payments were made. Important as the Institute was, its exist-

ence impinged only marginally on the lives of most of Earth's
nine billion people. Merely a minority could afford the costs of
escaping oblivion. There was a stiff fee for registration; the fee
payable each time one recorded one's persona was not small; a
registrant was expected, though not required, to make a new
recording at least once every six months. The cost of receiving a
persona transplant was formidable—more than the average man
could hope to earn in a lifetime. In theory, anyone who had the
money and was certifiably stable could receive a new persona
each year of his adult life, superimposed above the earlier ones.
But in practice most people were content with two or three transplants, if they could afford that many. No one, to Kaufmann's
knowledge, had ever taken more than nine. Though he could
well afford any number of additional identities himself, he had
not applied for a new one in more than a decade. He found three
quite enough—not counting the youthful indiscretion that had
had to be erased.

It was anything but cheap to erase a persona, also. The Institute turned its profit at every stage of the process.

Kaufmann followed Santoliquido into the vestibule of the main
storage vault. It was a long, low-roofed tunnel whose far end
was plugged by a security door almost comical in its paranoid
massiveness. Through apertures in the glossy blank roof came
colored lights of scanners: a blue ray, a green, a turquoise, a
pale yellow.

"What are they checking?" Kaufmann asked.

"Everything imaginable. Your blood type's going on tape, your
retinal pattern, your DNA-RNA, and several other matters too
intimate to mention. If you ever came through here bent on lar-
ceny, you'd be picked up within minutes after you left the building."

"What if the scanners get through and find I'm too disrepu-
table to admit?"

"It'll be unpleasant."

Kaufmann envisioned a cage of pressure tape springing from the ceiling and trapping him. Whirling blades slashing him into hamburger. A trapdoor opening to hurl him to limbo. But in fact the colored lights vanished, and with solemn ponderousness the great door began to open. Santoliquido nodded. They stepped out onto the grand concourse of the main storage vault.

It was a room perhaps a thousand feet high and three hundred feet wide from wall to wall. At the very top, far above his head, Kaufmann saw banks of light-globes affixed to the fabric of the building; but only a fraction of that light made its way down to the midlevel on which they stood, and below him were levels of Stygian bleakness. Motes of dust hovered in the vast central cavity of the room. Along the walls were ladders, catwalks, a spiderweb of metal pathways. Staring across the gulf, Kaufmann made out racks of shelves, paneled urns, shadows in the darkness. All this has been done for effect, he told himself. Surely the Institute could afford better lighting, if it wanted it.

"Come," said Santoliquido.

They moved along the tier. Silent figures in white smocks traversed private paths on other levels, and robots with blunt heads rolled on soundless treads from tier to tier, inserting something here, withdrawing there. Santoliquido paused in front of a sealed bank of urns and dialed a computer code. The bank opened. Reaching in, he withdrew a shining coppery casket some six inches wide, four inches long, two inches high.

"In this," he said, "is the persona of Paul Kaufmann."

Kaufmann took it from him and examined it with more awe than he cared to reveal.

"May I open it?"

"Go ahead."

"I don't see how—ah. There." He pressed a projecting lever and the casket's top rose. Within lay a tightly coiled reel of black tape, smaller across than Kaufmann's palm, and a stack of data flakes. "This?" he said. "This is Uncle Paul?"

"His memories. His experiences. His aggressions. His frailties. The women he loved, the men he hated. His business coups. His childhood ailments. The graduation speech; the cramped muscle; the wedding night. All there. This was recorded in December. It takes him from childhood to the edge of the grave."

"Suppose I reached over the balcony and hurled all this down there," Kaufmann said. "The flakes would scatter. The tape would he ruined. That would he the end of Uncle Paul, wouldn't it?"

"Why do you think so?" Santoliquido asked. "Your uncle was here every six months for more than thirty years. We have many replicas on file of what you hold in your hand."

Kaufmann gasped. "You keep the old ones after a re-recording?"

"Naturally. We have an extensive library of your uncle's personae. You have the latest one, the most complete; but if anything happened to it, we could make use of the last but one, which would lack only six months of his life experience. And so on backward. Of course, we always use the most recent recording for transplant purposes. The rest are kept as emergencies, a redundancy control, so to speak."

"I never knew that!"

"We don't make a point of announcing it."

"So you have sixty-odd recordings of Uncle Paul in this building! And a couple of dozen of me! And—"

"Not in this building, necessarily," said Santoliquido. "We have many storage vaults, Mark, well decentralized. We guard against calamities. We have to."

Kaufmann considered that. It had never occurred to him that such surrogate recordings existed, or even that there might be supplementary soul banks elsewhere, but both were logical enough. An implication struck him.

"If there are duplicates," he said slowly, "then it should be possible to transplant one man's persona into more than one recipient at the same time, yes? You could give Uncle Paul to Roditis, and Uncle Paul minus the last six months to someone else, and so on."

"Technically possible. But wholly unethical and unlawful. We keep the reserves as reserves. They've never been used that way and never will." Santoliquido looked agitated at the possibility. "*Never.*"

Kaufmann nodded. The intensity of Santoliquido's reply unsettled him. He closed the casket and handed it back.

"Now do you believe he's dead?" Santoliquido asked.

"Well, of course, I've got no evidence that the tape in this box has anything to do with Uncle Paul."

"Would you like to sample it?"

"Me? Are you proposing a temporary transplant?"

"I'll give you thirty seconds of Uncle Paul," Santoliquido offered. "Just as if you were shopping for a new persona. Then you can decide for yourself whether he's on that tape. Come along. In here."

They entered a cubicle with dark translucent walls. It contained a reclining seat, a console of equipment, a row of jeweled scanners. Santoliquido removed the tape from the box and clipped it into the grips of one of the scanners. He beckoned Kaufmann to the reclining seat.

They were in a sampling booth now. This apparatus was used strictly for checking and testing. What Kaufmann would experience was not in any way a transplant, not even a temporary; Santoliquido was just going to tune him in on the recorded thought waves of his late uncle and let him swim in them for half a minute.

Kaufmann watched, chilled and apprehensive, as Santoliquido adjusted his scanners and placed cold electrodes against his forehead. The plump man looked somber too; he had already tasted this experience, thought Kaufmann, and obviously it had been no pleasure for him. An amber warning light went on. Santoliquido tugged at a knife-switch.

Mark Kaufmann winced as his uncle came flooding into his brain.

It was a torrent, an avalanche, a cascade. Uncle Paul swept through his synapses with violent impact. A tide of raw sensuality came first; then a sudden stab of gastric pain; then a set of precise, instantaneous, all-encompassing calculations for the purchase, lease-back, and depreciation of a four-square-mile area in Shanghai's northern suburbs. On top of that came an overlay of family scheming, a nest of intricate and poisonous interpretations of taut relationships. In the first ten seconds of contact with his uncle's soul, Kaufmann thought his mind would burn out. In the second ten seconds he struggled for equilibrium like a man caught in rough surf and dashed again and again to the sand. In the third ten seconds he found that equilibrium, gaining purchase of sorts and discovering a strength within himself that he had not suspected. He realized that he could meet his dead uncle as an equal. The old man had the advantage of greater age, but not really of greater force; the Kaufmann genes had traveled from uncle to nephew in a knight's move of inheritance, and for all the unshackled power of Paul's furious mind, Mark knew that he could handle it indefinitely, if he had to.

The contact broke.

Kaufmann's eyes opened. He slipped the electrodes free and put his hands to his temples. Phantom calculations danced through his skull—the old man's arbitrage schemes, realty enterprises, testamentary codicils, percentage plans, all whirled together in a wild dance of dollars.

"Well?" Santoliquido asked. "Do you know your uncle better now?"

"The ruthless old bastard!" Kaufmann said in admiration. "The wonderful pirate! What a tragedy that he's gone!"

"He'll be back."

"Yes. Yes." Kaufmann clutched the arms of the chair. "I'd give anything to have him myself," he said in a low voice. "I'm the one best qualified to have him. Paul and I were a superb team, these last few years. Think how much better we'd be, working together in one mind!"

"I hope you're joking, Mark."

"Not really. Paul and I belong together. I know, I know, it's against the law to transplant a persona to so close a relative."

"Don't forget that your uncle directly requested in his will that he not be transplanted to any member of his own family."

"As though he didn't know about the law," said Kaufmann.

"Or as though he expected that someone like you would circumvent it."

Kaufmann flushed. "But what *are* you going to do with him? Give him to Roditis? Put those two together and they'll steal the universe!"

"Roditis can handle your uncle's persona," said Santoliquido. "He's got the strong personality that's necessary. What we must guard against is giving Paul to someone who'll be overwhelmed. The host must always remain in command. Roditis would."

"But he's got no scruples. He's nothing but an unprincipled buccaneer. And Paul was a principled buccaneer. Bring them into harmony and—"

"No decision has been taken," Santoliquido said brusquely. "Do you wish to inspect the three potential personae your daughter has selected?"

"Yes," Kaufmann murmured. "I might as well."

Santoliquido opened an information line and uttered a request. Moments later three persona caskets clattered out of a delivery slot. Santoliquido inserted Paul Kaufmann's casket in the same slot and sent it on its way back to storage. Then, turning, he said, "All these three young women died violently before the age of thirty. All three were quite beautiful, I understand. Risa had certain very specific anatomical and sexual qualifications, which of course we were able to meet, since the range of available personae is so great. To preserve the privacy of the dead, I'll call these three simply X, Y, and Z. Thirty seconds of each should be enough to gratify your curiosity. Have you ever sampled a female persona before, Mark?"

"You know I've never done anything like that."

"Of course. Of course. Well, it's an amusing novelty. I often think our prejudice against transsexual transplants is foolish. If a man could incorporate at least one female persona, or a woman at least one male one, there'd be far less anguish in this world. But I suppose we're not yet ready for that radical a step. And I suppose few people are really eager to allow their personae to come to life in a body of alien sex. Oh, they'd like to try it for a few days, but as for making it permanent—" As he spoke, Santoliquido was deftly inserting one of Risa's choices into the scanning equipment. Once more the electrodes touched Kaufmann's skull. He felt vaguely uncertain about doing this, but then he reflected that his exhibitionistic daughter would certainly not mind his peeking into her personae, and also that he had already spied on his daughter in many matters nearly as intimate.

The apparatus hummed.

"This is X," said Santoliquido. "Killed last year in a power-ski accident at St. Moritz, age twenty-four."

In the thirty seconds that followed, Mark Kaufmann learned a great many surprising things. He discovered what it was like to have breasts; he sampled the sensations of the penetrated instead of those of the penetrator, he felt the ebb and flow of feminine biology impinge on him; he scented a new perfume of flesh; he experienced the texture of his own smooth female body. He also generated an instant and electric dislike for the personality of the unknown X.

Giving him no pause for evaluation, Santoliquido said, "And now Y. Drowned off Macao last summer, age twenty-eight."

More of the same: the slow throb of the flesh, the lazy tremor of vaginality. In his brief contact with the mind of the dead girl,

Kaufmann ran imaginary hands over silken imaginary thighs, yawned, stretched, yearned for pleasure. This was a more relaxed spirit than X's; in that first persona there had tingled some disturbing undercurrent, some sort of hunger for an unclear vengeance, while in this girl was merely a generalized appetite for gratification, far less intense, far less vivid. Her recorded soul winked and glittered and was gone.

"Z," said Santoliquido. "Twenty-six years old. Pushed or jumped, eighty stories up."

Pushed, Kaufmann decided, after only an instant of contact with Z. This girl had not had the vitality to commit suicide. She was placid, passive, soft within and without. Now that the novelty of peering into female souls had worn off, Kaufmann found himself swiftly bored by this one. She was a void, a hollowness, and the thirty seconds dragged abysmally.

"You may find yourself slightly impotent tonight," Santoliquido was saying. "I suppose I should have warned you. There's a kind of sexual confusion that sets in after you've done some transsexual sampling. But it wears off in a day or so. How did you find it, being female?"

"Interesting. Not very appealing, though."

"Well, of course, these were young, shallow girls. I could find you female personae that would give you a real jolt of character. But the outward manifestations are unusual, aren't they? You never dreamed it was like that, so different, to belong to the other sex?"

"I'm glad to have had the opportunity. I can't say I'm impressed by any of my daughter's choices."

"Which would you prefer her to take? She's going to pick one, you know."

Kaufmann nodded. "Z was nothing but a cow. Risa would be as bored with her company as I was. Y was neutral, good-natured, most likely fun in bed. And X was utterly hateful. Vicious, nasty, selfish, hardly human. Risa wouldn't want a bitch like that in her head. I suppose that Y is the least of the three evils."

"She's going to pick X," said Santoliquido.

"Did she tell you that?"

"She didn't. But X is the obvious one. She's got the right combination for Risa—strength of character and voluptuousness. Why
did you hate her so?"

"I don't know. I can't find any particular reason. Just an absence of sympathy. Looking back, I can't pinpoint any single ugly
thought from her, but yet I know I loathed her."

"A pity," said Santoliquido. "From Tuesday on, she'll be living
in Risa, unless I miss my guess. Do you want to withdraw your
consent for the transplant?"

Kaufmann thought it over. It was within his power to prevent
Risa from taking this persona on; but he saw the futility of the
attempt at once. If thwarted, Risa would merely apply more pressure, and she was an expert at getting her way. He knew he had
to adjust to the changed Risa that would come forth, that it was
idle to try to block and control her.

He waved his hand. "Let her do as she likes. But I hope she'll
take Y."

"Your hope will he disappointed," said Santoliquido. He looked
at his watch. "I'm afraid I must leave you now, Mark. I'll turn
you over to a technician who'll see to it that your new persona
recording gets made right away. That *is* why you came here today, I'm sure you remember."

"Yes," Kaufmann said dryly. "All this spying was only the ap-
petizer. Now for the main course."

Santoliquido produced a young, earnest technician named
Donahy, with black hair so dark it seemed to have purple highlights, and startling, bushy eyebrows slashing across his too white
forehead. Kaufmann bade Santoliquido farewell, thanked him
for his favors, looked forward to his presence on Dominica the
next day.

"If you'll come this way—" said Donahy.

Shortly Kaufmann was out of the storage section of the building and back on familiar ground, in the public area where persona recordings were made. Here there was none of the carefully cultivated gloom of that great central vault. Everything was bright, glowing, radiant; the tiles gleamed, the air had a vibrant tingle. This was the place where one came to purchase one's claim to immortality, and its gaiety mirrored the moods of those wealthy enough and determined enough to preserve their personae for future transplants.

He had been here many times. He had left a trail of recordings stretching back to the youthfully restless, ambitious Mark Kaufmann of twenty. And, he now knew, all those recordings still existed in some remote but accessible archive. A biographer, given the right influence, could trace the unfolding of his development from youth to decisive manhood, stage by stage. Now the latest Mark Kaufmann would be added to the cache. Since he had been neglectful about reporting to be taped, nearly a full year's experiences were to be incorporated in the file now. It had been a more eventful year than usual, marked by his uncle's death, by his own increasingly complex relationship with his daughter, by several turns of his dealings with Elena Volterra, and now—in the final hours of the record—by this quartet of new experiences, his moment of entry into his uncle's persona and the three samplings of female personae. Those most recent events had left their imprint on him most clearly, and they would now become the potential property of the future recipient of his persona.

"Will you lie down here?" Donahy asked.

Kaufmann reclined. The Scheffing process had two phases-record and transplant—and the recording phase was the essence of simplicity. The sum of a human soul—hopes and strivings, rebuffs, triumphs, pains, pleasures— is nothing more than a series of magnetic impulses, some shadowed by noise, others clear and easily accessible. The beautiful Scheffing process provided instant mechanical duplication of that web of magnetic impulses. A spark leaping across a gap, so to speak: the quick flight of a persona from mind to tape. A lifetime's experience transformed into information that can be transcribed, billions of bits to the square millimeter, on magnetic tape; and then, to play safe and provide an extra dimension of realism, the same information translated and inscribed on data flakes as well. There was nothing to it. A transplant, involving the imprinting of all this material on a living human brain, was much more difficult, requiring special chemical preparation of the recipient.

The telemetering devices went into position. Kaufmann looked up into a tangle of gleaming coils and struts. Sensors checked his physical well-being, monitored the flow of blood through the capillaries of his brain, peered through the irises of his eyes, noted his respiration, digestive processes, tactile responses, and vascular dilation.

"You haven't been with us for a while," observed Donahy, making an entry in his dossier.

"No, I haven't. I suppose I've been too busy."

The technician shook his head. "Too busy to preserve your own persona! You must have really been busy, then. You know, you never would forgive yourself if you suddenly woke up as a transplant and found a year-long chunk of your life missing from your package of experience."

"Absolutely right," Kaufmann said. "It's unutterably stupid to neglect this obligation."

"Well, now, at least you'll be up to date again. But we hope you'll come to see us more regularly in the future. Here we go, now—lift your head a little—fine, fine—"

The helmet was in place. Kaufmann waited, seeking as always to determine the precise moment at which his soul leaped from his brain, impressed a replica of itself on the tape, and hurried back into its proper house. But as ever, the moment was imperceptible. His concentration was broken by the voice of the technician, saying, "There we are, Mr. Kaufmann. Your central will be billed, as usual. Thank you for coming, and I hope we have the pleasure of recording you many more times in years to come."

Kaufmann left the building and entered his hopter. According to the ticker, the market had risen sharply; he had profited not a little while wandering within the maze of the Scheffing Institute. And he had fulfilled his obligation to his future recipient by extending the unique and irreplaceable record of his life. Complete with a trifle of Uncle Paul's persona, and minute slices of the lives of three unknown girls.

Within his mind his own resident personae made their presence felt. They reminded him of other duties of this day, still undone. Planning for the party; a realty closing; a conference in Washington. Busy, busy, busy. But at least his conscience was clear for the moment. And tomorrow he could relax.

Chapter 5

The island of Dominica rises like a great many-humped green beast out of the blue Caribbean, well down the chain of the Antilles. Trade winds blow steadily; a tropic sun keeps watch; the lofty mountainous spine intercepts rainfall and keeps the island constantly moist. Here in this still unspoiled island the Kaufmanns had assembled a lordly estate. Industry had come to most of the neighboring isles of the West Indies, but the rain forests of Dominica remained as green and glistening as in primordial times, and in its humid lowlands the banana plantations spread from stream to stream. The arrangement, a quasi-feudal one, did not greatly please the Dominicans, who hungered for the prosperity experienced by Martinique and St. Lucia and Barbados and the rest. But their island was safe from defilement, whether they willed it or not.

The Kaufmann property lay in the northwest quadrant of the island, between Point Round and the thriving town of Portsmouth. There the family had purchased a series of waterfront tracts encompassing not only a majestic crescent arc of white beach, but also a string of the humbler dark beaches of black volcanic sand. Their holdings ran inland, up the rising slope of Morne Diablotin, Dominica's highest mountain, and so they sampled the available environments from the dry shoreline to the riverine interior to the mysterious cloud forest of the mountain. It had taken three generations of haggling and title search to put the estate together, and no one could venture to guess what its true value might be in a world where such tracts no longer could be had at all.

Risa liked to think of it as her own property, due to descend to her in time. In fact that was untrue; the estate belonged communally to the Kaufmann family association. It was administered

on behalf of the family by her father, but that did not put her in
line to inherit it. Each of her many cousins and aunts and uncles
and more distant relatives had a share in the property. But Risa
thought of herself as belonging to the main line of the Kaufmanns,
and since she was her father's only child, she saw herself as the
point of convergence toward which all the family wealth flowed.

It was midday, now: the most dangerous hour under the hostile sun. She stood nude in hip-deep water on the crescent beach,
relaxing before more guests arrived. About a dozen were here
already. Risa and her father had flown down from New York late
the previous night to oversee the preparations for the party. Looking up and don the beach, she eyed the early arrivals. They were
scattered like flotsam on the pink-white sand, sunning, dozing.
Four Kaufmanns, a pair of Lehmans, and a trio of Kinsolvings.
Some of them bare, others-not modest but aware of the esthetics
of ungainliness-covering selected portions of their bodies. Not
one was less than fifteen years her senior. Risa wished her cousins would arrive.

Turning her back to the beach, she waded seaward.

Her body glistened. She had oiled it to protect herself from the
sun. Her eyes were lensed against the salt water. She dug her
toes into the sandy bottom, kicked forward, and began to swim,
cutting a lean swathe through the green, glass-clear water. She
liked the touch of it against her breasts and belly. The sunlight
made sparkling patterns on the ocean floor, five feet below her.
Soon she was past the sandy zone and out above the coral reef
that lay a hundred yards off shore. Gnarled, twisted coral heads
jutted from the bottom. Fish of a thousand hues danced and
played between the stony orange and green slabs. Malevolent
black sea urchins twitched their spines hopefully at her. Risa
sucked air, dived, plucked a sand dollar from the bottom.

In time she lost interest in the reef. When she swam back to
shore, she found that another dozen guests or more had arrived-
among them, finally, someone of her own generation. Her cousin

Rod Loeb stood at the water's edge: eighteen, brawny, tanned, vain. She knew him well and liked him. He wore only a taut red loinstrap. His eyes passed easily over her slender nakedness as she emerged from the water.

"Just get here?" she asked.

"Half an hour ago. There was hopter trouble at the airport and we were delayed. You're looking good. Risa."

"And you. Let's walk."

They strolled through the slapping surf toward a cluster of jagged, metallic-looking rocks piled at the north end of the beach. Risa felt the noon warmth probing her skin for some vulnerable place to singe and blister; but the molecule-thick coating of cream protected her. She reveled in her nudity. She broke into a trot, her small breasts barely swaying. If Elena tried to run like this, Risa thought, she'd hit herself in the face with all that swinging meat.

They reached the rocks, neither of them short of breath. The white turrets of barnacles sprouted on the lower surfaces, licked by the waves. Rod said, "I hear you've had a transplant."

"News travels fast if it's reached Majorca already."

"Gossip moves at the speed of light in this family. Is it true?"

"Partly. I've applied for one. Mark gave his consent a few days ago. I went to the soul bank and tried a few personae out, and on Tuesday I'll have the transplant."

"Who'll it be?'

"I'm not sure yet. I'm deciding between some different types. Whichever it is, it'll be a girl who died young and sexy. Maybe even someone you've slept with."

Rod laughed. "Is that incest? If you pick up a persona with a memory of having been to bed with me, I mean?'

"I don't know. I don't care- Is there anything so special about going to bed with you?"

"Try me and see," Rod said. "Without filtering it through a transplant."

She eyed his loinstrap. "Right out here on the beach, or should we go to your cottage?"

"Why not right here?" he asked.

"All right," said Risa. She stretched out on a flat palm of stone, flexed her knees, drew her legs apart. Anyone on the beach could see them from here. She propped her fist against her chin. "Go ahead," she said. "I'm waiting."

"I almost think you're serious," Rod said.

"I sin. And you are too, aren't you? That strap doesn't hide much. You want me. You've been hinting about it long enough. So here's your chance. Get on top of me."

His eyes sparkled maliciously. "I wouldn't take advantage of a child."

"Monster! I'm past sixteen."

"Chronologically. But only a child would want to put on a sick exhibition like that in front of everybody. It's tasteless, Risa. If you really want to have sex with me, get up and we'll go somewhere private and I'll oblige you. But just to show everyone that you're old enough to sin a little—"

"Would I be the first to make love at one of these parties?"

"Stop it," he said. He swung himself down beside her and lightly slapped the outside of her left thigh. "Can I change the subject? What do you know about Uncle Paul's transplant? Who's going to get him?"

Disgruntled by his casual disregard of her wanton mood, Risa closed her thighs and said, "How should I know?"

"The story I hear is that he's going to go to John Roditis."

"Not if my father has anything to say about it"

"That would be a blow, wouldn't it?" Rod said. "Roditis is big enough as he is. With Uncle Paul, he'd be a titan. He'd have the business mind of the century."

Risa yawned. She swiveled around, dipping her toes in the water. A gray ghostly crab scuffled along the sand and vanished, digging down with startling swiftness. Risa said, "My father doesn't want Roditis to have Uncle Paul. My father's a good friend of Santoliquido, and Santoliquido decides. See?"

Rod nodded. "You make it sound very open and shut."

"It has to be. Why, if Roditis got Uncle Paul, he'd be able to come to our family gatherings, he'd have a wedge right into our whole group. Wouldn't that be horrible? That nasty, aggressive little man sitting right there on the beach, sipping a drink, making us be polite to him for Uncle Paul's sake? But it won't happen."

"Perhaps. Perhaps not."

"It won't."

"If it isn't going to happen," Rod said, "what's Roditis' private secretary doing here?"

"*Where?*"

"Look," Rod said, pointing.

Risa peered back and saw a group of new arrivals descending to the beach from the cabanas. Leading the way came Elena Volterra, wearing next to nothing, her oiled body agleam, fusion nodes glistening in her skin, her heavy breasts artfully cantilevered into position by a wisp of sprayon support. Beside her, pink and fleshy, walked Francesco Santoliquido. A pace behind them came an attractive couple whom Risa recognized as David and Gloria Loeb, and on Gloria's right was a very tall, very thin, extremely pale and fair-haired man who indeed closely resembled Charles Noyes, a well-known associate of John Roditis.

His appearance on the beach was exciting comment from many quarters. Heads were turning; whispers buzzed. Noyes himself looked ill at ease. He was thickly lathered to protect his skin from the sun, but even so he continually wrinkled his back as if to make sure he was suffering no harm.

"What could *he* be doing here?" Risa muttered.

"Maybe Roditis is here too," said Rod. "Having a little discussion with your father in the main house."

"No. No." Risa looked for Mark Kaufmann and failed to see

him. This was impossible, she told herself. Then she recalled: "Noyes is Gloria's brother. He must have just come along for the ride. This doesn't have a thing to do with Roditis."

"Let's hope you're right. But it seems odd, having a Roditis man right in our midst. Like Death at the feast."

"I want to go over and find out more?"

"Go ahead," Rod said. "I'm going swimming. I'll get all the gossip from you later."

He sprang from the rocks and hit the water in mid- stroke, heading outward toward the reef. Risa, disturbed, crossed diagonally to the new little group standing on the sandy crest of the beach at the midpoint of the crescent. She greeted Elena curtly and took Santoliquido's hand. She smiled at David Loeb, a tall, courtly-looking man of about forty-five to whom she was related in some incomprehensible way, and embraced his lean, leggy blonde wife Gloria. Risa had never known either of them very well. Gloria looked tense and somehow irritated; but she turned smoothly and said, "Risa, I don't think you know my brother. Charles Noyes. Risa Kaufmann. Mark's daughter."

"A pleasure," Noyes said. It didn't sound to Risa as though he meant it. His large blue eyes raced in all directions, as if trying to avoid any direct confrontation of her girlish nakedness; then, with an obvious effort, he smiled at her.

"I've heard so much about you from Gloria," Risa lied sweetly. "It must be so exciting to work with Mr. Roditis. Tell me, is he coming to our party too?"

"No, he-ah—won't be here," Noyes said.

"Pity. I'd love to meet him. Will you excuse me?" Risa grinned icily and went jogging across the hot sand, up onto the lawn and into the main house, where the servants were programing the buffet lunch. She looked for her father and found him, as she expected, in the bamboo- paneled study, on the telephone. She could not see the face in the screen. He hung up after a moment and looked at her.

"Do you know who's here?" she asked.

She could tell from his sour, hooded expression that he did. "Yes. Gloria's little surprise package. She should have had better taste than that!"

"Why'd you let him in?"

"He's her guest. I can't refuse him, even if he is Roditis' right hand. It's permissible to bring one's brother to a party like this."

"But what does he want here? Spying for Roditis? Trying to soften us up?"

Kaufmann relaxed and allowed himself to laugh. "Why are you so worked up over it, Risa? It's my problem. You go out in the sun and have a good time."

"If I'm a Kaufmann, it's my problem too. We have certain family standards to uphold!"

"They'll be upheld, love. I'll deal with Mr. Noyes."

It was a dismissal. Mark still refused to accept her as an adult. He was patting her on the head and telling her to run off and play. Risa's nostrils flared, but she kept her anger unvoiced and quickly left the building, narrowly avoiding tripping over a robot crawler that was polishing the patio floor.

Hands on hips, she stood at the edge of the patio, looking down at the guests. Rod had emerged from the water and was talking to Noyes and the Loebs. Santoliquido and Elena, oddly, were off by themselves near the rocks where Risa had tried to seduce her cousin with so little success. Overhead, three huge brown pelicans wheeled and folded their wings, plummeting into the water to snatch up fish; they had been treated with adrenergic drugs, Risa knew, so they'd stay hungry all afternoon and stage a good show for the guests. Suddenly furious, Risa whirled and ran toward the small cottage, one of thirty behind the main house, where she was staying on this visit. She flung herself down on the bed, sobbing sulkily.

Minutes later the doorscreen announced a visitor. She looked up and saw Rod's image.

"Come in," she called.

The door slid open. He stepped in, sticking his feet into the vibrator to rid them of sand. "I've got the word on Noyes," he said. "He's not here on account of Roditis. He happened to drop in on Gloria and Dave just as they were leaving for the party, and they couldn't get rid of him, so Gloria had to say, sure, get in the hopter with us, and here he is. Your father must be burning."

"I'm not concerned with my father's feelings just now," Risa said thinly. "Or with Noyes. Or with Roditis. They can all go to hell."

"Hey—"

Tears ebbed from her eyes. "And you can go there with them!"

"What's wrong? What did I do?"

"It's what you didn't do," Risa said.

Rod stared at her strangely. His eyes traveled the length of her body as though he had never seen her before. Risa trembled expectantly. It was almost time for lunch. But first—

His eyes met hers. Her gaze was steady. He nodded.

He stepped toward the bed.

Noyes thought his brain would melt under that hellish sun. He recited mantras of self-possession and liberation, dug his toes into the scorching sand, watched the nude and near-nude Kaufmanns, their friends, and relatives, flit by, and wished fervently that he were almost anywhere else. It was bad enough that Roditis had pitchforked him into this gathering where he was so little wanted; he also had to tolerate tropical heat, and that was beyond the call of duty. Would the protective cream really protect him? Or would he be parboiled by nightfall?

He felt Kravchenko's jeers.

—Take it like a man, friend.

"Very amusing. But you won't feel the sunburn."

—That's part of the business of being dead. You don't feel the pain, you don't feel the pleasure either. Say, say, say, what's

Santoliquido up to?

Noyes looked down the beach. He hadn't noticed it, but his persona had; Santoliquido was deep in conversation with Elena Volterra. And Elena was known to be Mark Kaufmann's mistress. In the midst of his discomfort Noyes analyzed this situation in terms of Roditis' needs. Was Elena at this moment doing a hatchet job on Roditis, filling the soul bank administrator's receptive mind with reasons why the Paul Kaufmann persona should not go to him? Or, contrariwise, was Santoliquido attempting to bring Elena into his orbit while Mark was elsewhere? The first possibility held no promise of leverage, but the second did.

Trying to seem casual about it, Noyes edged toward the distant pair. That Elena was certainly a splendid woman, he thought: all that tawny flesh, so well tanned, so opulent, so nicely displayed. He suspected that Elena might easily look sloppy with her breasts unbound, and that if she gained another five pounds her ampleness would turn to grossness. But as she was, she was quite attractive. And Santoliquido's sensual tastes, Noyes realized, inclined toward women of Elena's sort, Latin and statuesque. It would be quite useful to Roditis' cause if Santo worked himself into some kind of compromising position with Elena this weekend.

He got no closer than a hundred yards—still beyond lip-reading range. Then a robot carrying trays of refreshments rolled across his path, and, as he turned to help himself, Noyes was intercepted by a short, gushing woman with golden eyes and an aggressively jutting chin. "Charles," she said. "I haven't seen you in a thousand years. Come meet my new husband!"

He sorted through foggy family memories. She was an Adams, yes, that was clear, and she had attended his sister's wedding to David Loeb, and he remembered dimly that she had been married for a while to one of the Schiffs. He smiled uncertainly.

"You don't remember me?" she asked.

"It's been a long time—Donna, Donna Adams, is it?"

"Donna's my sister. I'm Rowena. How could you forget a name like that? You should take your memory drugs more often, Charles. I don't believe I'll ever forget the way you carried on at Gloria's wedding! You—"

"I didn't catch your mated name now," Noyes cut in quickly.

"Owens. Yes, you were going to meet my husband. Nathaniel Owens. He's right over here. A most extraordinary man. Can you imagine it, Charles, he carries seven personae! *Seven!*"

But he doesn't carry them very well, Noyes decided a moment later, when he had been introduced to Nathaniel Owens. Owens was burly and barrel-chested, flaunting a thick mat of body hair as though perversely proud of its ugly coarseness, and his square, harsh-planed face looked as though it had been constructed from random components. He was about sixty, Noyes guessed. His eyes were black and not quite focused, and when he spoke his voice soared confusingly through an octave or more before settling on its pitch.

"My wife been telling you a lot of nonsense about us?" Owens demanded truculently.

"Not at all. She simply said you're carrying seven personae."

Owens blinked and twitched. "Damned right I am! You see anything wrong with that?"

"If you can handle the strain—"

"He can handle anything, chum," Owens said in a strangely altered voice, a basso growl. "He's the original *übermensch*. You just have to ask and he'll tell you."

Noyes was still attempting to understand why Owens had suddenly spoken of himself in the third person when Owens blurted in a much higher voice, "Shut your goddam mouth!"

"It's your goddam mouth I'm talking through," came the deeper voice.

"*Our* mouth, you sniveling idiot!" It was a third voice, bland, silky. "We're all in this cage together!"

Noyes realized, stunned, that Owens' personae had seized control of the man and were carrying on an argument through his vocal apparatus. Owens himself stood stupefied, long arms dangling at his sides, shoulders lifting and hitching in oddly automatic motions. His eyes rolled. His wife, seeing what had happened, grabbed a drink from a roboservitor's tray and plunged it, dagger- fashion, against Owens' thick-muscled arm. His twisting facial muscles subsided. He looked abashed.

"Nathaniel hasn't had much sleep lately," Rowena Owens explained to the little group that had gathered. "Sometimes he finds it difficult to exert the proper authority when he's tired. Feeling better now, darling?"

"I'm all right, yes," Owens said. "I'm in full command again." His voice was neutral; he had ceased to twitch.

Noyes stared, stricken with horror. It seemed to him that he saw his own fate mirrored in Owens' eyes. The man's personae had for the moment ejected him from control of his body and had transformed him into a prisoner in his own skull, assailed by dybbuks. Just as James Kravchenko ceaselessly attempted to do to him. Kravchenko had not yet succeeded even in grabbing the power of vocalization; when he spoke, it was still only an Inward murmur. But he was trying all the while. It did not soothe Noyes to reflect that he had merely the problem of keeping one persona under control, while Owens wrestled with a whole team of them.

Owens took Noyes' shocked silence for disapproval, evidently. He said with belligerence, "What's the matter? Don't you believe in Scheffing transplant?"

"Well, I—"

"I know. You're one of the Erasure people. You feel it's all an evil, sinister manifestation of cultural decay, and you want all the personae rubbed out. Right? And here I stand with seven of them under my roof, and to you I'm the embodiment of Satan. Right? Right?"

"It isn't that way at all," Noyes murmured.

"As a matter of fact, my brother isn't part of the Erasure group in the least. Are you, Charles?" Gloria had appeared from somewhere and now stood at Owens' elbow, looking fair and lovely, as much a willowy girl as she had been on her wedding day.

"Of course not," Noyes managed to say. "I've got a persona myself, you know. What gives you the idea I'm against transplant?"

Owens looked mollified. "I suppose I leaped to the conclusion. You know, there are so many of me that I tend to make snap judgments. We assess the evidence as a team, and sometimes we assess it too fast." He thrust out his hand. "Who are you, anyway?"

"Charles Noyes. I'm with Roditis Securities."

"Oh. Yes. Sure." The hand enfolded his. Just as contact was made, Owens twitched again, and a kind of convulsion ran the length of his arm, forcing him to pull his hand back. Noyes watched uncomfortably as the spasm traveled down the entire right side of Owens' body.

Gloria said quickly, "Charles is also an authority on Buddhist reincarnation theory. He and Mr. Roditis have just returned from a pilgrimage to the lamasery in San Francisco. He—"

"You believe in that crap?" Owens asked.

Noyes faltered, astonished by the hairy man's capacity for starting trouble. Rowena Owens bit her lip. As quietly as he could, Noyes said, "I think the teachings form a valuable guide to existence in a world where reincarnation is a practical fact. We must know the art of dying if we're to master the art of living."

"I say it's crap," Owens repeated loudly. "It's an artificial movement grafted onto a materialistic society for reasons of guilt. Those of us who take part in the transplant program are set apart from ordinary humanity, from the clods, if you like, and because in effect we've become immortal we need to console ourselves with a new religion. So we've borrowed this prayer-wheel garbage from the Himalayas, only we've turned it upside down, since in its original form it's inapplicable to our society. It—"

"You sound a little like Mr. Roditis now," Noyes began. "He—"

"Let me finish! The whole idea of the Buddhists is to break the chain of incarnations and go off to nirvana, isn't it? Born no more? And our whole idea is to grab as many incarnations as possible, down through the centuries. For us, good karma leads to rebirth. Is that Buddhism? That's a perversion of Buddhism! I know. I've got a guru right here inside me, one of the best, a real theologian. Murtaugh, from the Baltimore group. You know of him?"

Awed, Noyes said, "Why, of course. He wrote *The Art of Right Dying.*"

"And he died right himself, and I got him! So you better not argue theology with me. I've got it straight from the source, Noyes. *Om mani padme hum.* And I know how cynical the entire movement is. I've got collective karma." Owens twitched again. He was losing control once more. "I tell you, only a tired persona wants off the wheel of sangsara. The rest of us hunger to go round and round and round again. We—" A scabrous obscenity slipped from Owens' lips. He paused, astonished, and hammered his fist against his left cheekbone. He trembled.

It was sickening to watch him being pulled apart this way.

Recovering, Owens. said, "Sometimes it's difficult to hang on to the reins."

"Why did you set such a challenge for yourself?" Noyes asked. "Seven transplants—"

"Actually, only four transplants," Owens said. "Murtaugh's persona brought two transplants of his own along, and one of my others already had one. Three hitchhikers, four transplants. Quite a crowd. Quite. A. Crowd."

Noyes understood. Such hitchhikers were known as secondary personae: those that existed as part of the recording of someone subsequently transplanted to another person. The problem of the secondary personae was becoming acute, now that the Scheffing process was more than a generation old. Everyone who carried a persona in addition to his own now handed it on when he was recorded, and some of these crowded minds were being picked up by recipients. In another few years, virtually every transplant would bring the recipient two or three secondary personae for each primary one. Then every transplant would create a babbling mob within the brain, even though the secondary personae were much less vivid than primaries.

There were ways around it, Noyes knew. The simplest was to accept as a transplant only a persona with no secondaries attached, as he had done. Kravchenko had not gone in for the Scheffing process until quite recently, and the recording of him that had been on file at his death had been made before the transplant, so it included no trace of Kravchenko's inherited persona. But of course that method soon would be impossible, since everyone took a transplant young these days, and incorporated the persona in his earliest records.

Another way was to have any secondaries deleted from the persona before adopting it. The erased secondaries thus went back into the soul bank and could be rerecorded as primaries for new recipients. Noyes preferred that idea. However, personae meant prestige, and multiple personae meant multiple prestige. People nowadays seemed to want to clutter their minds. When one took on a transplant, one desired to take that persona's whole package of secondaries, thus getting the full benefit of the transplanted soul in all its complexity.

Which was fine if one could handle it, Noyes thought. But it would be instructive for each potential transplantee to spend five minutes with Nathaniel Owens and find out what it was like to be too greedy.

"—it might be better if none of this transplanting business had ever begun," David Loeb was saying. "And no, I don't believe in erasure either. I've got my personae too. But still—"

"It's our salvation. It's our hope of immortality." That was Owens, speaking in one of his milder voices. "I've recorded myself with this entire tribe of passengers, and I look forward to my next turn on the cycle, in another body, when—"

"Nat! Your arm!" Rowena yelped.

As he spoke, his left arm had reached out in seeming independence of his body to seize Gloria Loeb's thigh. Gloria winced as the stubby fingers dug in. Owens blurted something apologetic, but did not let go. David Loeb and Noyes went to the rescue simultaneously; Noyes grasped Owens' wrist, and his brother-in-law pried at Owens' fingers. The hand came away. Purpling blotches appeared on Gloria's pale flesh.

Owens did not seem to comprehend what he had done. There was a long moment of silence while this group of well-bred people struggled to find a well-bred way of covering the gaffe. Owens solved the problem himself. He said hoarsely, "I think I better go swimming now. Work off this charge of energy and get everything in order."

He ran down toward the water, a lumbering, clumsily powerful figure, stumbling once as some subsidiary persona fought him for control even while he ran. But he managed to hit the water in a smooth dive. Head down, arms pinwheeling, he swam like a torpedo out to the reef.

Noyes closed his eyes. The sun suddenly seemed immense over his head, a great molten ball, dripping flame. Within him Kravchenko sounded his silent mocking laughter.

—Take a good look, Charlie. That's what I'm going to do to you one of these days. I don't need six pals to push you aside. I'll do it myself.

Noyes turned away from the others. In order to speak directly to Kravchenko he had to vocalize his words, and he did not want anyone aware that he was talking to himself. He murmured, "You won't get away with it. The instant you start trouble I'll kill both of us, Kravchenko."

—Ah. The carniphage threat again. Where's the flask, Charlie? In your swimsuit?

"Let me alone."

—Why don't we go over and talk to Elena? *There's* a woman! You're hungry for her, and I'll sit back and watch. I knew her when I was carnate. She wasn't Kaufmann's mistress then. Elena and I can reminisce. Put me in control, Charlie, and I'll seduce her for you.

"Stop it!"

—That would be a good deal for both of us. I'll make Elena, and your body will enjoy the fun.

Noyes shivered. Instead of threatening, Kravchenko now sought to tempt; but the goal was the same. It might happen at any time: the persona winning command of the shared body, even a countererasure that would wipe Noyes out entirely and leave Kravchenko in undisputed possession, a dybbuk. That was the true rebirth: to take over your host, to have a body of your own again, to walk in the world, freely sampling the sensory intake. Noyes was determined not to have Kravchenko victimize him in that way.

The sun was turning into a flask of carniphage.

Reach up, Noyes thought. Grab it, bite on it. Show him a thing or two.

Trails of sweat ran down his body. He felt his skin puckering and blistering, his bones beginning to melt into rubber. People looked at him worriedly as he swayed. Smiling, bowing, Noyes grinned at his sister, at Elena, at Rowena Owens. I'm all right. Perfectly all right. Maybe a touch of the sun, but nothing serious, quite all right, no need for fear.

Someone screamed.

Noyes thought at first that they were screaming about him, that in his weakened state he had collapsed or split apart or melted or seized the sun. But no, he was still on his feet, and no one was looking at him. They were all pointing toward the water. With colossal effort he swung himself around to see what the matter was.

"He's out of control !" Rowena Owens cried. "Help him, somebody, help him!"

Noyes saw that Nathaniel Owens had reached the reef, swimming to that patch of brownish coral a hundred yards off shore that lay just beneath the surface and broke it to jut up in several places. And there, the warring, incompatible personae within him had rebelled. Now Owens thrashed and leaped about on the reef like a hooked tarpon, flying from the water, smashing down on the razor-keen coral, kicking his legs in the air, vanishing from sight for a moment,, then erupting again to crash into another part of the reef. Already long red gashes streaked his skin. Again and again he flung himself at the reef, now mounting one strip of it and doing a wild, frenzied dance along its upper rim.

"He'll cut himself to bits," David Loeb said.

"And the blood in the water-there'll be sharks soon," Santoliquido observed.

Within Noyes, Kravchenko laughed.

—See? See? Just wait!

"No," Noyes whispered. "You'll never do that to me!"

Risa Kaufmann broke from the group. She had been standing silently by, visibly disturbed by Owens' irrational behavior, and now, a tanned nude streak, she ran lithely across the beach, entered the water, and sped toward the reef, swimming nearly submerged, now breaking the water with a kicking ankle, now with an upturned buttock, now a shoulderblade. She reached Owens. He stood upright in water only a few feet deep, readying himself for another lunatic dash against the reef. Deep-hued blood welled steadily through the coarse mat of hair on his body. Risa clambered up beside him, caught him, spun him around, gripped him tightly. The contact of her bell-like little breasts against his hairy fleshiness seemed revolting. But, with brisk efficiency, the girl propelled the dazed, bleeding man away from the coral knives of the reef and drew him into the clear green water closer to shore. He was safe. A cheer went up.

In that same instant Noyes felt the heavens explode and the sun fall at his feet. He snatched it up and devoured it, and as the hallucination overwhelmed him he plunged to the ground, jerking and yammering, seized by an uncontrollable attack. The world grew dark. His limbs lashed the ground. Kravchenko howled in pleasure.

He felt warmth against him. Tender female flesh.

"Easy, easy, easy. You'll be all right." ·

Elena Volterra was cradling him. He pillowed his head against the ripe, lush mounds of her breasts and sobbed.

"Give him air," a voice said.

Noyes closed and opened his eyes several times. He clung to Elena desperately. "My name's Kravchenko," he said. "James Kravchenko."

"Kravchenko is dead," Elena told him. "You're Charles Noyes."

"Yes. Yes. Charles Noyes. Kravchenko's dead."

"Rest now," Elena whispered. "Easy, easy, easy."

"Rest. I am Charles Noyes. Yes."

"You'll feel better in a little while."

A cool ultrasonic snout touched his arm. Not a drink but an anesthetic, Noyes realized. He saw the Buddha-Heruka, with three heads, six hands, and four feet firmly postured, the right face being white, the left red, the central dark-brown; the body emitting flames of radiance; the nine eyes widely opened; the eyebrows quivering like lightning; the protruding teeth glistening and set over one another. "I am Charles Noyes," Noyes said.

—Give Elena a great big kiss for me.

Noyes' eyes closed. He felt no more pain.

Chapter 6

It was Tuesday morning. Risa entered Francesco Santoliquido's office and stood just within the door. He was busy, using a data machine with his left hand while tapping out computer instructions with his right.

At length he looked up and said, "There she is. Our little heroine. Come in, come in, sit down."

"You got a good tan this weekend," Risa observed.

"There's nothing like the tropical sun. It was a splendid party, Risa. My congratulations to you and your father. Of course, there were some unusual events—"

"They've taken Owens to the therapy satellite. He'll be there a month, floating in nullgrav until he's healthy."

Santoliquido scowled. "Sad, very sad. But nullgrav's not the therapy for him. He's a candidate for erasure."

"I didn't think you used that word here!"

"I'm not speaking in the political sense," said Santoliquido. "Strictly the medical. That man's got more than he can handle under his skull."

"Much more." Risa was flattered that busy Santoliquido would take the time to discuss Owens' problems with her. It was a tacit recognition that she was now an adult. She said, "Is there any provision in the law for mandatory erasure?"

"Well, yes, when the presence of the persona threatens the security and integrity of the host."

"Certainly that's true here."

Santoliquido's eyes twinkled. "But Nat Owens has influence. I'd hesitate to ship him off for erasure against his will. We'll see how he feels when he gets back from his float. Possibly we can get him to give up two or three of the least compatible personae, the ones at war with one another."

Solemnly Risa said, "That would be best. It was scary, out on the reef. Big strips of skin hanging loose on him, and he didn't even seem to know what he was doing, just hurling himself against that sharp coral again and again."

"It was brave of you to rescue him."

She giggled. "I didn't stop to think. Maybe if I had, I wouldn't have done anything. But it just seemed like the right thing to do. I mean, I knew I could get out there and pull him away from the reef, and so I went and did it, and then there was time to be nervous afterward. Especially when I came ashore and found the other man having a fit too, Charles Noyes—"

"It was a wild moment," Santoliquido agreed. "Noyes has been in stasis these last two days, hasn't he?"

"I think they let him out. He's calm again."

"Tell me, Risa. Now that you've seen two men run wild at once, because they found their transplants too difficult to control, have you changed your mind at all about your own transplant?"

"Of course not," she said instantly. "Oh, I admit I've been a little uneasy, but I wouldn't be here unless I meant to go through with it. What happened to them isn't any concern of mine. Owens was asking for trouble when he took on that mob of personae. And Noyes is an unstable character, they tell me. I'm ready."

"Good girl." Santoliquido pressed a buzzer. "We'll get going, then. You've chosen the persona you want?"

"Yes."

"Tandy Cushing?"

"How did you know that?"

"I knew," said Santoliquido. "Ask your father. I predicted the choice you'd make." He opened his desk, came through it, took her by the hand, and lifted her to her feet. "I won't be seeing you again as you are now, Risa. You'll leave my office as Risa Kaufmann, but the next time we meet, you'll be Risa plus Tandy. I hope you find it an enriching experience."

"I know I will," she said.

Her lips brushed his. She liked him; he was so much like a jolly uncle to her. Though of course she knew it was a mistake to take a patronizing attitude toward a man as powerful as Francesco Santoliquido. He was so kind to her only because she was Mark Kaufmann's daughter, and it was rash to forget it.

A black-smocked technician appeared at the office door. "This way, please, Miss Kaufmann."

She waved goodby to Santoliquido.

Here we go, she thought. Hello, Tandy Cushing!

She followed the technician toward the transplant room. It was a long trip, spanning many levels of the building, and tension grew within her as the moment drew near. She eased her fears by studying the technician. He was young, hardly any older than her cousin Rod, and he seemed plainly in awe of her. It was his job to deal with the rich and mighty, to pump new personae into their receptive brains, but Risa suspected that he himself left this palace of wonders each night to return to some dismal little hovel, full of cockroaches and squalling babies, where he waited tensely for the next day's excursion into fantasy. How brutal it must be to live in the real world, she thought, earning perhaps a thousand dollars fissionable a month, never able to afford anything, and faced with the terrible knowledge that after death comes ...nothing!

"We go in here," said the technician.

"What's your name?" Risa asked.

"Leonards, Miss Kaufmann."

"Is that a first name or a last?"

"Last."

Last. No doubt he had a first name too, but wasn't supposed to give it. He was merely a piece of walking equipment. Leonards. He was good-looking, in his own worried way, too pale, pinch lines already forming between his eyebrows, but tall and sturdily built. Are you married yet, Leonards? Where do you live? What are your dreams and ambitions? Isn't it frustrating for you to work in the soul bank and never have any hope of receiving a transplant yourself, or of being recorded? Wouldn't you like enough money so you could put your persona on file, Leonards? Suppose I had your account credited with half a million dollars fissionable. Would that be enough? I'd never miss it. I'd tell Mark I gave it to charity. Your life would be altogether different. Or how would you like to meet me when this is over, Leonards, and go to bed with me? Would that please you, sleeping with a Kaufmann? I'm good, too. Ask Rod Loeb. Ask a lot of people. I'm young, but I learn fast.

Together they entered the booth.

She kept her face rigid, masklike, hiding her thoughts from the young man. It would never do for him to know what she had been thinking. He might get upset and bungle the transplant somehow. Let him stay calm and cool at least until the work is done. Afterwards, maybe, I'll have a little fun with him.

The transplant room was a rectangular cubicle, perhaps nine feet by twelve, warm, well lit. It had windows along two walls, one facing the outer corridor, one looking into an inner access room that was part of the spine of the building. Risa saw a couch, a computer terminal, and a cluster of gleaming equipment.

Opaquing the hall window, Leonards said, "Please lie down. Make yourself comfortable."

"Shall I remove my clothing?" Risa asked.

Her hands went to the discard stud. Leonards' facial muscles rippled in shock at the mere suggestion that she was willing to disrobe before him, and it was a moment before he recovered his poise and said, "That won't be necessary. Kick off your shoes, if you like."

She stretched out, shoeless. Leonards grasped a bronze knob and a mass of equipment swung free of the wall. He drew it toward her. "This is a diagnostat," he told her. "We simply wish to check your physical condition before we proceed with the transplant. It's important that your health and body tone be at the top of their cycle. This part just takes a minute—there." The diagnostat hummed and clicked and was silent. Leonards pressed an eject stud. A copper-colored capsule dropped out, and he flipped it into a transfer hatch that would take it to some scanning instrument within the building's computer bank. He looked more nervous than she was. After a moment a light went on in the access room, and through a slot in the wall came a yellow slip. Risa craned her neck but could not see what it said.

"You're in fine shape," Leonards reported. "Where did you get those skin abrasions, though?"

"In the West Indies on Saturday. A man was in trouble on a coral reef and I pulled him free and got cut up a little. They're healing fast."

"In any case, there's no effect on your receptivity to the transplant. Now, I suppose you're familiar with the Scheffing process, but I know you want to keep up with me on each phase of the transplant, so I'm likely to tell you a few things you already know. For example, the first step is the drug treatment, to enhance your memory receptivity. We inject a nucleic acid booster, coupled with one of the mnemonic drugs. A mnemonic drug—"

"Am I getting picrotoxin or one of the pentylenctetrazol derivatives?" Risa asked.

Leonards looked shaken. "You've been doing some homework!"

"Which do I get?"

"It'll be the pentylene," he said. "We get better response curves on it with women under thirty. Picrotoxin blocks presynaptic inhibition, and some of the others block postsynaptic inhibition, but pentylenetetrazol doesn't interfere with either. It excites the nervous system by decreasing neuronal recovery time, without reference to inhibitory pathways. Thus it prevents memory decay and significantly increases the response latencies. Still following me?"

"Yes," Risa lied. She was damned if she'd let his deliberately accelerated flow of gibberish upset her. "The result is to make me more receptive to the imprint from the recording. All right. I'm ready whenever you are."

He produced a thick, stubby, phallic-looking ultrasonic injector. While he fumbled with the dial settings Risa casually disengaged her tunic, baring the lower part of her body to the groin. Leonards was slow to notice, but when he finally looked at her he was so rattled he nearly dropped the injector.

Staring rigidly at her chin, he said, "Why did you uncover yourself?"

"I understood that the injection was given in the upper part of the thigh."

"No."

"In the backside, then?" She grinned kittenishly and rolled over.

"The arm will do."

She pouted. "Well, all right."

He was sweating and flushed. She figured she had paid him back well enough for that burst of postsynaptic inhibitions and response latencies. Chastely she covered herself again, not wanting him to jab the injector into the wrong place while he was so shaken. He took a deep breath and put the snout to her arm. There was an ultrasonic whirr.

"We allow one hour for the nucleic acid booster to reach the brain. By then the mnemonic drug will have already taken effect. I'll leave you to relax until the next phase can begin. Perhaps you'd like to look through this information leaflet."

He made his escape from the transplant room, looking visibly relieved.

Risa sprawled on the couch and examined the booklet.

SOME FACTS ABOUT THE SCHEFFING PROCESS, it was headed. She glanced through it without interest. It told her things she already knew: how her brain was prepared for the persona to come, how the recordings were made, how transplants were effected. Toward the back was some material of more direct importance: tips on making the transition after your first transplant.

You will have complete access to the memories and life experiences of your imprinted persona, the booklet told her. As with your own memories, some of the experiences you receive will be blurred or distorted and not immediately retrievable. During the period of adjustment you may feel occasional confusions of identity, particularly if the new persona was noted for strength of character in its previous carnate existence. THIS SHOULD NOT BE CAUSE FOR ALARM. After a few days you will establish a satisfactory working relationship with the persona. Your new companion will enhance and support your responses to your environment. You will have the advantage of extra perspective and an additional set of life experiences on which to base your judgments. Think of the persona as a guest, a friend, a partner. It is the most intimate possible human relationship, and represents the finest accomplishment of our era.

A few pages on, Risa found information on how to communicate directly with the persona. At any time, she could simply reach into the pool of experience and memory that was being transplanted to her brain, and haul out whatever was useful to her immediate situation. But if she-wanted to speak to the persona, to address her as an individual, she would have to talk out loud. At least at first, though the booklet said it was possible after a while to talk to the persona via the interior neural channels. Meanwhile the persona, having no other communication access, was able to key herself right into the brain and make her thoughts known.

Did a persona have thoughts, Risa wondered?

A persona was nothing but a set of memories. It didn't have real existence. You couldn't see a persona, any more than you could see an abstract concept. And the persona was dead, a closed account with all totals drawn. How could a transplanted persona think and react and have things to say?

Judging by the behavior of adults she had observed, a persona was not dead at all—merely suspended from the time of record-ing to the time of transplant. Then, jacked into the nervous sys-tem of its host, it could perceive and respond as if literally rein-carnated. That was the whole point of the Scheffing process. It assured the participants everlasting life, with occasional inter-ruptions between transplants. At the same time it provided the living with the benefit of the experiences of the dead. Nothing was lost, except the souls of the poor fish like Leonards who never took part in the rebirth game at all. That was ninety per-cent of mankind, at present. But did they matter?

As her final hour of independence ticked away, Risa inevitably began to wonder if she really wanted to go through with this enterprise.

No doubt everyone wonders about that, waiting for it to begin, she told herself. At least the first time.

And of course it would be eerie, carting about someone else's soul in her head. Risa was accustomed to privacy when she wanted it. An only child, wealthy enough to isolate herself from the world, never called upon to share anything with anyone-and now she'd have to make room in her head for Tandy Cushing. Strange, strange, strange! Yet appealing, too. She had been alone so long. In a world where everyone she knew carried two or three personae, Risa felt pallid and childlike in her solitude. Now she would be like the others. In one bound she'd shed the last vestiges of immaturity. Merely sleeping around hadn't brought her far enough into the adult world, but this transplant would, especially with worldly, sophisticated Tandy Cushing like an older sister inside her mind.

As the booklet pointed out, it was irrational to fear or mistrust the persona. The persona wasn't going to get any charge out of snooping on you, any more than you could snoop on yourself The persona would be you, and herself as well, a joined identity. Risa's mind whirled a little at that concept. She thought she un-derstood it, but of course she knew she did not, could not. No one who did not have a persona already transplanted could really comprehend what it was like. This was a new thing in the world, a fundamental break with the human condition. No longer were people walled up alone in their own skulls. They could have company.

What if she didn't care for Tandy Cushing's company?

Cast her out like a demon. That could be done, for a price. Her own father had had a persona erased when he was young. Of course, a lot of people preferred to suffer along with their personae even when incompatibility was obvious. Just the way, Risa thought, people will stick with a hopeless marriage, or fight to prevent the amputation of a diseased limb, purely because they can't bring themselves to give up anything that has been part of themselves, no matter how much harm it's doing them.

Look at that Owens man, for example. Driven twitchy by all his personae, and yet he brags about them.

Or Charles Noyes. Right there on the beach, he had almost been engulfed and ejected by his own persona. Why didn't he stop in for an erasure? Did he like to live dangerously, knowing that he might get kicked out of his mind at any moment?

Suppose Tandy tries that with me?

It happened, Risa knew. It was a bit improper to speak of it, but she was aware that powerful personae sometimes overwhelmed and destroyed weak hosts, and took possession of their bodies. Dybbuks, they were called, after some medieval myth. According to the law, a dybbuk who had completely vanquished his host was a murderer, and subject to mandatory erasure. But most of them were too clever to fall into that trap. They continued to use the name of the dead host, keeping their dybbukhood a secret. Someone like James Kravchenko, if he finally succeeded in countererasing Charles Noyes, would probably go on calling himself Noyes for his own safety, and nobody might ever be the wiser.

Risa shuddered. Tandy, will you try to be a dybbuk?

Very strong individuals went in for such things. Waking up in a stranger's brain, they found it intolerable to be relegated to the status of a mere persona. So they pushed the host out and took over. Essentially, they lived again, body and soul, real rebirth, if they got away with it.

Tandy was a strong individual, Risa knew.

But so am I. So am I. If I were in Tandy's place, I'd try to take over. But I'm in my place, and I won't let her win if she tries anything like that.

The door opened. Leonards returned, carrying the oblong metal box that contained the persona of Tandy Cushing.

"How do you feel?" he asked.

"Fine. Impatient."

"I'm supposed to ask you if you'd like to cancel at this point."

"Don't be silly."

"Well, then. Here we go. I want to check to see how well the drug has worked."

"I haven't felt anything," Risa said.

"You shouldn't." He wheeled the diagnostat over and ran a test on her. When the report came, he nodded and smiled encouragingly. "You're in maximum recept now."

"That sounds dirty."

"Does it?" he asked, embarrassed again. He leaned toward her and slipped a cool metal band around her forehead. "This isn't for the transplant," he said. "It's merely to let you sample the persona. We take every precaution against an error. You've got to tell me that this persona is actually the one you've requested."

"Go ahead," Risa said.

This part was familiar. He activated the sampler and Risa found herself once more in contact with Tandy Cushing. The memories were unchanged. After perhaps half a minute, Leonards disconnected the sampler.

"Yes," said Risa. "You've got the right one."

"Please sign this release, then."

Risa grinned and thumbed the thermoplastic. Leonards dropped the sheet in the access hopper.

"Lie back," he said. "Relax. Here we go on the actual transplant."

Panic seized her. Leonards was a step ahead of her, though, efficiently shackling her wrists and ankles to the couch, and telling her in a low, soothing tone, "We do this for your own safety, you understand. Some people find it a big impact and start thrashing around. You'll be all right."

She was stiff with fear, and that surprised her. Forcing a laugh, she looked down at her spreadeagled body and said, "How do I know you're not going to torture me? Or rape me? This is a good position for a rape, isn't it, Leonards?"

His laughter was even more forced than hers.

He was in motion, never pausing, adjusting electrodes, manipulating scanners, balancing switches. Risa thought about the booklet she had read. Odd: it had been completely secular. No mantras, none of the Tibetan stuff, not even a quotation from the Book of the Dead. Nothing about sangsara or nirvana, the cycle of karma, all the other fashionable words people tagged to the Scheffing process. She realized the fundamental truth of something Nathaniel Owens had said on the beach Saturday at Dominica: the whole religious part of the rebirth business was external. It came after the fact, a moral justification, a dodge, a blind. The work of the Scheffing Institute went on serenely in a spiritual vacuum, and the mumbo-jumbo of the rebirth religion had no place within this building.

"Look up, please," the technician said. "Open your eyes wide."

Twin spears of white light stabbed at her pupils.

She could not close her eyes. She was frozen, immobile, penetrated by those sharp beams of brightness. It seemed to her that she heard a voice intone, "Now thou art experiencing the Radiance of the Clear Light of Pure Reality. Recognize it. O nobly-born, thy present intellect, in real nature void, not formed into anything as regards characteristics or color, naturally void, is the very Reality, the All-Good."

She had summoned out of memory the words to welcome the newly dead into death. Surrender to the Clear Light and attain nirvana. Yes. Yes. So her words were directed to the persona of Tandy Cushing, emerging from that spinning reel of tape, but what she offered Tandy was not oblivion but rebirth. Yes. Yes. Now and at the hour of our birth. Come on, Tandy. I'm ready for you.

If only the light wasn't in my eyes!

Time ceased Eons passed between heartbeats. Risa could feel the blood creeping along her veins and arteries, impelled by the last spasm and not yet at its destination. She could not see. She could not hear.

The tension broke, and she heard a stranger's voice whispering in her skull.

—Where am I? What happened?

"Hello, Tandy. Welcome aboard."

—Did I die?

"Yes."

—When? How? Why?

"I don't know. I'm Risa Kaufmann. I'm your host."

—I know who you are. I just want to know how I got here. How long have I been dead?

"Since last August," said Risa. "You were killed in a power-ski accident at St. Moritz."

—That's impossible! I'm an expert skier. And I had every safety device! I'm not dead! I'm not!

"Sorry, Tandy. You must be."

—I can't remember anything past June.

"That's when you made your last recording. Two months before you were killed."

—Stop saying that!

"If you're not dead, what are you doing in my mind?"

—There's been a mistake. They can transplant a persona even when the donor's still alive. Sometimes they slip up.

"No, Tandy. Get used to it."

—It isn't easy.

"I'll bet it isn't. But you've got no choice."

—If it's a mistake?

"Even if it is, that doesn't affect you. Assuming Tandy Cushing is still walking around alive somewhere, you're still where you are. A persona in my skull. You aren't Tandy, you're just an identity of Tandy's memories up to the day she recorded you. Well, now you're off the shelf and in a body again. You're lucky, I'd say. And in any case Tandy *is* dead. You're all that's left of her."

There was silence within. The persona was digesting all that. Risa, too, made adjustments. She still lay shackled. The light had gone out, and she could not tell if Leonards was still in the room. Cautiously, gingerly, she made contact with the persona at a variety of points. She picked up a memory of her late body, tall, dark-haired, with high, firm, heavy breasts. A man's hand ran lightly over those breasts, hefting them, savoring their bulk. His fingertip flicked across her nipples. So that was what it was like, Risa thought. You're less aware of them than I expected. Suddenly she darted back along Tandy's timeline and was eleven years old, staring in a mirror at her budding little chest and frowning. And then, coming forward five years, Risa saw Tandy soaring on personnel jets eighty yards above the Sahara, a strong, dark-haired man beside her as they flew.

I have never done that, Risa thought. Yet I know what it's like. I am Tandy!

She did not go deeper. There was time to explore the depths of the persona later. For Risa the world was suddenly tinged with wonder, all objects taking on new hues, extra dimensions. She saw through four eyes, and she had never seen such colors before, such greens and reds and yellows, nor had she tasted wine so sweet scented flowers so pungent.

"Tandy?" she said. "How is it now?"

—Better. So you're a Kaufmann?

"Yes. Lucky you."

—Why did you pick me?

"You seemed interesting."

—You're very young for this.

"I'm past sixteen, you know."

—Yes, I know. But I was twenty-four, and I hadn't had my first persona yet.

"Don't you wish you had?"

—I was waiting until I was twenty-five.

"I never wait," Risa said. "Not for anything."

—I see that. We've got so much to talk about.

"We've got all the time in the world. You'll be with me forever, Tandy."

—Forever?

"Of course. The next time I record myself, your persona will be added to mine. Someday I'll need rebirth, and you'll be going along to the next carnate with me."

—People can get awfully bored with each other like that.

"*We* won't," Risa said. "I promise you, we won't."

The shackles dropped away. Risa sat up, feeling a little shaky. Leonards was eyeing her hesitantly.

"You've made a good adjustment," he said.

"Is that so? Fine."

"How does it go?"

"I'm very pleased," said Risa. "What happens now?"

"We take you to a rest booth. You can lie down, relax. get to know your persona. After an hour you can leave the building."

"You've been very kind, Leonards."

"Thank you."

"Maybe we can get together after hours."

He looked smitten with confusion. "I'm afraid-that is —I mean to say—"

"All right. Take me to the rest booth."

She lay down on a comfortable webfoam cradle, closed her eyes, sent her mind roaming through the treasury of Tandy Cushing's experiences. Risa felt faintly uncomfortable, seeing the older girl so nakedly exposed. But she told herself that she had every right to explore that material. At this very instant, wasn't Tandy peering into her own soul? By definition they now were one person. They would share everything.

Risa felt no regrets. Her fears had evaporated. She felt only tremendous relief, for she had accepted a transplant and it was good.

She smiled. She said softly to Tandy, "I'll record the two of us in a week or two. Just to be on the safe side."

—Good. And then I want you to help me find out how I really died.

Chapter 7

"Come to Jubilisle!" the barker called. "Games, thrills, pleasure! Three bucks fish, the round trip! Jubilisle, Jubilisle, Jubilisle!" And globes of living light drifted free over Battery Park, soft indigo bursts tipped with yellow, reinforcing the shouted message with subtler pleas, many- hued whispers, *Jubilisle, Jubilisle, Jubilisle...*

It was night. The hydrofoil ferry waited at the pier. Crowds shouldered past, hustling toward it, people in rough, low-caste clothes, some of them even waving cash in their fists. Watchful quaestors stood by, ready to make arrests if the mob got out of hand. Charles Noyes experienced a sudden dizzying spasm of resistance. Everything about this outing repelled him all at once: the shouts of the barker, the faces of the people rushing past him, the too sleek hull of the waiting ferry, the quaestors. He turned to the handsome woman at his side.

"Let's not go," he begged. "I'll take you somewhere else, Elena."

"But you promised!"

"Can't I change my mind?"

"I've wanted to go to Jubilisle for months. Mark won't take me. And now you—"

Sweat rolled down his face. "I've only been out of stasis for a few days. The noise, the tumult—it's upsetting me."

She looked at him, wounded. "Before you say yes, now it's no. That's your name, isn't it? No-yes? Don't disappoint me like this, Charles!"

—Pull yourself together, man, came Kravchenko's voice. She won't like it if you back out.

"Ferry leaving now for Jubilisle," roared the barker. "Hurry, hurry, hurry! Thrills! Gaines! Pleasure! Three bucks fish, that's all it costs!"

Elena silently pleaded. She looked radiantly beautiful, her opulent body sheathed in glittering scales of some dark green material that followed every contour of her majestic thighs and breasts and buttocks. Her black, glossy hair tumbled to her bare shoulders. In this crowd she stood out so vividly that even the jostling plebs stepped back in automatic deference. Noyes peered into the dark, large, soft eyes. He observed the small, flawless nose, the full, shining lips.

Kravchenko obligingly sent one of his own choice memories bubbling up from the storehouse: Elena nude in Kravchenko's bachelor apartment in Rome, sprawled on a divan like a Venus by Titian, one hand coyly resting on the plump mons, the eyes beckoning, the breasts heaving, the dark-hued nipples erect, the firm flesh tense and taut with anticipation.

—You'll never get anywhere with her if you let her down now, pal. It's now or never, and she holds grudges.

"All right," Noyes said. "I won't go back on my word. Jubilisle for us, Elena!"

"I'm so glad, Charles."

He slid his arm around her waist. The scales of her gown pricked his skin. He felt the roll of meat at her hip. Sweeping her forward, he joined the flow of pleasure-seekers rushing aboard the ferry. A robot ticket-vendor held out a hand as though expecting Noyes to put cash in it. Noyes shook his head and offered his thumb instead. The robot, adapting smoothly and without comment, rang up the credit transfer, billing Noyes' account for six dollars, and the barrier dropped, admitting them to the ferry. Minutes later they were speeding across New York Harbor toward the pleasure dome. Ahead lay the bright glow of Jubilisle; behind rose the majestic black-capped somberness of the Scheffing Institute tower, with the rest of the Lower Manhattan skyline behind it. Noyes looked from island to tower. Those who could not buy rebirth at one could purchase distraction at the other.

He and Elena found a place at the rail for the ten-minute journey to the anchored artificial island. She stood close to him. The warmth of her body on this cool spring evening was welcome, and the fragrance of her perfume helped obliterate the rank stench of the mob all about them. She had been kind to him last week at Dominica, when he had had that awful convulsion at Kaufmann's beach party; a touch of the sun, she said, deftly concealing the truth, which was that he had suffered a sudden and nearly successful rebellion by Kravchenko. She was kind, yes. Tender, almost motherly, though she was several years younger than he was. That vast bosom of hers, he thought. It makes her seem the mother of us all.

But his interest in her was not at all filial. He had Kravchenko's testimony that Elena was seducible, and her own willingness to make herself available for this night on the town backed him up. Furthermore, she was Kaufmann's mistress and probably Santoliquido's as well, so that it enhanced Noyes' own sense of self to be out with her. Lastly, Roditis approved. In the final analysis, what mattered to Noyes was how well or how poorly each of his actions served the interests of John Roditis, and in squiring Elena Volterra to Jubilisle he was in a position to serve Roditis handsomely.

Elena said, "I imagined you came here often. Isn't Jubilisle one of Roditis' properties?"

"Yes, of course. One of his most successful. But I don't think I've been here more than three times in the ten years it's been open."

"Don't you like amusement parks?"

"There are amusements and amusements," Noyes said. He lowered his voice. "It happens that Jubilisle is designed mainly to please plebs. I'm not being snobbish when I tell you that; it's the truth. That's why we put it here, right in the shadow of the Scheffing building, so these people could look up and see the tower and think deep thoughts about rebirth. Which, since they can't have it unless they've got lots of money, will inspire them to gamble heavily here, making John Roditis a little wealthier."

"Very clever." Elena glanced around. "Now that you mention it, I see that we're a trifle out of place here. Most of them were paying cash to get aboard."

"You noticed that."

"It fascinated me. I don't think I've ever touched cash myself, not even once. I wouldn't recognize a bill if I found it in the street. Why do they bother?"

"They like the feel of money," Noyes said. "The central computer balance is a little impersonal for them. Here—I always carry a bill with me, just for luck. Would you like to see it?"

He slipped his wallet out and found his hundred-dollar bill. It was a slender plastic card which bore the atom symbol, a serial number, the Arabic numeral 100 in black type, and the inscription, *The Bank of the United States Government has on deposit One Hundred Dollars Fissionable Material as security for this note. Legal Tender.* Elena studied the bill as though it might be a mounted butterfly from another planet. "Fascinating," she said at last, handing it back. "Can you get me one?"

"Of course," he said.

He took her by the hand and led her across the deck to a refreshment stand where an automatic servitor was dispensing soft drinks. When the scanner beam flashed in his direction Noyes said, "Give me a hundred-dollar bill." He put his thumb to the charge plate. A bill popped through the slot and he handed it gravely to Elena, who examined it a moment grinned dazzlingly, and slipped the little card into the deep valley between her breasts. Onlookers gaped in astonishment.

"Thank you," she said, as they returned to the rail. "I'll treasure this little souvenir."

"You'll certainly keep it warm," Noyes said, and they both laughed.

The ferry was nearing Jubilisle's approach slip, now. The great arching dome of the pleasure island rose precipitously before them, topped with a layer of living light that pulsed from one end of the spectrum to the other. A hundred acres of area, six separate levels, the capacity to amuse half a million people at once—that was Jubilisle, and Noyes could not deny it was an impressive sight. Even Elena looked moved.

"Roditis owns it all?" she asked in a whisper.

"Through a nominee corporation, yes. I helped plan the financing soon after I joined his organization. It was his first great coup."

"It must have cost *billions*!"

"It did. And of course Roditis didn't have that kind of money yet, so we had to juggle. He pledged everything as collateral. Paul Kaufmann was willing to put up a construction loan of two billion, but he wanted a fifty-percent equity. Roditis said no. Kaufmann was so astonished he lent the two billion anyway. At ten percent, but he lent it. And Roditis kept the full equity. He owns the place outright. The last debenture was paid off in January. He's thinking of arranging a mortgage, now. Say, about seven billion, from a consortium of banks, and using the money to finance Jubilisle Canton and Jubilisle Rio. Eventually he'll have a dozen of them on every continent. Am I boring you with all this money talk?"

"Not at all," Elena said. She did look genuinely enthralled. "I'm very much interested. Roditis must be a terribly exciting man. I'd love to meet him."

"You never have?"

"Never. We just haven't crossed paths. You know, I spend so much of my time with Mark, and Mark is so hostile to Roditis."

"Yes. Yes, of course."

"But I think one day I will happen to meet Roditis. And he and I will both find the meeting rewarding."

"Powerful men intrigue you, eh, Elena?"

"Why not?"

"Mark Kaufmann—Santoliquido—"

She looked startled. "Santo and I are just good friends."

"Is that all?" He saw the color rising in her cheeks. Laughing, he said, "*Very* good friends, I imagine."

"What are you getting at?"

"Nothing. Nothing."

The ferry was at rest. The gangways extruded themselves and the crowd started ashore. Noyes and Elena let the flow carry them along.

A brilliant directory board in at least six colors confronted them. Twenty feet high, thirty feet wide, the board provided a detailed map of Jubilisle's offerings. Noyes paused to study it, but Elena tugged him along. "Let's just wander," she said. "One level's as good as another."

"That's not true. They're aimed for different sectors of the population."

"What does that matter? We're slumming tonight!"

He shrugged and yielded, and they stepped aboard the moving ramp leading to Level D. Noyes was hazily familiar with the structure of Jubilisle from his past visits; he recalled that the island was cunningly laid out in a series of mazes and dead ends, so that the bemused visitor might roam for hours without arriving at any clear knowledge of how much remained to be seen. The intention was to prod the clientele into realizing that it was impossible to see more than a small fraction of Jubilisle on any one visit, and thus one must return again and again.

The island was devised to offer something to every economic stratum, from those who lived off government credit to those who could afford a dozen persona transplants. Generally, the pull of Jubilisle was stronger in the lower middle brackets, those people who could not afford to traffic in the Scheffing process but who had enough disposable income to part with some here. There was no admission charge at Jubilisle; Roditis made his money, partly from the ferry ride, but mainly from the income of the booths and concessions. Noyes had seen the analysis: each visitor spent some fifteen dollars fissionable per trip, on which Roditis' net profit was about thirty-five percent. With half a million visitors at any one time, and perhaps three or four million on a busy Saturday night between sunset and dawn, it was easy to see the source of Roditis' affluence. Jubilisle had competitors now, of course, but it was the first of its kind, and the most successful. The powerful Kaufmann interests, having missed their chance to gain an equity investment in the original Jubilisle, had not deigned to open an imitation, much to Roditis' pleasure. Officially, it was because they had no desire to pander to the debauched tastes of the ignorant, but Noyes thought it was more likely the Kaufmanns stayed out of the pleasure-island business out of fear that they would not meet Roditis' level of success.

The inner core of the island provided the highest-priced delights. Those who came specifically to gamble large sums, to purchase costly sexual experiences, or to indulge in the illicit sensory stimulations of forbidden drugs, generally proceeded by a direct route to that area of Jubilisle. But Noyes had come merely as a casual sightseer, as had Elena, and they moved without plan down the glowing halls and galleries and chambers.

At a gambling pavilion, close to the perimeter of the island, the rhythms of exploding atoms determined the payoffs. A barker claimed that the process was completely random and so must be utterly honest. "Everyone stands an equal chance, folks. I don't mind telling you that some games favor the house, but not here, not here, not here! Step right up ..."

"Can that be so?" Elena asked. "A truly random game of chance?"

"Maybe so," Noyes told her. "Notice that it's on the outside of the island. If people win steadily here, they're encouraged to try the games within. Which are not quite so impartial."

"But Roditis must lose money on this, even so."

Noyes shook his head. "Not if it's truly random. He'll break even, and all he'll lose is his overhead, which isn't consequential. Call it a promotional loss. Let's try it?"

"All right."

They stepped up. You could pay cash, and most did, but of course Elena had no cash except the souvenir nestling between her breasts, and Noyes thumbed the plate to establish a gambling balance for her. The game was intricate; he scarcely understood its workings himself, and those about him must be wholly baffled by it. In the center of the platform lay what purported to be a block of polonium, flanked by a comically ornate gamma detector; an array of tubes and pipettes emerged from it, filled with scintillating colored fluids. A turquoise fluorescence paid off at 3 to 1; carmine yielded 8 to 1; a yellow streak in the ebony fluid produced a 10 to 1 payoff. The barker chanted rhythmically; the polonium atoms disgorged their component particles; the lights lit and went out. The crowd pressed close. A bell rang and a certificate dropped from a hopper.

"You've won ten dollars," Noyes said.

"Glorious! I want to play again!"

"There's much else to see," he reminded her.

They moved on. At a fortune-telling booth a spectral hooded figure predicted long life for them both, and numerous children. Then, looking Noyes over cunningly, the prophet added, "You will have many rebirths." Noyes tapped the plate and added a dollar to the soothsayer's credit balance.

"How did he know we were recorded?" Elena asked.

"He guessed. He saw how well-dressed we were and figured we were wealthy, and if we were wealthy we must be on file with the Scheffing people. In any case, it's flattery to wish us rebirths, even if we're not in the class that lives again."

"Perhaps he recognized us," Elena suggested.

"I doubt it."

"I'd like a mask, in any case."

"Many of the fairgoers were masked, particularly the women. Girls bare to the hips tripped along, cloaked only by striped dominoes. At Elena's insistence Noyes took her to a masking booth and purchased a concealment for her: a dark band of pseudoliving glass that took possession of her face in a kind of caress, slipping snakelike into place from ear to ear. They laughed. She pulled him close and kissed him fleetingly on the lips. "Buy a mask yourself," she said.

He did. Hidden now from the stares of the curious, they moved through the gallery, taking a dropshaft to the one below on a sudden whim. Noyes felt buoyant, relaxed. Within him Kravchenko was dormant for once, and Elena, warm and exciting on his arm, seemed to promise eventual ecstasies. The evening was going well after a poor start. The giddiness of Jubilisle had broken through his habitual melancholy. Yet there was always the memento mori not far below the surface; they paused in a closed arcade to embrace, and Noyes drew Elena so tightly against him that the soft mound of her left breast felt the impress of the flask of lethal carniphage that he carried always with him. When they separated, she touched the bruised place tenderly and said, "You hurt me. Something in your pocket—"

"I'm sorry. I didn't realize you'd feel it."

"What do you have there, a gravity bomb?"

"Just a flask of carniphage," he told her pleasantly, "In case a suicidal mood hits me."

Of course she did not believe that, and so she showered a silvery cascade of laughter over him.

A flamboyant sign declared: WELCOME TO THE HOUSE OF HALF-LIFE.

"What's this?" she asked. "More radioactive games?"

"I have no idea. Shall we go in?"

They entered. A fee of a dollar fissionable was extracted from each of them. Swiftly they discovered that the House of Half-Life, despite its name, did not traffic in neutrons and alpha particles; the half-life offered here was biological, hybrid creatures raised from fused cell nuclei. Behind an electrified barrier stunted beings shuffled around, while a pre-programed speaker recited their identities. "Here we have mouse and cat, folks, one of the most popular hybrids. And this is dog and tiger, believe it if you can! Next you see snake and frog."

The hybrid animals bore little resemblance to any of their supposed ancestors. They tended to be neutral, unspecialized in form, evolutionary prototypes lacking in clear characteristics. Most were less than two feet in length, moving about on small uncertain legs. The dog-tiger had patches of gray fur. The snake-frog was squat and glistening, with pulsating pouches of flesh. "Man and mouse, ladies and gentlemen, man and mouse!" came the disembodied voice. "You think the Scheffing people work miracles? What of this? Infect them with the Sendai virus, blend the nuclei in a centrifuge, toss in a dash of nucleic acid, yes, yes, man and mouse!" A dozen distorted things, neither mouse nor man, moved into the arena. Their eyes were pink and beady, their hands were claws, they could not walk erect. Elena stared in rigid attention.

A shill sidled up to them, proffering a handful of explosive darts. He said silkily. "You look like expensive folk out for a night's fun. Would you like to kill some of the hybrids? A hundred bucks fish a dart."

"Sorry," Noyes said. "No, thanks."

"Try your aim. Some folk your class come back often. We've got a room in back, lots of hybrids to throw at. They aren't rare, really."

"Shall we?" Elena asked him.

Noyes looked at her in amazement. Her eyes were gleaming.

Kravchenko awakened and offered a warning:

—Don't refuse her anything if you're smart.

Sighing, Noyes gave in. They went to the back room. He lowered his credit balance by five hundred dollars fissionable and

Elena took a cluster of darts in her delicate hand. On a platform before them, half a dozen pitiful bluish things, half squirrel, half otter, moved in ragged circles. They were slow, awkward animals with lengthy hairless tails and large flippered feet.

Elena aimed and threw. Her breasts quivered beneath the covering of green scales; her arm moved jerkily, a stiff throw from the elbow. To Noyes' relief, she missed, and missed also on the second and third casts, the darts landing and igniting in quick incandescent puffs. But on the fourth she struck one of the hapless hybrids at the base of its twisted spine, and the odor of singed fur drifted toward them. When the smoke cleared Noyes saw the remnants of the creature. Elena looked exhilarated; a deep crimson flush appeared beneath her dark, tawny skin, making her appear disturbingly more sensual than before. She handed him the remaining dart. He thrust it back at her.

"Go on," she cried. "Throw it! It's fun!"

"To *kill?*"

"Those things come out of test tubes. They're not really alive. They're better off dead." She joggled his arm. The nearness of her perspiring flesh maddened him. "Throw it!"

Desperately Noyes hurled the dart. It cleared the platform by ten feet and smashed harmlessly against the backdrop. Then he seized her by the hand and pulled her through a side exit lip ahead, a cocktail lounge could be seen, and they entered it.

"Don't you care for hunting?" Elena asked him.

"Not really. But hunting is sport. There's nothing sporting about throwing darts at mutated monstrosities."

She laughed. The tip of her tongue flicked out. "There was a grand hunt in Italy six years ago. We chased partridges across the campana south of Rome. You must have a memory of it."

"I?"

"Jim Kravchenko was there. If he's truly your persona, you have the memory."

Kravchenko promptly thrust the memory up into view. A misty

October morning; the shattered remains of a Roman aqueduct gaunt against the gray sky; handsomely dressed young men and women, riding power carts, pursuing the terrified birds across the rolling plain. Laughter, the occasional burst of needlefire, the squawk of the prey, the autumn fragrances. Elena beside him, looking a trifle slimmer, chastely garbed in hunting attire, wielding her needlegun to deadly effect and hissing with delight each time she registered a kill. Then, afterward, the tang of iced champagne, the pleasure of spicy foods imported from the outworlds, the easy flow of light conversation in a palazzo at the edge of the city. And Elena in his arms, still clad in her hunting clothes, the pleated skirt pulled up, the white thighs exposed, the hips thrusting, thrusting ...

"Yes," Noyes gasped. "I remember now."

"You must have many interesting memories. Jim and I were quite fond of one another."

"I haven't done much checking," said Noyes. "Somehow it seems unfair. It overbalances our relationship, Elena. I mean, I carry intimate recollections of you, so you have few secrets from me, but you have no such insight into me."

She looked startled. "Why do we take on personae if not to gain advantage? I don't understand you, Charles. If in your mind you hold Jim's memories of me, why not enjoy them?"

—Because you're a damned masochist, Kravchenko suggested.

Noyes winced. To Elena he said, "You're right. I'm being foolish."

He searched the archive Kravchenko had brought with him into his mind. He was lying, in a way, for he had already done a good deal of peering at Elena's relationship with Kravchenko. He knew that they had been lovers for about two years, on and off, nothing serious on either side. Kravchenko had many women, and, Noyes gathered, Elena rarely confined her attentions to one man at a time. Within his mind was Elena's entire repertory of passion; he had merely to sort it out and study it.

Elena said, "I find it hard to believe that Jim's really dead. He was such an exciting man. Do you and he get along well?"

"No."

"So I've understood. Why is that? Why did you select him, if there were incompatibilities?"

Noyes ordered drinks for them. "We came from the same general background," he explained. "I was playing it cautious when I picked a persona. I could have had a financier, a university professor, a starman. Instead I chose a rich playboy, because I was just a rich playboy myself, and I wanted more of the same. Well, I got it. He gives me no peace."

"You don't have to keep a persona you don't like," she said.

"I know. Perhaps one day I'll ask for erasure and start all over."

—That'll be the day, Charlie-boy.

"It might be best for both of you," said Elena. "It would give Jim a second chance too. Is he your only persona?"

"Yes. I didn't think I ought to risk another."

"Possibly a second one would have calmed him a little."

"Possibly. What about you, Elena? You're such a mystery woman. How many personae are you carrying?"

"Four," she said coolly.

He was dumbstruck. He had calculated her for one, or perhaps two personae, no more. Few women undertook four. But Noyes realized he had made the mistake of assuming that because she was beautiful, she must also be of limited intellect. Evidently Elena could handle four personae, since she spoke clearly, with no signs of internal conflict.

"One secondary, three primaries," she amplified. "It's an amusing group. We get along well. I took on the first ten years ago, the last only in November. I may add others. I've talked to Santoliquido about a possible new transplant."

"Someone in particular?"

"No," Elena said. "Not yet. That is, if I can't have Paul Kaufmann—"

Noyes sputtered. "You want him too?"

"I'm merely joking. They haven't legalized transsexual imprinting, have they? But I imagine it would be fun to have him. I know
Mark would be astounded. Mark worshiped that terrible old man.
Strong as he is, Mark never could withstand his uncle's wishes
in anything. And if I walked into the house one day and opened
my mouth and spoke to him with the Words of Paul Kaufmann—
" Elena giggled. "A delightful picture. It calls for another drink."

Noyes found it difficult to see the humor in it. He summoned
the drinks; then, slowly, he said, "Do you have any idea who's
really going to get the Paul Kaufmann Persona?"

"How should I know?"

"You spent time with Santoliquido at Mark's party."

"I don't discuss Santoliquido's administrative decisions at parties," Elena said. "Why do you ask? Are you thinking of apply-
ing?"

"For Paul Kaufmann? He'd burn me out in ten minutes. But
John Roditis is interested."

"*Interested* isn't the right word, from what I hear. *Desperate* is
more appropriate."

"Desperate, then. It's no secret. Roditis feels he's qualified to
handle a potent persona like Paul Kaufmann, and he also believes that the two of them acting together can have much to
offer society. The two greatest business minds of the century,
blended into a dynamic team. Honestly, I think so, too. I profoundly wish Roditis would be granted the persona."

"Do you know who else wants Paul?" Elena asked.

"Who?"

"His nephew Mark."

"That's impossible! A transplant within the family—"

"Illegal, I know. Mark knows it too. He has no hope of actually
getting the transplant. But he has business ambitions too, and
they'd be well served if he had the use of his uncle's experiences. Besides, he's eager to keep the old man out of Roditis'

possession.

"Why does Mark hate Roditis so much?"

"He regards him as an upstart. It's quite simple, Charles. The Kaufmanns are aristocrats by birth. They have ancestry. As do you. As do I. As does Santo. We have more than wealth; we have pedigrees back into the twentieth century, even to the earlier centuries. Roditis can tell you his father's name, but that's all. Now, with a Kaufmann persona, he'd have social access to our group, access that he can't buy with all his billions. Mark is determined not to let Roditis force his way in. He regards it as blasphemy for a man like that to have his uncle's persona."

"We were all upstarts once," Noyes pointed out. "Take the Kaufmann line back far enough and you find peasants. Go back farther and you find apes."

Elena's laughter tinkled across the lounge. "Of course, of course! But it's the distance between the peasant and the banker that marks the social prestige. Your Roditis is too close. Perhaps his great-grandchildren will rule society, but Mark won't tolerate it now."

"Mark can't have his uncle's persona. He'd be wise to give in gracefully and let Roditis have it. Bury the hatchet, forge a mighty alliance of wealth."

"That's not how Mark operates," said Elena.

"He could. Elena, I'd be grateful if you'd suggest that to him. Point out the advantages of combining with Roditis instead of battling him."

"You want me to serve as a go-between, passing Roditis' messages?"

He colored. "You put it very bluntly."

"We are on the island of truth, Charles. This is what you want from me, is it not? To push Roditis' case with Mark?"

"Yes."

"And perhaps even to talk to Santo?"

"Yes."

"Is there anything else you want from me, Charles?"

He could barely look at her. The carniphage flask throbbed against his breastbone. He felt bitterly ashamed that she would humiliate him before Kravchenko this way. But he had asked for it.

"There's one more thing I want," he said.

"Name it."

He touched the warmth of her shoulder. "An hour with you in the bedchambers of the inner level."

"Certainly," she said, as though he had asked her to tell him the correct time.

They left the cocktail lounge and passed through a hail of gaudy nightmare fantasies, and crossed an arena in which the products of teratogenetic surgery performed a grotesque dance, and rose on a circular ladder leading beyond a pool of slippery cephalopods engaged in a stately ballet, and at length they came to one of the blocs of bedchambers that were scattered at frequent intervals through the galleries of Jubilisle. For fifty dollars he rented an hour's use of a room.

Within, Elena activated a device that cast a kaleidoscopic pattern on the ceiling above the circular bed. Then she disrobed. Beneath the scaly gown she wore only an elastic strip around her hips, and another that bound her breasts, thrusting them upward and close to each other. His hundred-dollar bill was wedged in that deep cleft. She snapped the elastic strips; her massive breasts tumbled free, and the banknote fluttered to the floor. Ignoring it, she faced him, displaying her nudity for his inspection, and without a word arranged herself on the bed.

—Your big moment, Kravchenko told him.

Furiously Noyes dug into the darkest corners of the persona to learn the secrets of unlocking Elena's passion. The information was all there: the proper zones, the proper words, the timing. Kravchenko had most diligently done the research for him years ago.

Noyes joined Elena on the bed. Their bodies met. Their flesh touched and exchanged warmth.

He made the rewarding discovery that she was easily aroused and that she was satisfying in her frenzy. At the climactic moment she dug her heels into the backs of his legs and shivered in authentic ecstasy, but then, amid the stream of wordless syllables of joy that issued from her lips, it seemed to Noyes that he heard her saying, "Jim, Jim, Jim, Jim, *Jim*!"

Chapter 8

John Roditis listened with flickering patience to all that Noyes had to tell him. They sat at the edge of a wide veranda overlooking Roditis' Arizona ranch; before them stretched an infinite acreage of harsh brown turf, tufted here and there by grayish-purple islands of sage. Roditis had been in Arizona all week, supervising the preliminary negotiations for a power project encompassing the region south of Tucson and well over the Mexican border. He had had Noyes fly to him that morning, four days after Noyes' interlude with Elena Volterra.

Noyes said, "Elena will speak to Santoliquido on your behalf. Probably she's spoken to him already."

"Is she his mistress?"

"She's everybody's mistress, sooner or later. Mainly she lives with Mark Kaufmann. But she spends time with Santoliquido too. She's quite intimate with him."

Roditis knotted his thick fingers together and peered past Noyes into the cloudless, harsh blue sky. "Is Kaufmann aware that Santoliquido is trifling with his woman?"

"I imagine so," Noyes said. "Neither of them bothered to conceal it much. And Mark's no fool."

"Has it occurred to you, then, that Kaufmann has deliberately winked at that relationship-so that by lending Santoliquido Elena, he can influence the destination of his uncle's persona?"

"You mean, making Elena the price for Santoliquido's cooperation in keeping Paul Kaufmann out of your clutches, John?"

"Something like that"

Noyes took a deep breath. "I've considered it, yes. But I don't think it's the case. What's going on between Elena and Santoliquido isn't happening at Mark's instigation, any more than Mark had anything to do with what took place between Elena and me. And I believe that Elena will serve your interests in dealing with Santoliquido."

"Why should she?"

"Because I asked her to."

"How much money did she want?"

"Elena's not interested in money," said Noyes. "At least, not in any realistic sense. She's got all she needs, and any time she wants more she can get it from Kaufmann just for the asking. What fascinates her is power. She likes to be close to strong men. She likes to be at the core of intrigue."

"She's not unique in that," Roditis remarked.

"Elena wants to meet you, John. I suspect that she wants to become your mistress. And she knows that the best way to make an impression on you is to help you get the one thing in the universe you most want and can't obtain by yourself, which is Paul Kaufmann's persona. So she'll use her influence with Santoliquido to get it for you, and then she'll try to cash in by throwing herself into your bed."

"It would infuriate Mark Kaufmann if I took away both his woman and his uncle, wouldn't it?" Roditis said quietly.

"It would madden him."

"I'm not sure I want to madden him that much," Roditis said thoughtfully.

"You want the persona, don't you?"

·   "Of course."

"Elena will help you gain it. What happens after that between the two of you is entirely up to you."

"Why are you so confident that Elena will cooperate?"

"I've explained," Noyes said. Rising, he stepped off the veranda and scuffed at the desert sand beyond its margin. "There's another reason that I haven't mentioned yet."

"Go on."

"Elena knew Jim Kravchenko very well. They were lovers in Italy five or six years ago."

"Yes," Roditis said. "So?"

"Elena was very fond of Kravchenko. She wants to please him, now that she's found him again inside me. She believes that by helping me win status with you, she'll be doing her old friend Kravchenko a good turn."

"That's an intricate line of reasoning, Charles. Kravchenko's dead. If she's reaching through you to him, she can't have a very high opinion of you."

"She doesn't. She hates me. And this is how she shows it."

Roditis spat. "There are times when I wonder why I work so hard to get involved with you society people. You're nothing but beasts, really. You disembowel one another like ballet dancers with tusks, and you find the most complicated possible reasons for doing what you do."

"Inbreeding, perhaps," Noyes suggested.

"Yes, that. And more. Mere money doesn't interest you; your great-grandfathers have made enough for the whole tribe. Mere status is of no importance; you had that before you were old enough to be housebroken. You inherit power and rank. So you turn your lives into a kind of Byzantine intrigue to keep from going crazy with boredom. Rebirth makes it all the more interesting. You can switch back and forth across the generations, opening old wounds, keeping ancient feuds alive, scarring each other, using sex like a dagger." Roditis' eyes glittered. "Let me tell you something, Charles. I'm a *real* Byzantine. I don't practice intrigue for intrigue's own sake. I'm looking to put it to practical ends. And so while the whole bunch of you go on backstabbing and clawing, I'm going to move right in and take everything over. Just the way my ancestors moved in and took over Rome. By and by, the language of the Roman Empire was Greek, remember? That's how a Byzantine works. Watch me."

"I've never stopped watching you, John."

"Good. We'll see about Elena's conference with Santoliquido in a little while. Come take exercise with me, now."

"I'm a little tired, John. The flight from New York—"

"Come take exercise with me," Roditis repeated. "If you kept in shape, you wouldn't be worn out by a little thing like a flight from New York."

They entered the house, passing through corridors lined with smooth white stucco walls, and descended to the cool basement where Roditis had installed a gymnasium. Quietly he adjusted the gravity control to a boost of ten percent. That was unfair to Noyes, but no matter; Roditis had little desire to waste his exercise session by imposing an insufficient challenge on himself. Usually he boosted the pull by twenty percent or more. When things went badly, he had sometimes worked under double grav, straining every fiber, pushing heart and lungs and muscles to their limits for the sake of extending those limits another notch.

Stripping, Roditis said, "Would you like to recite a mantra of exertion, Charles?"

"I'm not sure there is one.

"Give us a pious phrase or two, at any rate. Then get out of your clothes."

Noyes said, "When, by the power of evil karma, misery is being tasted, may the tutelary deities dissipate the misery. When the natural sound of Reality is reverberating like a thousand thunders, may they be transmuted into the sounds of the Six Syllables."

Roditis belched. "*Om mani padme hum.* Excuse me."

"It's all nonsense to you, isn't it, John?"

"Western Buddhism? Well, it has its place. I've studied the arts of right dying, you know. I mean to leave a well- prepared persona for my next carnate trip."

"How will it feel, I wonder, being a passenger in someone else's brain?"

Roditis stared levelly at Noyes. "I won't be a passenger for long, Charles. You must realize that, of course. I play the game to win, all the time. If I can't win trough to dybbuk, I don't deserve rebirth."

"I pity the man who picks your persona."

"He'll live comfortably enough. He just won't be supreme in his own body, is all." Roditis laughed boomingly. "All this is sixty, seventy years away, though. Right now we're here for exercise, not speculation on my discorporate existence. *Om mani padme hum*. Wake up, Charles!"

Roditis activated the vertical trampolines. They were two flexible screens, mounted upright about fifteen feet apart and moving in a flagellatory oscillation on their mountings. He stepped between them and jumped diagonally against the left-hand screen, keeping his ankles pressed close together. The screen batted him away, and he pivoted neatly in midair, directing his feet at the other screen, striking it squarely, rebounding, pivoting again. For twenty cycles he let himself be shuttled back and forth between the screens, never once touching the floor despite the enhanced pull of gravity. Then he resisted the elasticity of the screens by tensing his body, and dropped lithely to his feet at his staffing point.

"Your turn," he said to Noyes.

"John, I—"

"*Come on!*"

Noyes looked dubious. He stepped between the pulsating screens and leaped. His feet touched the center of the webwork to his left, and the screen hurled him away, slamming him shoulder-first to the floor. He stood up, rubbing himself.

"Again," said Roditis. "You're growing fat, Charles. Sleek-headed, and you sleep o'nights. Let me have men about me with a lean and hungry look."

Noyes leaped again, angrily. As he struck the screen, he flexed his knees, trying hard to achieve the correct propulsive effect that would send him arcing toward the opposite screen. But his feet came in contact with the screen a fraction of a second apart from one another, and he gathered no momentum. Instead he trickled to the floor, striking his cheekbone and the side of his lower lip. He was bruised and bleeding when he arose.

"I'm sorry, John. I'm simply not in shape for this kind of thing, and by the time I get in shape it'll probably kill me," he said thinly.

"I'll make it easier for you."

Roditis seized the gravity control and cranked it to half level. Beneath the floorboards there was a rumbling sound as the straining magnetodynamic field made the adjustment, and shortly Roditis felt the pressure lift.

"Try again," he said.

Noyes moved into position and jumped. In the suddenly lighter gravity, he hit the screen too high, but it made no difference; he was hurled across to the facing screen, landing belly first, bounced back, made another cycle, all the time floundering, kicking his long legs about, waving his arms desperately, like a giant Sancho Panza tossing on his blanket. Roditis watched for more than a minute as Noyes slammed back and forth through the air. Then, feeling irritated and amused all at once, he restored the gravity to normal plus ten, and Noyes dropped heavily to the floor. He was slow to get up this time. His face was reddened and his chest heaved.

"Enough of that," said Roditis mercifully. "Should I call an ambulance, or will you try other exercise?"

Noyes shrugged. Roditis picked up a medicine ball and gently tossed it to him, underarm. Noyes caught it and flipped it back, and for a few minutes they played catch, Roditis surreptitiously stepping up the force of his throws until the heavy ball traveled with considerable velocity. At last Noyes' trembling fingers failed to hold it, and the ball rocketed into the pit of his stomach, rolling away while he gagged and retched. Roditis did not smile.

They played power-shuffleboard, which Noyes found more to his liking. They swam. They climbed ropes. Roditis took another turn on the trampolines. Then he relented, and they went upstairs to dress. Lunch followed.

Roditis was in a restless, surging mood. His business enterprises were going well; but the one thing that was of highest importance, the Paul Kaufmann project, seemed stalemated and stagnant. He wished he did not need to act through intermediaries in gaining Santoliquido's favor. Especially intermediaries he did not even know, such as this woman Elena Volterra, famous for her beauty and for her promiscuity as well, an unlikely ambassador indeed. He had sent Noyes off to Dominica to make contact with Santoliquido; instead, Noyes had reached this Elena. Perhaps she would serve him well, after all, if Noyes' tortuous reasoning had any merit to it. But Roditis itched to be handling the deal himself. The groundwork had been laid; now was the moment to fly to New York, corner Santoliquido in his den, and make full, formal, and final request for the transplant of the Kaufmann persona. Time was passing. It was unreasonable of Santoliquido to withhold his decision any longer, and Roditis did not know of any other qualified applicant. Possibly Mark Kaufmann had the capacity to handle the persona of his uncle, but Mark was barred by law and the old man's direct wish from taking it. Which leaves only me, thought Roditis.

That afternoon he closed the power transaction with the Mexicans. His computer produced the final specifications for the transmission pylons; the Mexican computer produced the final estimates of allowable cost. There was brief negotiation between the computers, and by three o'clock the contract was ready for signing. Roditis affixed his thumbprint, the chairman of the Mexican Power Authority delivered an eloquent speech in confused English, and substantial quantities of tequila were served.

An hour later, Roditis was eighty thousand feet in the air, bound for New York.

The world had become a strange and infinitely complex place for Risa Kaufmann in the eight days since she had acquired the persona of Tandy Cushing. At a single stroke, her stock of life experiences had been more than doubled; her perceptions of human relationships had become more intense; her attitude toward herself, her father, and the world in general had grown more tolerant. The presence of the persona had provided her with a sense of parallax. She had two viewpoints from which to observe events, and that made a vast difference.

She felt a trifle guilty about her former self's wanton bitchiness. Risa plus Tandy looked upon Risa alone as an insufferable little minx, obsessively self-indulgent, petty, exhibitionistic, with a wide streak of sadism in her makeup. Together, they understood what had created that constellation of undesirable character traits in her: her impatience to erupt into the adult world, which had seemed in no hurry to accept her. Now that she had made that passage safely, it ceased to be important for her to externalize her frustration by tormenting those about her.

Tandy, too, had had her shortcomings. Risa clearly recognized the persona's flaws: laziness, shallowness, lack of discipline. Tandy came from a moneyed family, one of the old New England lines, but it was a family in which no one had done any work in at least five generations. To a Kaufmann such an attitude was abhorrent and almost incomprehensible. Kaufmanns worked. They might flit about the world to a dozen parties a week, they might go off to Venus for a month if the mood took them, they might spend a fortune on clothing or furnishings or illuminated portraits of Uncle Paul or additional personae. Their great wealth entitled them to any luxury they chose, save only the luxury of idleness. Risa's father devoted many hours of his day to business activities that could just as easily be run through hired managers, or even left entirely to the computer services. Risa herself had a keen understanding of the uses of the business cycle, and had every intention of taking her place in the Kaufmann banking hierarchy. But Tandy had no training, no interest in anything but sensuality, no marketable skills. If for some reason the Cushing estate had failed, she would have had no choice but to go into prostitution.

Risa disapproved of Tandy's flightiness. Tandy disapproved of Risa's aggressiveness. They had much to offer one another, by way of countervailing forces.

During their first few days of life together they spent long hours sorting through each other's memory files. Risa withdrew to her apartment for what would have seemed to an outsider as passive meditation, but which was in fact an exciting, vivid, and unending colloquy of the most intimate kind. All in a rush she entered Tandy's backlog of events, the love affairs, the trips, the parties. It was like gaining eight extra years of past in a moment. Tandy, at twenty-four on the date of her final persona recording, had done everything that Risa in her first sixteen years had done, and had gone beyond those first tentative experiments to a full-blown erotic career. Risa had had a few affairs, impulsive, fragmentary, hesitant, the fleeting curiosities of a girl on the edge of womanhood. Tandy had known love, or what she regarded as love, and the record of emotional storm and fervor, of sunrise and sunset, lay accessible to Risa.

She knew now the sensations of lying naked to couple in the Antarctic snows. She tasted strange cocktails in a hotel on the slopes of Everest. She experienced orgasm in free fall. She quarreled with lovers, raked their faces with clawed hands, kissed away the salty tricklings of blood.

Risa sensed that it would not take her very long to exhaust Tandy's stock of incident. Oh, there would always be interesting formative events to return to, yes, and there would always be the useful presence of a second mind within hers, but Risa knew that the present keen stimulation of having Tandy with her would wear off in a year or two, and their relationship would settle into coziness, a marriage that had consumed its passion. Tandy simply did not have the complexity of personality that would permit indefinite mining of her experiences, colorful as those experiences had been. By the time Risa reached Tandy's final age, she would be far beyond the point Tandy had reached at her death.

Then it would be time to add another persona. An older woman, Risa thought. From Tandy she had acquired voluptuousness, a sense of physicality that her own lean body would never provide for her. From the next persona Risa wanted an advanced course in avarice and shrewdness. It would be useful to have the benefit of age to draw upon as she entered the larger world of conflict and achievement.

But that was for the future. For now, Risa had exactly what she wanted.

"You're satisfied?" her father asked her.

Spring sunlight flooded Risa's apartment. She wore an airy gown that might have been made of woven cobwebs. "Very satisfied. It's all I dreamed it would be."

"The change in you is very pronounced."

"A change for the better?"

"I think so," Kaufmann said.

"Then why did you fight me, Mark? Why couldn't you have given your consent when I asked for it the first time?"

He looked sheepish, an expression she had never seen on his face before. "Sometimes I miscalculate too, Risa. It seemed to me you weren't ready. I was wrong. I admit it. You and Tandy are good friends, eh?"

"Extremely."

"What's she like?"

"Very much like me, only eight years older, and much more relaxed about things. With one exception."

"And that is?"

"The manner of her death. Tandy's obsessed with that. She's convinced she was murdered."

"She died in a power-ski accident last summer, didn't she?"

"That's the official verdict," Risa said. "Tandy tells me that it couldn't have happened that way. She was an expert skier, and her equipment had safety devices anyhow."

"Safety devices fail. Does she have any recollection of her last moments?"

"How could she?" Risa laughed. "She recorded her persona two months before she was killed! They don't take recordings of dying girls at the scenes of accidents!"

Mark looked sheepish again. "Stupid of me. But does she have any basis for thinking she was murdered, or is it simply an irrational obsession?"

"Since she's got no evidence, it has to be considered irrational," Risa said. "But she's asked me to do a little checking, and I will."

"Checking? What sort of checking?"

"Detective work. Reconstructing her last day of life. Finding the man she was skiing with."

Frowning, Mark said, "You could get yourself into trouble doing that, Risa. If you like, I'll have a man assigned to—"

"No. I'll handle it, Mark. I'm curious about it too."

It was time to get started on that project, Risa told herself. She had hesitated to make any outward moves, in this week of orientation; but now there was no further reason for waiting. She prodded Tandy for details of her final memories.

"Who would you have gone to St. Moritz with?"

—I'm not sure. Perhaps Claude. Or maybe Stig.

"They were both power-skiers?"

—Yes. And I was seeing both of them last spring. You know that much already.

"Did you have any plans for power-skiing with either of them at St. Moritz?"

—How would I know?

Risa studied Tandy's recollections of her two escorts. Claude Villefranche was a Monegasque, a citizen of that anomalous little Mediterranean principality that so stubbornly retained its sovereignty in a day when such notions were long obsolete. Filtered though Tandy's eyes, he was tall, wide-shouldered, dark, moderately sinister-looking, with a tapering sharp nose and thin, easily scowling lips. He was about thirty, it seemed, athletic, wealthy, a man of strong tastes and a somber, brooding nature.

As for Stig Hollenbeck, the Swede, he was Claude's complement: sunny and open, a slender, lithe man in his late twenties, blond, fair, looking somewhat as Risa imagined Charles Noyes must have looked when younger, though not so tall and lanky. His family had shipbuilding money; Stig himself, like nearly everyone in the late Tandy Cushing's orbit, was a non-worker.

Tandy had been sexually intimate with each of them on many occasions in the last two years of her life. Each had been aware of her interest in the other; neither had shown any flicker of jealousy. There was nothing in Tandy's view of either one that led Risa to think they were capable of murder. Yet Tandy had a powerful conviction that one or the other of them had accompanied her to St. Moritz last August and had chosen to sabotage her equipment with intent to kill.

"I'll look them up and find out if they can tell me anything about your final two months," Risa said. "Which one should I begin with?"

—Stig.

"Why?"

—Because Claude's got such an ominous face. He's the kind of man who *looks* like a murderer. So we ought to begin with the less obvious suspect.

Risa was amused by that. But she humored Tandy; this entire enterprise struck Risa as frivolous, and so there was no point in trying to impose rational judgment on any segment of it. Murder was a rarity in the world Risa knew. Since everyone had a recent persona recording on file, and thus could be said always to be in transition from one carnate existence to the next, it was pointless to risk erasure by committing that crime. If you took life intentionally, your own recordings were destroyed and you were barred forever from participation in the rebirth program. Who would risk such a dread punishment? Why jeopardize one's own eternal life for the sake of bringing a temporary interruption to another's span?

Yet Tandy was convinced she had been murdered, doubtless because she could not accept the notion that some clumsiness of her own had led to her early death in the snows of St. Moritz. Risa dialed the master directory and requested information on the whereabouts of Stig Hollenbeck. To her surprise and relief, it turned out that Stig was currently living on his family estate just outside Stockholm. She placed a call to him the following morning, when it was early evening in Sweden.

His calm, appealing face smiled out of the screen at her, the eyes friendly, a little puzzled. He looked much like Tandy's image of him, though younger and a trifle more lean.

"Yes?"

"I'm Risa Kaufmann. I'd like to talk to you about Tandy Cushing, if I might."

He lowered his eyes. "Tandy, yes. A great tragedy. Were you a friend of hers?"

"I've obtained transplant of her persona."

Hollenbeck's reaction was vivid: a sudden spasm of the muscles of the throat, a lifting of the eyes, a quick and involuntary turning of the head several inches to the left Risa, watching closely, wondered whether this was the response of a guilty man taken by surprise, or whether, perhaps, he simply was startled by the knowledge that Tandy's persona was at large in the world again and looking at him through Risa's eyes.

At length he said, "I had not heard that she was back."

"Quite recently. Last week. She suggested I get in touch with you. There are questions I'd like to ask."

"Very well. If I can be of any service—"

"Not by phone. May I visit you in Stockholm tomorrow?"

"As you wish. It would be a great pleasure for me to meet— ah—Tandy's new friend. Shall you be coming from America?"

"From New York, yes." As she spoke, Risa requested a time-table over her data line, and discovered there was space available on a flight leaving at nine the following morning. "We could have lunch together," Risa said.

They arranged to meet at the airport. When she stepped through the immigration scanners, he was there, looking pale and rather more fragile than she had imagined. They embraced in the courtly manner prescribed between strangers at their first meeting. As he held her, he peered into her eyes, and it seemed to her that his cold blue eyes were trying to stare through her at the Tandy lurking within. A muscle throbbed in his cheek. Risa doubted that this man had committed murder.

—He's changed, Tandy commented. He looks older, quieter. Almost shy.

"I have reserved a lunch for us," he said to Risa. "My hopter is waiting."

Within minutes they were in a sumptuous building many hundreds of years old that stood at the edge of a lovely park in metropolitan Stockholm. He had arranged for their meal to be served in a private chamber, upstairs, at the inn. At face value, that might seem to be an invitation to a seduction; but Risa sensed that he had no physical interest in her. She was good at detecting the radiations of desire, and there were none forthcoming from him. Evidently he preferred the more robust, fleshy physique of a Tandy. She wondered if he knew Elena Volterra.

A robot servitor brought them cold aquavit and tapering flasks of chilled golden beer. Then a table of delicacies was wheeled into their room, and she followed him about selecting bits of aromatic herring, snippets of smoked reindeer, lush strips of salmon. A huge window admitted a maximum of sunlight: a scarce commodity at this latitude, and so highly prized.

Tandy fluttered and palpitated within her. It excited her terribly to be in the presence of her former lover. She seemed eager to go to bed with him once more, even vicariously. Without speaking, Risa attempted to communicate to the persona Stig's lack of yearning for her.

As they ate, Stig said, "You wish to ask questions about Tandy?"

"You were very close to her, weren't you?"

He smiled. "Surely you must know that I was."

"Yes. I do. I'm sorry to have voiced the obvious. Can you tell me when you last saw her?"

"Last summer," he said. "Some time before her-death."

"How long before?"

"Let me think. In the spring we were together at Veracruz. April and part of May. Then she returned to Europe, to Monte Carlo and Claude. You know of Claude?"

"Of course."

"Well, then. It must have been at the end of June that I saw her again."

—After I made my last recording, said Tandy.

"Where was this?" Risa asked.

"We met in Lisbon. We traveled together as far as Stockholm, where I had family obligations. She continued on into Suomi— into Finland. I joined her there in mid- July. We journeyed through the arctic regions together, down to Kiev again, and flew to Zurich. In Zurich I left her. Several weeks later she was dead."

"You didn't see her at all after the end of last July?"

"Unhappily, no." He indicated Risa's empty plate. "Shall we proceed to the warm food, or do you wish more fish?"

"I'd like to try some of the other kinds of herring."

"As do I." He grinned, the first sign of warmth she had had from him. They filled fresh plates. At a signal, the robot produced more beer. Risa resisted more aquavit.

"About Tandy—"

"When she left me in Zurich, I understand she met Claude again. They went to St Moritz" His countenance darkened. "I did not hear of her death until October. I assumed she was still traveling with him."

"What can you tell me about her death?"

"This is a wintry subject for such a sunny day."

"Please," Risa said. "It's important for me to know. For—us to know. Don't you see, Tandy has no information about it. Her last recording was made in June. She's trying to reconstruct her final eight weeks, and particularly the events of her—of her death. Can you help?"

"As I say, my information is secondhand. I'm told she was skiing with Claude. They were on the high slope, making a rapid descent, one of the long jumps. She was crossing a crevasse, one hundred meters in the air. Suddenly her equipment failed. The gravity repulsors failed to hold. She fell. I understand they did not recover her body until the following week."

Risa felt a quiver of shock. "I hope it was a swift death."

"One can hope so, yes.

They were silent. Risa saw Stig searching her face, and knew that he must still be seeking some way to speak through her, directly to Tandy. But of course it was a grievous breach of etiquette to address someone's resident persona. One spoke only to the living, not to the merely carnate. Stig could not possibly commit a blunder so gross; yet clearly he ached to seize Risa's arms and find himself embracing Tandy.

"I loved her very deeply," he said after a while. "I doubt that she realized it. We were always so elaborately casual, after the approved manner. I would have wanted to have a child by her. I would have wanted to share her life. But I never let her see any of that, and so all we shared was a bed. I regret that."

"Will you be offended if I tell you that Tandy was more aware of your feelings than you thought?" Risa asked.

He smiled faintly. But he did not look convinced.

They scarcely touched the rest of their meal. Afterward, they walked in the garden of the inn, both of them quiet. The indirect conversation between Stig and Tandy had left Risa drained and numb. She had, at least, settled one thing to the satisfaction of herself and the persona within. If Tandy had indeed died through malevolence, Stig Hollenbeck had had nothing to do with it.

At the airport, he said as she dismounted from his hopter, "I wish I could have been of more assistance to you."

"You were extremely helpful. We're both grateful."

"Where will you go now?"

"To see Claude," Risa said. "We didn't know which one of you had been with Tandy at the end, you see. Things are much more clear now. Do you happen to know where I'm likely to find him? By this time I suppose he's over the shock, and willing to talk about the accident."

Stig winced, reacting almost as sharply as he had when Risa had told him she possessed Tandy's persona.

"You do not know?" he asked.

"Know what?"

"Claude is dead too. He died in December, swimming at night on the Great Baffler Reef. He can tell you nothing. Nothing. Unless you can get information from his persona, wherever it may be."

Chapter 9

Francesco Santoliquido said with obviously forced heartiness, "It's good to see you again, John. I'm always delighted when you drop in."

Roditis took the proffered hand. It was soft, warm, not precisely a flabby hand but certainly the hand of a man who welcomed all comforts. The door of Santoliquido's office did not argue that he had spartan tastes.

"Drink?"

"Certainly, Frank."

They touched ultrasonic snouts to their arms. Santoliquido beamed. "You've kept well, John. Still a demon for exercise, are you?"

"I get only one body to inhabit," said Roditis. "I keep it with respect."

"Naturally." A wary expression crept into Santoliquido's eyes. Roditis suspected that the older man was afraid of him, and he liked that, for Santoliquido was very high in the system of the world, very high indeed. He wondered just what Elena had been saying to Santoliquido about him, and what the response had been.

Roditis said, "The statue looks as splendid as ever."

"The Kozak? Yes. Yes, a masterpiece." Santoliquido chuckled. "Don't think I've forgotten you have Anton Kozak sitting back of your eyes. Has he led you to take up sonic sculpture yet?"

"He tries," said Roditis. "But I know my limitations."

"A wise man."

"I lack the skills of Kozak. I would not defame him by plying his art. His mind cannot drive my muscles."

"Of course not," conceded Santoliquido.

"He is glad to see that piece again. He tells me it's one of his favorites. A brilliant artist, Frank. I compliment myself many times for having chosen him. You know, a man like me, a man of dollars, I didn't get much chance to learn how to appreciate beauty. Kozak has taught me. Now I know what the balance of line means: what the harmony of form is. I'm much richer."

"That's the purpose of the Scheffing process," Santoliquido said sententiously. "To enhance, to enrich. Doubtless he's greatly widened your horizons of perceptions. But tell me, John: how does Kozak find it, seeing the world through the eyes of a billionaire financier?"

"He enjoys it, I believe. He makes no complaints. His world is enriched too. He moved much too much in the company of esthetes; now he sees a different facet of existence. I'm sure that when he makes his next carnate trip he'll try to express some of that new knowledge in art, if he's lucky enough to be acquired by someone with the right skills for practicing sonic sculpture."

"That's far in the future," said Santoliquido nervously. "You look quite healthy, John, and there'll be no new carnate trip for you or your personae for a long time to come, I'm sure"

"I hope so."

"And Walsh? Old Elio? He's thriving too?"

"Oh, yes," Roditis said. "We're kindred spirits. He built a network of power-transmission stations; I've built a network of a different sort of power. He finds his present place quite rewarding. And I regard him as indispensable." Roditis smiled, and held the smile just slightly too long, intentionally. Then he said, "I'm sure you realize that I didn't ask for this appointment so I could discuss my existing personae."

"Of course."

"You realize why I'm here?"

"Naturally."

"Shall I name it or will you?'

"Paul Kaufmann," Santoliquido said. "Yes?"

"Yes. The old man's been dead since the turn of the year. It's nearly May now. There's no reason for keeping him in storage any longer, is there?"

"We're nearing a decision, John."

"I've been hearing that phrase for weeks. I'd like to know how long you plan to go on nearing that decision'

"I'm approaching it rapidly," said Santoliquido.

"And asymptotically?"

"John, you don't appreciate the complexity of what's involved. Here's the persona of one of the world's most powerful men, perhaps *the* most powerful of his age, a uniquely vigorous personality, a man of colossal wealth, of the highest family connections. It takes time to evaluate the applicants for his persona. The decision can have far-reaching consequences."

"How many other applicants are there?" Roditis asked.

"Hundreds."

"And how many of them do you seriously think are qualified to handle a persona of such force?"

"Several," Santoliquido said.

Instantly Roditis knew that he was lying. But he did not dare force the situation beyond this point. Obviously Elena's ministrations had clinched nothing yet. Santoliquido was still reluctant to surrender the Paul Kaufmann file.

Roditis said, "It's not my intention to put pressure on you. I feel you owe it to the world to restore Paul Kaufmann to carnate existence, and I'm offering myself as the vehicle for that. As time passes, you know, his persona gets out of touch with the flow of events. We'll forfeit his abilities to evaluate situations if we let the world become incomprehensible to him."

"But do you think you're an adequate vehicle, John?"

Surprised, Roditis answered, "Has anyone ever doubted that I am?"

"The Kaufmann persona is a powerful one."

"I realize that. I'm prepared and capable. You've tested my capacity."

"Yes. Even so, I remain uneasy. A man like Paul Kaufmann could so easily break through to dybbuk—"

"No one," said Roditis stiffly, "is going to reach dybbuk at my expense. Not even Paul Kaufmann."

"There are times," Santoliquido murmured, "when I feel it would be best to leave that old man in storage forever."

"That would be a crime against his persona! You have no right!"

"I didn't say I would. But it's a temptation. Otherwise we run the risk of loosing him on the world again. A buccaneer. A cannibal. A marauder."

"He was merely a shrewd and aggressive businessman," Roditis said. "Give him to me and he'll be under control every minute of the day. I'll harness him."

"You're very confident of yourself, John. Come with me."

"Where?"

"To the main storage vault. I'll give you a closer view of Kaufmann."

Roditis had been in the storage vault before. But yet it never failed to strike pangs of awe in him as he moved through the low-roofed vestibule with its assortment of wary scanners and into the huge gloomy cavern of canned souls. They reached a sampling booth. Santoliquido requisitioned one of the storage caskets and cradled it firmly under one arm.

Looking about the colossal room, with its tier upon tier of racks and urns, Roditis said softly, "Do you know the eleventh book of the *Odyssey*? Odysseus goes to the Halls of Hades to seek advice of the soul of Teiresias." His hand swept along the dully gleaming balcony. "Here we are. The Halls of Hades, the City of Perpetual Mist. We beach our boat and make our way along the banks of the River of Ocean. Odysseus draws his sword, digs a trench, pours libations to the dead. Honey and milk, wine, water. He sprinkles white barley. He cuts the throats of sheep. The dark blood pours into the trench, and now the souls of the dead come swarming up from below. He sees his unburied friend

Elpenor. He is approached by his mother, but waves her away to speak with Teiresias. Then he meets others. The mother of Oedipus. The wife of Amphitryon. Ariadne. Poseidon. These are the Halls of Hades, Santoliquido. We can summon up departed souls."

"You know your Homer well," Santoliquido said.

"I am a Greek," said Roditis calmly. "Are you surprised?"

"You don't usually seem so-literary, John."

"But this is Hades, isn't it? Not a place of punishment, not Dante's Inferno, simply a storage vault. As Homer tells it. Standing here looking into that darkness, Frank, don't you feel it?"

"I've felt it many times. Though not in Homer's terms, exactly. We Romans have a poet of Hades too. Remember? "The descent into Hell is easy. Night and day lie open the gates of death's dark kingdom.'"

"Virgil?"

"Yes. Aeneas also sees the dead. He plucks a golden bough and inquires after his comrades. A deep, dark cave, with fumes coming up from its throat; he follows a path, he takes the ferry across the river, he encounters the shade of his steersman Palinurus. He finds Dido, weeping. And his father, Anchises. I've often thought of it, John."

"Open Hades for me, then. Show me Paul Kaufmann."

"Come inside the booth."

They entered. Roditis was in a dark mood now; he stared at the coppery casket containing the persona of Paul Kaufmann, and a terrible desire came over him to seize it from plump Santoliquido and run off. But that was foolishness. He waited while Santoliquido set up the equipment.

"What are you going to do?" Roditis asked finally.

"Allow you to have a thirty-second peek at Paul Kaufmann. It's a standard scanning. Once it begins, I'll let it continue no matter how you react, and afterward we'll know how eager you really are to have him with you forever."

"You don't frighten me."

"I don't mean to. But I want you to realize that there are risks."

"Go ahead," said Roditis.

He accepted the electrodes. Through slitted eyes he observed the final preparations.

"Now," Santoliquido said.

Roditis jerked and quivered in the first impact of union with the persona of Paul Kaufmann. It was as if he had plunged into a boiling, sulfurous lake, dropping straight to the bottom, engulfed in it, fighting for breath. But he did not drown. Within moments he was rising, finding his level, learning the art of swimming in this medium.

Incredible!

Such strength, such vitality, such intensity that old man had had! Roditis examined strands of memory; not tangled knotted ones, but firm hawsers of recollection, stretching across the void of years. He acknowledged a formidable mind when he met one. Had old Kaufmann ever forgotten anything? Had he ever blundered? Roditis stared in delight at serried rows of archives, at a comprehensive and flawlessly arranged memory bank. Kaufmann must not have been human, but some sort of computer. But no, he was human enough: here were lust, rage, avarice, triumph, all the passions, throbbing chords of emotion slashing in bright primary hues across the purpled backdrop of that powerful mind. To and fro Roditis moved, examining everything, passing freely down the frozen canyons of that awesome persona, admiring stalactites and stalagmites of desire, glittering crystals of achievement, the ropy fabric of maturity. Kaufmann at seventy had been a phenomenon, but not a sudden one; roving backward, Roditis saw the unity of the man, saw the same unbending purpose at forty, at twenty, even at ten. How could there be a man like this, all fire and ice at once? Having entered that realm of wonders, Roditis could not leave. He heard the sound of distant music, resonant, somber, a chromatic symphony of great power. He saw towering Gothic arches receding to infinity. In his nostrils was the scent of grandeur. Roditis planted his feet firmly on a broad plain beneath a black sky. He threw his head back and roared joyous laughter at the heavens.

The images dissolved. He sat in a small room, electrodes on his forehead, Santoliquido studying him with interest

"Give him to me," Roditis said at once.

"The risks—"

"There are no risks. I can handle him. He belongs to me! He must be mine!"

"You're shaking all over," Santoliquido pointed out.

Roditis discovered that it was so. He stared at his trembling fingers, his quaking knees. The harder he tried to regain muscular control, the more violent the tremors became. He said, "It's nothing but a reaction to tension. I don't pretend it was like nothing, scanning that mind. But I am well. I am strong. I have the right to receive that persona."

"How do your own personae feel about it?"

Roditis realized that he had lost contact with Kozak and Walsh. He had to grope uncertainly in the recesses of his own mind a moment before he located them. Walsh seemed dazed; Kozak, sullen, withdrawn, wounded. As he probed them they stirred gradually; as if thawing after a freezing bath. They had not enjoyed their brief exposure to Paul Kaufmann, it appeared. Roditis tried to cheer them. They would get used to their new neighbor in his mind.

He said to Santoliquido, "Well, they're a little shaken up, I suppose. He was a rough dose for them. But it'll wear off."

"I'm worried, John."

"About them?"

"About you. If you took on Kaufmann, what the long-term effects might be. You're an important man nowadays, with plenty of responsibility. If you should cave in under the weight of this new persona you want—"

"I won't."

"*If,*" said Santoliquido. "There could be serious economic consequences."

"How many different ways do I have to put it? I'm capable of bearing up. Do you know, Frank, I feel such exultation now, having seen that man's mind—such a sense of *widening*, after only half a minute. You've *got* to give him to me!"

Santoliquido's tongue appeared and made a slow circuit of his lips." After a moment's silence he rose and beckoned to Roditis. "Let's take a walk," he suggested. "If you've recovered from those tremors by now."

Roditis stood up with exaggerated agility. Santoliquido put the Kaufmann persona back in its casket and stuffed it in a hopper slot; it vanished from sight, to Roditis' sharp regret. They left the sampling booth. Santoliquido led him out on the catwalk that rimmed the circumference of the storage vault.

"We're going to take a tour of Hades," he said. "I want to show you some possible alternate personae."

"I don't—"

"At least consider them," said Santoliquido. He tapped out digits on a data terminal. One of the sealed storage banks opened and he pulled out an urn, examined it, frowned, replaced it, removed the adjoining one. He held it up. "Elliot Sakyamuni," he said. "You know him? An outstanding guru, one of the architects of the new religion, a truly powerful man. He died in March. We've had him here, waiting for the right recipient. John, if you were to take him on, you'd have the added spiritual depth, the extra dimension of wisdom, that only a fully trained guru of the highest degree could offer. You're the first person I've suggested giving him to. Consider it."

"In addition to Kaufmann?"

"In place of Kaufmann," said Santoliquido. "I think the guru would be better for you."

"No," said Roditis. "I can get along without extra spiritual depth.

I've got Noyes to recite mantras for me. Put Sakyamuni back."

Santoliquido sighed and put the urn away. They climbed to another catwalk. Indicating a frosted glass panel, Santoliquido said, "The world-famous mathematician Horst Schaffhausen. He has waited nearly two years now to return to carnate form. A mind like yours would be well- suited—"

"Stop it, Frank."

"You oughtn't turn away from Schaffhausen that lightly. His unique powers would be of great value to you in—"

"I'll take him three years from now," said Roditis. "Give me a chance to digest Kaufmann first."

Beads of sweat burst out on Santoliquido's forehead. Hoarsely he said, "Won't you get off that obsession, John? Kaufmann's a burden for anyone. He'll weigh you down."

"I want him."

"You and he are too much alike. In the Scheffing process we should seek for complements, not supplements. There'll be war between you and Kaufmann over every business decision. He'll want to do it his way, you'll want to do it yours—"

"And I'll win," said Roditis. "I'm alive, he'll just be carnate. I'll use his judgment, but I won't let him call the tunes for me."

"If he goes dybbuk—"

"Impossible."

Santoliquido said, "I offer you your free choice of any persona we have here, but that one."

"Are you trying to torture me?"

In a low voice Santoliquido said, "It might even be possible to arrange something slightly irregular. Would a transsexual transplant interest you? What if I made available to you the persona of Katerina Andrabovna, say. An extraordinary combination of sensuality and intellect, a truly blazing woman—"

"Is it that bad?" Roditis asked. "Are you in such a mess, Frank, that you have to consider breaking the law? What hold do they have on you, anyway?"

"Who?"

"The Kaufmanns!"

"No one has any hold on me whatever," said Santoliquido with obvious strain. Roditis was amazed at the anguish visible on the plump face. "I make my own decisions."

"Mark Kaufmann doesn't want me to get his uncle's persona. He's fixed things so I won't. You're willing to offer me the whole vault, if I please, so long as I keep away from old Paul. You've even offered me an abomination. So you must be really trapped. You'd like to make me happy, but you're afraid to offend Mark, and that leaves you ripping in half." Roditis put his hand on Santoliquido's shoulder. "I know what it must be like for you," he said more gently. "But all I ask is that you do your duty. I'm the logical recipient of Paul Kaufmann. Mark would get reconciled to the idea after a while, once he finds out I'm not a monster."

"We can't talk about such things out here."

"In your office, then."

But even amid the Babylonian splendor of his office Santoliquido was ill at ease. He took several drinks in quick succession, paced the floor, stood for a long moment before the Kozak sonic sculpture. Finally he said, "I need more time, John."

"You're just stalling."

"Maybe so. But I'm not ready to move. You know. I'll have to live with my decision forever. Give me a few more weeks. By May 15 I'll announce the disposal of the Kaufmann persona, all right?"

"I have no way of holding you to that," Roditis noted.

"I pledge my word."

Roditis let his eyes linger on Santoliquido's. He knew that such a pledge meant a great deal to a man like Santoliquido, who had centuries of ancestors peering down at him all the time. A Roditis, a *condottiere*, might break a solemnly given word when it suited his needs; but not a Santoliquido. Or so Roditis tried to persuade himself.

"Very well," he said. "Weigh your decision carefully, Frank. Don't let Mark pressure you into doing something shortsighted."

Outside the building, Roditis gave way to an access of rage. He sat in his hopter a long while, burning with fury, while angry spasms of heat ripped through him. So much for Elena's help! So much for all Noyes' scheming! The situation was right where it had been since Paul Kaufmann's death... a stalemate. Santoliquido still equivocated. The administrator was all facade; beneath, he quivered with fright at the possibility of offending someone mighty, and so took no action.

When ten minutes had passed, and Roditis felt somewhat calmer, he ordered the hopter to lift and head out over the ocean, due east. The machine throbbed into the air.

"Is there any specific destination?" the robopilot asked.

"Just keep going east till I tell you to go somewhere else."

Roditis closed his eyes. Instantly there came flooding into his mind the renewed presence of Paul Kaufmann. Just that tiny tantalizing taste of Kaufmann's persona had been enough to leave Roditis unalterably convinced that the old man must be his. It was more than mere desire now. It was destiny.

What if Santoliquido should rule against him?

That was hard to imagine. Roditis knew of no one else who could handle the high-voltage mind of Paul Kaufmann. Of course, Santoliquido could take the coward's way out, and simply leave Kaufmann in the storage vault, as he had hinted he might do, as he seemed to be doing with that mathematician, Schaffhausen. But Santoliquido was a man of honor. He could not expose himself that way to shame. He would have to allot Paul Kaufmann to someone.

What if, at Mark's prodding, Santoliquido found some innocuity and impressed the persona on him?

Roditis smiled. Instantly a dybbuk would be created. His investigators would demand the penalty of the law. Erasure would be imposed. Kaufmann would go back into the soul bank, and Roditis could reapply.

On the other hand, Roditis reflected, suppose Santoliquido discovered a person who was strong enough to cope with the Kaufmann persona?

That would be awkward, but it could be handled. Roditis saw that in that event it would be necessary to arrange a discorporation. There would be an accidental death; Paul Kaufmann and his late host would both revert to the soul bank; Roditis could begin the quest anew. One way or another, he would obtain that persona. Having tasted it, he could not now relinquish his need.

He opened his eyes. The small hopter was far out over the Atlantic now. Though spring had formally arrived, the water far below was gray and ominous. High waves surged like mobile mountains, rising and crashing. Through the audio Roditis picked up the sound of that baleful sea. He ordered the hopter to dip low, skimming no more than three hundred feet above the water. The vehicle was meant for short-haul transport, and it was unsafe to have come out here, alone, in such a fragile craft, but Roditis felt soothed by the dangers. The fusion pack below his seat could power the hopter all the way to Europe, if he chose.

On the face of the water the dull tubular bulk of a whale appeared suddenly. Roditis studied the fleshy mass, observing the gray-white spout of water that flumed abruptly from the broad forehead. There was strength! There was power! The tail came up; the flukes lashed the waves. The whale sounded and was gone. A Paul Kaufmann of the seas, Roditis thought. A watery titan.

"Return to New York," he ordered the hopter.

Stormy winds sped the craft landward. As he neared shore, Roditis put through a call to Noyes and found him, tense and knotted, in his apartment.

"It was no good," Roditis said. "Santoliquido still hesitates."

"But Elena said—"

"Elena is a worthless slut. Santoliquido is terrified of Mark Kaufmann, and Mark still refuses to let me have the old man. We're stuck. Santoliquido was willing to give me any persona in the place, except that one. Even a woman."

"You're joking, John!"

"I could have had Katerina Andrabovna. That's how panicky he is."

Noyes bowed his head. He muttered, "I was sure it was all fixed up. Elena was positive too."

"Santoliquido promised to make a decision by May 15," said Roditis. "He didn't promise that the decision would be favorable to me. If it goes some other way—"

"It won't, John."

"If it does, there'll be work for you to do. We can't let that persona slip away. Do you know, Charles, he let me sample the old man! I saw into that mind. I would do anything to have it now. *Anything.*"

"Perhaps I should talk to Elena again," Noyes ventured.

"It can do no harm. But probably little good, either."

"I'll try. I'm in this as deep as you are, John. I've got a lot staked on success. I'll speak to her and get her to put the screws on Santo all over again."

Roditis nodded. He made a dismissing gesture. The screen went blank.

Behind him an ocean storm was rising. He felt the winds buffet his hopter, and ordered the craft upward to safer altitudes. It was late in the afternoon when he landed. He went at once to his nearest office, mind churning with half-conceived ideas. The storm broke in full impact and, as he looked from his tower window, it seemed to him that he saw the gigantic and powerful figure of Paul Kaufmann raging in the dark sky.

Chapter 10

"Where is Risa today?" Elena asked.

"Chasing about Europe," said Mark Kaufmann. "Doing some detective work on behalf of her persona. Last I heard of her, she was in Stockholm, but that was a few days ago."

"You don't worry about her?"

"She can look after herself. Besides, I have her under surveillance."

Elena laughed. "How typical of you! In one breath you tell me that she's self-reliant, and that you're having her watched anyway. You never leave anything to chance."

"I have only one daughter," Kaufmann said quietly. "My dynastic urge won't allow me to leave Risa's welfare to chance."

"Would you have wanted a son?"

He shrugged. "The name won't die. Only my line of it. And I'll be right there, watching the future unfold." Kaufmann got easily to his feet. They were lying on the resilient tile beside his private swimming pool, a hundred feet beneath the Manhattan streets. Warm pinkish light filtered down. "Shall we swim?"

"I'll watch you from here," said Elena languidly.

Leaping into the pool, he swam three lengths in some sudden furious haste, then, more calmly, let himself drift back and forth across the width. The pool had been designed for Elena's tastes. The water contained a fluorescing compound, so that his body left vivid streaks of gold and green as he sliced through it. Below, sparkling globes of captive living light glowed on the pool's floor. The sides of the pool were studded along the waterline with silicaceous thermotectonic gems. The entire installation had run him into many thousands of dollars fissionable. Elena rarely used the pool her whims had created; she was content to lie naked beside it, soaking up warmth from the battery of overhead lamps. Kaufmann disliked the decorative effects, but he humored her.

He surfaced. His hand came up over the margin of the pool and seized her thigh, inches from her groin. He began to draw her to the water. Elena shrieked. Her buttocks bounced and skidded over the tile, and her free leg poked futilely at him.

"Mark!"

He tugged her in. She landed with a radiant fluorescing splash and came up sputtering and blinking, her ebony hair in disarray, her tanned skin shining. *"Birbone,"* she muttered. *"Scelerato!"*

"Sticks and stones will break my bones." He pulled her to him and kissed her, standing upright in the shallows of the pool. Her body resisted him stiffly for a moment, but only for a moment, and then she flowed against him, and her rigid nipples drew a tickling line across his chest When he released her, she was pouting with what he knew to be mock rage. He watched the sparkling water stream from her skin as Elena hauled herself out of the pool and flounced to a vibrator to dry. She stood with her back to him, combing out her hair. His eyes followed the supple line of her spinal column downward from her long neck through the widening hips, the delightful dimples, the fleshy blossoming of her rump.

"I'll get even with you for that." she told him. "I'll make Santo give your uncle's persona to an Arab."

"Better that than to Roditis," Kaufmann said.

Elena stared at him over her shoulder. "I almost believe you mean that. You'd have Paul saying prayers to Mecca before you'd let him into Roditis."

"Yes. Yes, I'm sure of that."

She finished at the vibrator and sprawled on the tile again, well out of reach of his grasping hand. He remained at the edge of the pool.

She said, "Shall I do a three-dollar frood job on you, Mark? I'll tell you why you hate Roditis so much."

"Why?"

"Because he's so much like you."

"What do you know about Roditis? Have you ever met the man?"

"Not yet."

"I have," Kaufmann said. "He's a little thick coarse fellow with big muscles and no grace of soul. He's a walking bank account. He dreams money day and night, and if he's got any other interests they don't show."

"He gave more than a million dollars to a lamasery in San Francisco a few weeks ago," Elena pointed out. "The same one your uncle used to give so much to."

"And for the same reasons, too. You think Paul was a Buddhist? You think Roditis gives a damn about karma? He's looking for publicity, and maybe he'd like the guru to lobby for him with Santoliquido. I'm surprised you're taken in."

"And I'm surprised that you underestimate him so much," said Elena. "He's not quite the ugly dollar-chaser you say he is. One of his personae is the sonic sculptor Kozak. Roditis is a connoisseur of the arts. He collects rare books. Do you know, he's got an entire building full of editions of Homer?"

"How do you know all this?"

"I've been reading about him. I mean, he'll be practically a member of the family soon, and so I thought I'd better—"

Kaufmann was out of the water instantly. He rushed toward her, knowing that he must look absurd in his angry dripping nakedness. He dropped don beside Elena and shouted, "What's that? A member of the family?"

"After he gets your uncle's persona."

"There's no chance of that!"

Elena smiled sweetly She appeared to be enjoying his discomfiture. She placed one hand flat on the tile at either side of her, leaned back, inflated her lungs to give her breasts maximum display. Coolly she said, "I talked to Santo about it. Santo expects to award the persona to Roditis any day now."

154 . To Live Again

"No," Kaufmann said. "Impossible! I've talked to Santo also about this. He promised—"

"What did he promise?"

Kaufmann hesitated. "Well, perhaps not exactly a promise. But he indicated he didn't want to see Paul go to Roditis, any more than I did."

"That was some time ago. Santo is discovering that there's no other qualified recipient. Roditis is clamoring for the persona, and without a valid reason for denying it, Santo is going to have to give it to him. He's holding back only because he's searching for some way to break the news to you."

"No, no, no, no!"

"Yes, Mark!" Elena's face was strangely animated. "You're jealous, aren't you? Roditis is going to get him, and you want him yourself! You can't bear to see anyone else have Paul Kaufmann's persona."

"Stop it," he said.

"I offered you the three-dollar frooding. Take the ten-dollar job instead. It's as I said: you and Roditis are practically alike. The same drives, the same hungers. You have ancestry and he doesn't; that's the only difference. He came out of the dirt and you were born to the Kaufmann billions. Now he's going to grab himself a Kaufmann, and everything will be even. You can't bear that thought."

Kaufmann slapped her across the face. She jumped back, the meaty mounds of her bare breasts leaping toward her chin. Trembling but not in tears, she glowered at him.

"I'm sorry," he said after an endless moment. "You pushed me too far."

"Was I wrong in what I said?"

"I don't know. I don't know." He crouched on the tile and pressed his forehead against his knees. Looking up, he said, "How does it happen that you've been discussing all this with Santoliquido? And why are you suddenly so fascinated by Roditis?"

"Strong men have always interested me, Mark. I shouldn't need to tell you that. And I've neglected Roditis up till now. I should have paid more attention to him while he was on the way up. Now it's clear to me that he's the coming man."

"And so you're preparing to make the hop from my bed to his," Kaufmann said. "Eh?"

"That's an overstatement. But I mean to know him better. And I hope you'll bring yourself to get over your hatred of him. The two of you, working together, could control the world. Particularly with your Uncle Paul guiding him."

"*I* should have Uncle Paul."

"But you can't, Mark. So let him go to Roditis, and then make terms with them. Are you afraid you'll be outnumbered? Aren't you a match for Roditis and Paul together?"

"No," said Kaufmann. "No man ever born could be a match for those two in one mind."

"All the more reason for you to make peace," Elena told him. "He's going to get that persona, and if you haven't come to terms with him, he'll try to break you. Don't be stubbornly proud, Mark. Don't let anger get in the way of common sense. As of now you're richer and stronger than Roditis, but not by much, and the balance is going to tip."

"You sound so sure of that, Elena. Exactly what did Santo tell you, anyway?"

"You've heard it already. It's inevitable that Roditis will get your uncle's persona."

"I'll block it."

"You can't," Elena said in exasperation.

"I'll speak to Santoliquido! I'll—"

"Santo's been having a terrible enough time over this thing as it is, Mark. And you're the cause of all his trouble. Let him alone! It's not proper for you to interfere this way. He's trying to look at things objectively, and here you are in the background, throwing your weight around as a Kaufmann, threatening, cajoling—

"

"I can't let Roditis do this," said Kaufmann stubbornly, feeling more and more like a blind, obstinate fool, but unable to let himself turn back from his chosen course.

Elena yawned prettily. "I'm tired of this discussion. We're at a dead end. You're giving me a headache. Come swim with me."

"You don't like to swim!"

"What of it?" She sprinted past him, reached the rim of the pool, catapulted herself out into space. For an instant she seemed to hang there, for at her request Kaufmann had lowered the gravity of the room they were in, and he watched the heavy mounds of her breasts extend themselves into downward-pointing cones. Then she slipped sleekly into the water, leaving a bright streak that outlined her nudity in an appealingly sensuous way.

He went diving after her. She eluded him for several moments as they crisscrossed the pool. At last he caught her, and she struggled playfully in his arms. He pulled her toward the shallow end of the pool. His lips descended into the hollow between her cheek and her shoulder.

Panting, she slipped away and sprang from the pool. She went only a few paces, turning, going to her knees, then reclining to await him. Tense and uneasy, Kaufmann came after her. She drew him down against the soft cushion of her flesh, and he entered her quickly, fiercely, and together they shuddered out their ecstasies.

He was calmer afterward. He lay beside her, caressing her, apologizing for his loss of temper, for his shouted words, for the slap.

His busy mind prepared new plans.

He had no reason to doubt Elena's statements. He knew that she had been spending time with Santoliquido lately, both at the beach party at Dominica and in New York. It was no secret to him that she had seen the Scheffing administrator on several occasions. He had not objected, partly because he was not possessive toward Elena. and—he admitted to himself now—partly in the unconscious hope that Elena would influence Santoliquido in his favor. It appeared that Santoliquido inclined in the opposite direction. Kaufmann had sensed that, too, from the recent nervousness of Santoliquido in his presence. And he did have to concede that a rational, impartial verdict would award the disputed persona to Roditis.

It was time to stop fighting the inevitable.

There were other ways to keep abreast of Roditis' ambitions. He had tried subtle agitation, and it had failed. Now he would have to go beyond the law, or else he was lost.

Risa spent three days in Monaco before she learned anything of the fate of Claude Villefranche's persona. There were worse places to be hung up, she realized; but yet it was bothersome. Ancient traditions of secrecy interfered with her quest. She could not simply pick up a data line and demand the information she needed. She had to go through channels, and the channels were not always clear.

In late April the weather here was mild, almost balmy, bringing an advance taste of summer. Purple bowers of bougainvillea blossomed on the ramparts of Monte Carlo. The sun was dazzling against the white towers of the tiny principality. She stood in the princely cactus gardens and looked out across the blue Mediterranean, and it seemed to her that she could see Africa slumbering in the hazy horizon. Risa had never been here before. Of course, Tandy had, many times, and she was Risa's guide.

Little had changed in Monaco since the grand days of the nineteenth century. The Hotel de Paris still dominated the waterfront, with the baroque magnificence of the Casino alongside. Pavilions of feathery palm trees swayed in every breeze. Here were dandies and belles cast forward into time, as though this were some pocket of the preserved past. Some of these buildings had been continuously inhabited for more than five hundred years.

At the Hall of Records Risa learned quickly enough of Claude's death, confirming the story Stig had told. On December 18 last, he had been caught in a tidal surge on the Great Barrier Reef and swept out into the open sea. His body had not been recovered. Meat for the sharks, no doubt

Who had received his persona?

Nothing in the records about that. So far as the principality was concerned, the story of Claude Villefranehe had ended on December 18 through accidental discorporation. If his persona had moved on by now to a new carnate existence, it mattered not at all, officially; carnates paid no taxes, did not vote, held no passports. In the United States it was possible to obtain details of a persona's migration from body to body, but not here.

"What will we do?" Risa asked Tandy.

—Can't your family help you?

"Of course. Of course, that's the answer!" She hurried to the offices of Kaufmann et Cie, in a gilded building on the esplanade just below the Hotel de Paris. The bank was operated by the European branch of the family, and actually there were no Kaufmanns currently involved in its management; the directors now were entirely Loebs and Schiffs. Yet Mark Kaufmann's only daughter was certain to get a hospitable welcome. Risa, dressed chastely and sweetly, presented herself to M. Pierre Schiff, her cousin by some intricate prank of genealogy, and explained her problem.

The banker was fifty, portly, staid. He paid Risa the courtesy of addressing her in English; she felt obliged to speak to him in French, which made for an odd conversation.

"I remember the incident," he said. "Last winter, yes. I believe he was a client of ours."

"I've asked the soul bank in Paris for information on him. They wouldn't tell me a thing."

"You gave your name?"

"Yes. It didn't matter."

"Let me try," said Pierre Schiff. He asked his telephone for a number, and did not bother with the vision element. Quickly be made contact. He spoke in rapid, slurred French, pitching his voice so low that Risa could not follow the words. The soft flesh of his face creased into deepening frowns; after a few moments he dropped the phone into his cradle.

He said, "The persona of Claude Villefranche was taken from storage in February and implanted."

"In whom?"

"The name was not available. Even to me. Even to me." He studied his pudgy palm as though it held the answer. "They are quite secretive, those people. But of course there arc ways of dealing with them. They are in need of constant credit for the expansion of their services, and we—" He smiled eloquently. "My son will help you. Let me summon him."

An hour later, Risa found herself on a balcony overlooking the sea, lunching with Jacques Schiff, who was also her cousin, apparently, and far less portly than his father. She had changed from her chaste girlish clothes into something more likely to please Cousin Jacques: a scalloped shell of sprayon that lanced across her slender body to reveal a flawless shoulder, a small firm breast, and a rounded hip. Cousin Jacques was twenty-five, unmarried, tall, attractive. His eyes had a Gallic sparkle, brighter even than the sunlight dancing through the golden-yellow wine they drank with their oysters.

"I knew this Villefranche, yes," he said. "Was he a friend of yours?"

"Of my persona," Risa said.

"Ah! Yes, so. Do you think I knew her?"

"You didn't know her personally. If you did, she's got no recollection of you, and I doubt that she'd have forgotten you, Jacques. Tandy Cushing."

"Yes. So. I knew her by name. Claude described her to me. A

beautiful, beautiful girl, he said. With—ah—" He laughed awkwardly. "Very adequate body. She is dead?"

"She was discorporated at St. Moritz last summer. A skiing accident. Claude was with her at the time. She'd like to know more about what happened."

"But Claude himself has since been discorporated too," Jacques mused. "It is a sad world, even now. Dangers lie everywhere for the young, the strong, the rich. Only the poor live long lives."

"But they live only once," Risa pointed out.

"True. True." Jacques steepled his fingers. "After lunch," he said, "I will trace Claude's persona for you."

They ate well. For her main course Risa had a mousse of sole, and vegetables of some unfamiliar sort braised in a sauce that was clearly Venusian in origin. Yet the wine that flowed so copiously throughout the luncheon was quite Terrestrial, a lively Chablis four years old. Elderly men passing beneath the veranda paused and looked up at them and made mental calculations, wondering who it was who might be lunching with Pierre Schiff's son, that pale girl in the revealing costume. Did any of them realize that it was not Pierre Schiff's son but Mark Kaufmann's daughter who should concern them on that veranda? Risa enjoyed her anonymity here.

After they had eaten, Jacques suggested that they go to his office while he made the necessary calls. Risa nodded toward the nearby hotel.

"My room is closer," she said.

He looked startled for a moment, but only for a moment. At his insistence, though, they entered the hotel through different doorways. She left the door to her room unsealed, and he slipped through it a moment after she arrived. The large, cavernous room was dark. Jacques produced a portable cesium-powered MHD torch and set it on the ornate dresser. Then he settled in a chair before the old-fashioned telephone and punched out a number.

"This will take a while," he said.

She went into the bathroom, removed her clothing, and stepped under the vibrator. When she felt thoroughly clean, she wrapped herself in a cloud of grayish mist and emerged. Jacques still sat at the telephone, taking notes. At length he grunted in satisfaction and hung up.

"Any luck?" she asked.

He turned to look at her. He frowned, and his eyes pierced the quasi-concealing mist to survey the essential points of her body. "Yes," he said absent-mindedly. "I have the details. His persona was awarded to Martin St. John, a resident of London, several months ago."

"Who's he?"

"The third son of Lord Godwin. Here is his address. I have requisitioned his photograph, and it will be coming by slow transmission in a few moments."

"I'm very grateful to you, Jacques. You've done me a great service."

"Say nothing of it," he replied.

But he seemed willing enough to be rewarded for his activities on her behalf. His body was supple, lean, and skilled. It was the first time Risa had made love since taking on Tandy Cushing's persona, and when she slipped into Jacques' arms she felt a sudden wild surge of embarrassment, for there was something enormously public about this lovemaking, with Tandy watching everything through her eyes. Risa was not accustomed to feeling inhibited. After a moment she realized that it was not the lack of privacy that troubled her, but rather that she sensed the much more experienced Tandy sitting as a judge of her erotic performance. Tension gripped her.

—Loosen up, Tandy said. Are you always like this?

Risa felt a flood of encouragement coming from within. She ceased to think of Tandy as a critical observer; Tandy was a participant, a cooperative entity. That made it much more interesting for her. Risa wriggled prettily; she put her lips to Jacques';

she surrendered to him with that mixture of kittenish girlishness and precocious womanhood that she knew was the best weapon in her armory. Tandy guided her. Without her help, Risa might not have been so successful in meeting Jacques' sophisticated approach.

When it was over, and Jacques had donned his bankers solemn garb and was gone, Risa lay sprawled pleasantly on the rumpled bed, recapitulating with Tandy what had taken place, enjoying an amiable post mortem on her responses. It was wonderful to be able to speak so frankly and to know that every thought was perfectly understood.

"I feel so good having you with me," Risa said. "To know that I'll never be alone again. I wish I could reach out and hug you, Tandy."

—Why not?

Risa laughed. She thrust her arms about herself and squeezed tight, twisting on the bed as though she were in another's embrace. Then she relaxed. She waved her legs playfully about.

—We ought to get going, Risa.

"Where to?"

—London. To find Martin St. John.

"What's the hurry?" Risa asked.

But Tandy insisted. And so Risa phoned for reservations on the next flight to London, due to leave at five that afternoon. She just barely made it to the airport in time. En route, she studied the photo of Martin St. John that had come from the data file. Though only a flat, it gave a fair likeness: a man in his early thirties, light-haired, pale-eyed, with a soft face of no particular character. Flabby chin, loose sensual lips, pasty cheeks. Tandy was shocked. She sent up an image of the late Claude Villefranche for comparison: the hard face, the cruel eyes, the fight skin, the thin, curved line of the lips, all were the direct contradiction of the physiognomy of Martin St. John. Could Claude be happy in such a slack, soft-bodied individual?

Moments after she landed at London, Risa put through a call to Martin St. John. It was gratifying to find him at home. Peering at the three-square-inch screen of the airport telephone, though, Risa was struck by his lack of resemblance to the man in the photo. This Martin St. John looked tougher, harder, leaner. He's been sick lately, Risa guessed. He's lost a lot of weight. That must be it.

"Yes?" he said.

"I'm Risa Kaufmann. You don't know me, but we've got a great deal in common."

"How so?"

"You carry the persona of Claude Villefranche," she said. "I'm carrying the persona of Tandy Cushing."

Martin St. John's lips flickered, but he said nothing.

Risa went on, "I know it isn't proper to talk persona-to-persona. But Tandy's very eager to get some information from Claude. If we could meet, and transmit through ourselves the contact between them, it would make Tandy and me very happy."

"I don't know if we should do that."

"Please," Risa said meltingly. "I've chased all over Europe to find you. Don't refuse me now. Give me just half an hour of your time—"

"Very well."

"This evening?"

"If you insist."

"It's very kind of you."

He gave her the address of a coffee shop in the Finchley Road. Risa caught a hopter and was there within the hour. The place was a dark, oblong room, decorated in an arty fake twentieth-century style, with lots of plastic flowers and other foolishness. He sat alone at a table just within the door.

His appearance was unexpected. There was no trace of the flabbiness of feature and expression that characterized the photograph. This man was brusque, taut, and dynamic, His eyes, though a washed-but light blue in tone, were fixed and gleaming, and burned with a feverish intensity. His lips were tense, with the muscles poised in a way that minimized their natural fullness. There was little excess flesh on his face, and apparently none on his body, but about his chin and eyelids there were indications that he had recently lost perhaps forty pounds, for the skin had not yet completely adopted its new outline. When he rose to greet her, his motions were swift and aggressive.

He took her hand in the continental manner. His smile was the briefest of flickers, on and off.

He said in a harsh voice, "Claude Villefranche sends greetings to Tandy Cushing."

Risa was taken aback by the unconventionality of that welcome. "It's good to have located you finally. Mr. St. John. I won't trouble you for long."

"What will you drink?"

"Would you care to recommend something?"

"There's a filtered rum punch here. It's excellent I'll order two."

Risa said, "I'd love it."

He turned to place the order. But there were no servitors in sight. Then one appeared, moving behind their table without appearing to notice him. St. John called out, and still was ignored. He rose from his seat, turning, and his motion was clumsy for a moment, but then he seemed to change gears inwardly; he uncoiled and nearly sprang at the servitor, his hand pouncing down at the robot's nearest limb to spin it about.

"*Will* you give me some service?" he demanded.

It was an amazing performance, a show of temper, agility, and impatience that was as impressive as it was unexpected. Tandy had remained silent thus far in Risa's meeting with Martin St. John, but now she reacted. Waves of sheer terror rose from the persona and washed through Risa's mind.

"What's wrong?" Risa whispered.

—Can't you see? There's nothing left of Martin St. John!

Claude's ejected him! Claude's gone dybbuk!

It was only a guess, a quick flash of intuition. Yet Risa was convinced. Tandy seemed clearly to recognize the characteristic inflections and responses of Claude Villefranche, not veiled and distorted as they would be if Claude were only a persona reaching them indirectly through the mind of Martin St. John, but overt and definite, immediate, direct.

Still, caution was advised. Risa could hardly sound an alarm and call in the quaestors this early to arrest and mindpick the alleged Martin St. John.

Over filtered rum punches she said, "Tandy's memory line ends in June of last year. She died in August. What she wishes to know is how she came about her discorporation."

"Her skis failed as she was crossing a ravine. It happened rapidly and without warning."

"Claude was with her?"

"They started down the slope together. They were in the air together over the ravine. Then—suddenly—she was no longer with him. It was a terrible experience."

"It must have been," said Risa. "I can see that you're moved by it, and you weren't even there."

"My persona was there, though," St. John pointed out.

Risa nodded. It seemed odd to her that the memories of Tandy's death should lie so near the surface of St. John's mind. He did not give the appearance of reaching into a persona's crowded memory bank for the details, but rather of reading them right off his own backlog of experience,

She said, "What happened after the accident?"

"Claude saw that she had fallen. He turned upslope to find her. But she was gone from sight. It took a great deal of work to uncover her body. Claude was demoralized. He went off to Australia to forget what had happened. And there, as you perhaps know, he met discorporation last December."

"Can you tell me anything about Tandy's last few weeks with

Claude?"

St. John shrugged. His eyes never wavered from Risa's, making her feel acutely uncomfortable. "They met in Zurich at the end of July After ii week there, they went on to St. Moritz, for the summer skiing. They were both in high spirits. Occasionally they quarreled a bit, nothing serious, lovers' tiffs."

"They were in love?"

"Oh, yes. The second week in August Claude asked her to marry him."

—That's a lie, came Tandy's furious denial. Claude would never have married anyone!

"Did she accept him?" Risa asked.

"She hesitated. She told him she would have to wait until later in the year to make up her mind. But of course there never was any later in the year for her."

"I wonder if they would have been happy together."

"I'm sure of it," said St. John. His nostrils widened with some inner tension. "Investigate her earlier memories of him. You'll see how powerfully she was drawn to him."

That was true in its way, Risa knew. Certainly Tandy's feelings toward Claude had been far more powerful than what she felt for the detached, cool Stig Hollenbeck. But she had feared Claude as well as loving him.

"What about you?" Risa said. "Did you know Claude at all when he was alive?"

"We never met. It simply seemed to me his persona would be of interest to me. I needed someone more vigorous than myself, someone with athletic interests. It is always best to choose one's complement, of course."

"He seems to have had quite an effect on you."

"What do you mean?"

Risa hesitated. "Well—that is, when I began to trace you, I received a photo of you. With—I don't mean offense —a very different appearance. You looked softer, more plump."

"Do you have this photo? May I see it?"

She produced it. He studied it intently, his forehead furrowing, his lips curling in a feral scowl. At length he said, "It was taken about a year ago. I've lost a good deal of weight. I've been taking more exercise. Claude's helped me shed all that jelly." St. John glanced up and smiled for the first time. "I feel I'm the better man for having him aboard. Another rum punch?"

"I'd rather not."

"Must you be going?"

"I have-family to visit," Risa said lamely.

"They can wait. Let me show you London. We'll do the town tonight. After all, as you said, we have a great deal in common. Even though we're strangers, a bond of love unites us vicariously. We owe it to Claude and Tandy to come together."

Wavering, Risa felt herself captured. For all his ominous coldness and enigmatic intensity, this man had an undeniable appeal. She was always willing to have an adventure. And with Tandy's lover lurking behind those pale blue eyes—

St. John excused himself to pay the bill.

—Now's your chance. Get out of here, said Tandy.

"Why?"

—He's dangerous. You don't want to fool with a dybbuk. Find a quaestor and have him mindpicked!

"We've got no proof."

—Don't you think I know Claude? His way of speaking, his movements, his facial expressions? He can fool the whole world, but he can't fool me. He's done a countererasure on his host and taken over. First he murdered me, then he murdered Martin St. John. And if you give him a chance tonight, you'll be taking a new carnate trip too. Get out of here!

St. John was returning from the billing plate now. Abruptly, Risa scrambled to her feet.

She rushed from the coffee shop. St. John came after her, calling her name. But he did not pursue her beyond the front of the building.

A thin, acrid smell was in her nostrils: fear. Risa rushed to the corner, shouldering past pedestrians uncaringly. Time seemed to accelerate oddly for her, so that she was unaware of individual moments. In a blur of panic she came to a message box on the corner and opened the speaker hood.

"Quaestor!" she blurted. "I want to report a dybbuk!"

It took only an instant for the robots of the quaestorate to get a fix on the street. Two personnel hopters appeared, and gleaming figures dropped from them. Risa pointed tack toward the coffee shop. "Martin St. John," she said. "There he goes!"

The robots surrounded him. Risa saw the man struggling in vain.

—They've got him, Tandy cried. Come on! We'll have to testify.

"I'd better call my father first. I'm in this too deep."

—All right. Get him to ship a lawyer over. We'll post the challenge and demand a mindpick with me as the— injured party. And I want an autopsy report on my body, too. I'm beginning to figure this business out, Risa.

"What if we're wrong? What if it's all a mistake?"

—Then he'll sue you for false arrest and it'll cost your father some money. It's worth the risk. Do you want dybbuks walking around free?

"Of course not," Risa said softly. She began to walk like a figure in a dream toward the middle of the block. "Of course not. I'll call my father. He'll know what to do."

Chapter 11

"Send in Donahy," Mark Kaufmann said.

The door of his inner office flickered open, and the Scheffing-process technician stumbled in. He looked awed to the point of collapse. His huge bushy eyebrows were thrust up to the top of his wide pale forehead, and his hands plucked tensely at the fringes of his tunic. Within the confines of the Scheffing Institute building, men like Donahy taped the personae of the rich and mighty with little deference, blandly relying on their array of intricate equipment to give them the upper hand. But here, on the home ground of so potent a person as Mark Kaufmann, Donahy was devoid of confidence, a cipher, a twitching pleb smitten with terror, wholly unable to imagine why he had been singled out and summoned here.

Kaufmann said, "We're all alone in here, Donahy. There's no one with us, no one watching us, no mini- viewers, no monitor of any kind. Whatever's said in here remains absolutely private, between the two of us. Sit down."

Donahy remained standing. He shifted his weight from leg to leg.

"You don't trust me?" Kaufmann asked. He opened a panel on his desk and unclipped a microspool monad. "Do you see this? It's a spy detector. It's programed to set off an alarm if any outside entity taps into this room. So long as it quietly glows green like this, we can say what we please, we can plot to blow up the universe, and no one will know. So relax. Sit down and have a drink. I don't bite."

"I can't understand why you've asked me to come here."

"Because I want you to do something for me, obviously," Kaufmann said. He extended the tray of drinks as Donahy nervously lowered himself into the chair at last. Silently they went through the ritual of the drink. By every motion Donahy showed his fear and uncertainty. He'll be tugging at his forelock next, Kaufmann thought.

On Kaufmann's desk sat a small portrait of Uncle Paul, one of the many in his possession. He thrust it forward and let Donahy contemplate the patrician features, the sly, veiled eyes, the magnificent chin.

"Do you know this man, Donahy?"

A nod. "It's Paul Kaufmann, isn't it?"

"Yes. My late uncle. He'll soon be back in carnate form, I believe."

"I don't know anything about that, sir."

"The information I have is that Administrator Santoliquido intends shortly to approve the transplant of my uncle's persona to John Roditis."

Donahy looked blank. Kaufmann realized that he was speaking beyond the technician's comprehension; Roditis and Santoliquido and old Paul were simply not part of Donahy's world except as friezes on some titanic facade far overhead. They were demigods, and Donahy did not concern himself with their wishes, conflicts, or plans.

Kaufmann said, "How would you like to be earning twenty thousand bucks fish a year, Donahy?"

"*Sir?*"

"I need a favor. You're in a position to grant it. I could have picked any one of a hundred technicians to handle the job for me, but I've dealt with you before and I know you're capable and trustworthy. And I assume you could always use more money. What do you get paid, anyway?"

"Seven thousand, sir. With an annual increment of two hundred fifty."

"Which means that if you stick to your job and don't make any conspicuous mistakes, you're likely to be making as much as ten thousand by the time you're middle-aged, right? And there you stick until you retire and die. Well, I'm offering you an extra twenty thousand, on a lifetime annuity. Out of that you should be able to put aside enough money to make the down payment on a Scheffing persona recording. Would you like to live again, Donahy?"

The man looked utterly sick now. Rivulets of perspiration streamed down his face. He reached impulsively toward the tray of drinks, and then, as if deciding that it was impolite to serve himself without being asked, drew back, his fingers quivering.

Kaufmann smiled. "Go on. Have another. Have two. If you're tense, why not?"

Donahy jabbed the snout of a drink tube against his arm. When he spoke, he had difficulty framing his words.

"Could-could you be more specific, Mr. Kaufmann?"

"Certainly. I'm sure you know that the Scheffing Institute retains all persona recordings it makes, storing them in various depots around the world. For example, John Roditis is shortly going to receive a transplant of my uncle's persona recorded last December, but there's also a Paul Kaufmann persona that was recorded last spring, and one made the year before that, and so on over quite a span of time. And these previous recordings remain in dead storage. Are you aware of that?"

"Yes."

"Now, then, suppose you were to locate the whereabouts of my uncle's last-but-one recording, which shouldn't be too difficult for you to find, and remove it from storage. Then, suppose you were to bring this recording with you to a certain lamasery in San Francisco which is in the process of setting up its own soul bank. They've already installed enough equipment to do transplants and make recordings. What if you were to supervise the transplant of this borrowed persona at the lamasery? And then you'd undergo a blanking that would wipe all this incriminating evidence from your mind, so that no one could possibly prove that you had done any of these things. When you came to, you wouldn't know what you had been up to, but you'd discover you had suddenly become the recipient of an annuity which automatically transferred twenty thousand bucks fish into your credit balance each year. That's the equivalent of half a million dollars invested at four percent which is considerable capital. With that kind of stake, you'd be able to buy yourself onto the wheel of rebirth. The risk is very small and the reward is infinite. What do you say, Donahy?"

"I've always been a law-abiding man, Mr. Kaufmann."

"I know that. But would you give up your chance of eternal life for the sake of respecting the regulations? Look, Donahy, the rules about transplants aren't graven on tablets of stone. They don't represent basic moral commandments. If you kill a man, that's evil, I agree. If you molest a child and warp its life, that's evil. If you mutilate another human being for arbitrary amusement, that's evil. But the regulations governing the Scheffing Institute don't grow out of fundamental ethical constructs. They're just working rules set up to avoid confusion and possible conflicts. I don't say that they ought to be disregarded lightly, but they mustn't be looked upon as immutable. When there's a chance to have rebirth by winking at the rules for a moment it's suicidal to be a stickler for the letter of the law."

Donahy appeared to be impressed by that argument. But he was not altogether tempted.

"How can I be sure that this isn't some kind of trap?" he asked.

"Trap?" Kaufmann exploded. "*Trap?* You mean that I've had you hauled over here for purposes of entrapment? That I've given you this much of my time simply for the sake of finding out whether your loyalty to the rules is unshakable? Don't be absurd."

"I've got to look at this thing from my own viewpoint. You don't know me at all, Mr. Kaufmann, except that I've worked on your recordings at the Institute. All of a sudden you send for me and offer me a fantastic reward if I'll do something wrong. I can't begin to understand any of this."

"Let me spell it out for you, then. I'll give you some insight into my motives. The recipient of the transplant will be myself."

"*You?*"

"Me. I'm determined not to let John Roditis gain advantage on me by taking on my uncle's persona. I'll have a slightly earlier persona, slightly less complete, but good enough to match him anyway. That'll nullify what he gains by getting Uncle Paul."

Donahy was drawn back in his chair as though gripped by total panic. His eyes bulged; a muscle in his cheek danced about. Clearly he had no wish to be privy to these secrets of the great.

Kaufmann said, "Now you understand what's at stake, Will you help me?"

"What would happen to me if I refused?"

"I'd have you mindpicked and blanked to get all the details of this conversation out of your head. Then I'd send you back to your apartment and have another Scheffing technician brought here, and I'd make the same offer."

"I see."

"What's your answer, Donahy?"

"Can I have a little time to think things over, sir?"

"Of course." Kaufmann looked at his watch. "Take sixty seconds, if you like."

"I meant several days, Mr. Kaufmann."

"You can't have several days. You've heard the terms of the offer. I'll shield you from all consequences and give you an annuity that will make you a rich man. What do you say?"

Donahy let nearly a full minute spill away before he replied.

"Yes," he whispered. "Yes. I'll do it! But you've got to protect me!"

"You have my assurance," said Kaufmann. He stood up. "One of my associates will accompany you to your home. He'll remain with you overnight. In the morning you'll arrange to get access to the archive of old persona recordings. At the close of your working day you'll be picked up and taken to San Francisco with the recording. I'll meet you there tomorrow evening and you'll perform the transplant. When you report for work in New York the day after tomorrow, your part will be complete and you'll be blanked to protect you against possible interrogation. Your annuity payments will begin to accrue to your account that day. Is it a deal?"

Donahy nodded numbly.

"Your hand," Kaufmann said. He grasped the limp, cool fingers in his own. Then he buzzed for an aide to take the technician away. Donahy would not be alone again until the work was finished.

Moodily, Kaufmann let the tension ebb from his system. The interview had gone about as well as he could have expected. He disliked the shady nature of what he was doing; but at this stage he was compelled to take these protective steps. Above all else, a Kaufmann was bound by honor, yes. But if honor dictated that he preserve the family's position no matter by what means, he could hardly afford to boggle at shady doings. Normal concepts of honor were not framed to include the existence of a Roditis.

He flipped the retrofile, triggering it to see what calls might have come in while he spoke with Donahy. Risa's Image appeared. The file told him that she was waiting in London to speak with him.

"Put her on," he said, transferring the call to the large screen.

A moment passed; then Risa appeared, life-size, on the screen. She looked frayed and weary. It was after midnight in London. No doubt this legal business involving her persona was taking a heavy toll of her energy.

"Well?" he said. "How does it go?"

"It's moving very fast, Mark. The autopsy report on Tandy came in this morning."

"And?"

"She was almost four weeks pregnant at the time of her death.

That checks with the mindpick information they got out of Claude Villefranche's dybbuk."

"I see," Mark said. "She went to Claude and told him she was pregnant and wanted him to marry her, and he refused, and they had a fight over it and he killed her."

Risa laughed. "Oh, no! The way you tell it, it's straight out of one of the old melodramas. Tandy wouldn't have tried to use a pregnancy to blackmail a man into marrying her. Especially not a man like Claude."

"What's the story, then?"

"The gene tests show that she was pregnant by Stig The Swede, her other lover. Sometime between the time Tandy made her last persona recording in June and the time she died in August, she decided that it would be interesting to have a baby, I guess. So she stopped the pill and Stig filled her up. She knew that Stig would be willing to marry her. He's a decent sort. Claude excited her more, but she didn't trust him. Then she went off to Switzerland to have her last fling with Claude. At St. Moritz she broke the news to him that this was where he got off. He was furious and told her to have the fetus aborted, to forget about getting mated to Stig."

"But you said that Claude wasn't interested in marrying her," Mark said, puzzled.

"He wasn't. But he wasn't about to let Stig have her either. Or put a child in her. He saw that as an attack on his reputation for virility. He was wild with jealousy. So they had a fight, and finally they went out on the ski slope and he took the feeder pin out of her gravity repulsor, and down she went. If he couldn't run her life, she had to die. It's all there in the persona he last recorded. He made the recording two months after the killing."

"Didn't anyone think of examining her skis after the accident?"

"They were badly damaged, Mark. It was impossible to determine anything."

"And there was no autopsy?"

Risa shrugged. "When a girl is smashed up in a hundred- meter fall, there's no real point in an autopsy, is there? No one suspected she might be pregnant."

"What happens to this dybbuk now?"

"Claude? Well, they've got him on a double murder charge. The mindpick evidence shows that he killed Tandy, and there's also the little matter of what he did to his host. So the quaestorate has requested a complete erasure. They're going to blot him out entirely. He's being shipped to New York tomorrow and the job will be done at the Scheffing Institute. They'll clean him out of his host's mind and also destroy all his existing persona records."

"You must feel very proud of yourself, Risa, exposing this criminal."

"Well, actually, I could never have done it without Tandy. She was the one who guessed she'd been murdered, and she put the finger on Claude as a dybbuk. After that it was just a matter of seeing what was in his mind."

"And in Tandy's uterus," Kaufmann observed.

"Yes, that too. Well, now it's over, anyway."

"I'm glad. Risa, are you all through playing detective?"

"I think so. Why?"

"It would be nice if you'd stay closer to home for a while, with this business settled."

"I'll be home in about a week," she said. "Is that all right?"

"Fine," said Kaufmann. "Do you have enough money?"

"I'm drawing on the general family balance. All right?"

"Have mercy," he told her.

"I will. I'll see you soon."

Out of her tired eyes there twinkled a look of warmth, love, kinship He smiled at her. She was a fine girl, he decided. A credit to their line. She had the promise of true greatness. He blew her a kiss, and the screen darkened.

A pity she was a girl, he thought.

Of course, they had had an option to fix that. But Kaufmann's wife was delicate, and he hadn't cared to dabble in uterine adjustments. He had taken his chances, and had had a girl, and there had been no more children after that. Risa was masculine enough in her thinking, at any rate. A time would come when she'd enter the family enterprises as a full partner, and Kaufmann knew she'd do well. His only objection to her sex was an esthetic one: a woman in business was in some way an unattractive sight, no matter how beautiful she might be. That was archaic foolishness, he knew, but he could not escape the thought that it was somehow ugly to watch a woman at work in front of a data console, making executive decisions involving millions of dollars. Women should be gentler creatures. But there was nothing gentle about Risa, female or not. It would be interesting to follow her progress down the generations as they leapfrogged from one carnate trip to the next.

He turned back to his ticker. Three quick trades produced a handsome profit for him. A cheerful omen.

By the end of this week he'd have all the shrewdness of Paul Kaufmann to add to his own. At last. At last. Naturally, he'd have to go warily, lest anyone find out that he carried an illegal persona. But Roditis would be perplexed when he discovered that each of his new strategic thrusts, inspired by Paul's persona, was being countered by strategies just as shrewd. Would he suspect that a second Paul Kaufmann was at work to thwart him? Would it occur to Roditis that such a thing was possible—a duplicated transplant? Few people were even aware that old recordings were preserved. Mark himself had not known it, despite his wide range of information, until Santoliquido had told him. So Roditis, though he was naturally suspicious, would have no inkling of the truth. He would just wonder how it was that his rival stayed abreast of him. Of course, after Mark's death the next possessor of Mark's persona would discover the secret when he unexpectedly found Paul in his skull as well. But he was not likely to make the news public. Revelation of the irregularity would most likely bring about the erasure of both Kaufmann personae; the lucky man who had received two Kaufmanns for the price of one would make every effort to hide the fact.

Kaufmann laughed softly. His phone lit up. He keyed in, and the monitor said, "Francesco Santoliquido is calling."

Surprised, Kaufmann accepted the call at once. "Yes, Frank?"

Santoliquido looked younger, more carefree than he had appeared for many weeks. The living jewelry at his throat, the cage of tiny crustaceans, seemed to be leaping about jauntily in reflection of his changed mood. "I've reached a decision about your uncle's persona," said Santoliquido briskly.

Kaufmann remained calm. Donahy's assurance of co- operation was his bulwark against any possibility. "Yes?' he said easily. "Who's the lucky man? Roditis, as expected, eh?"

"No."

"*No?*"

"I've weighed this a million times, Mark. I've come around to your way of thinking: that Roditis has such power already that it would be a grave mistake to let him have Paul. That would set up an extraordinary concentration of ability in one individual, with unpredictable results."

"Of course."

"I've also taken into account the objections of the Kaufmann family, as voiced through you."

"Kind of you, Frank. But what will you do with old Paul, then? There can't be many others around you could safely award him to. I suppose it's best simply to leave him in storage a few years, until he's so far out of touch with events that he can be let loose again as someone's persona. I—"

"Oh, he'll be transplanted soon, though."

"To whom?" Kaufmann asked, taken aback.

"We have a rare event scheduled to take place here shortly," said Santoliquido. "The erasure of a dybbuk who's guilty not only of ejecting his host but of deliberately causing the discorporation of a young woman."

"The Tandy Cushing case. Yes, of course. Risa's given me all the details. But what does this have to do with—"

"Once Claude Villefranche has been obliterated, Mark, we'll be left with the empty but living body of Martin St. John, a young man of good family and decent health. Have you considered the status of a blanked-out body of that sort?"

"Why," Kaufmann said, "just take out one of St. John's own recorded personae and imprint it on his own brain. Isn't that the logical solution?"

"It's logical, but it won't work. That's called an autoimprint, and autoimprints can't be made. The brain rejects its own abstracted persona. There are complex reasons for this, partly having to do with the technique of the process, partly with the physiology of the autonomic nervous system, partly with the psychology of the persona. I won't trouble you with the details. But we can't put Martin St. John's persona back into Martin St. John's body. However, there's nothing stopping us from installing some *other* persona in that vacant, healthy body—"

Mark Kaufmann saw where Santoliquido was leading. The impact of comprehension was swift and violent.

"You'll put *Paul* in there?"

"Yes," said Santoliquido smugly.

"But that'll create an instant dybbuk! It'll be Paul Kaufmann operating Martin St. John's body!" Kaufmann cried hoarsely.

"True. However, there's no specific regulation prohibiting such a transplant. We have blank bodies so infrequently that there are no precedents. Paul himself is something of a precedent-setter, too, since his mind is uniquely dynamic and overbearing, and he's almost certain to turn any host he gets into a dybbuk. With a few possible exceptions, such as Roditis. And yourself. But we have a moral obligation to return Paul's persona to carnate form. If we give him an orthodox transplant, and a dybbuk results, the quaestors will insist on mandatory erasure again, If we put him into a wholly empty body, though, so that there's no charge of an unethical takeover of another intelligence, he won't be breaking any laws. In effect, your uncle will return to the world as an independent entity, truly reborn."

Kaufmann was staggered by the idea.

He saw the complacence in Santoliquido's face, and knew that the Scheffing administrator had engineered this most cunningly, as a way of immobilizing both Roditis and himself. Handing the disputed persona to a third party, a zero, a blank, neatly cut the ground from under both of them. Roditis could storm and rant, but unless he found some legal flaw in the transfer, he could not oppose it. And Mark, having put up a successful battle to keep Paul out of Roditis' mind, could not now very well presume to interfere with Santoliquido's further freedom of action.

It was ironic that Risa had provided Santoliquido with the solution to his dilemma. Very conveniently, she had helped to make a blank body available to him at the critical moment. Zip, zip, and Paul Kaufmann would walk the earth again, not merely as a silent persona, nor even as an unlawful dybbuk that had wrested control from a victimized host, but as a true rebirth, given a body of his own with the blessings of the Scheffing Institute!

"What do you say, Mark?" Santoliquido asked coyly.

Shaken, Kaufmann replied, "This is very sudden. It brings up all kinds of complications. What, for example, would be the legal status of this carnate form? Paul's dead. His estate is going through probate."

"Legally, the new entity would assume the property and status of Martin St. John," said Santoliquido. "I've already had a ruling on that. He'd be St. John, carrying the Paul Kaufmann persona. Of course, in effect he'd simply be Paul in St. John's body, but that doesn't give him any title to Kaufmann status. I assume that you'd accept him into your family circle as Paul and find room for him in your business enterprises, but that's strictly up to you. You could just as easily let him try to make his way as St. John.

Knowing Paul, I think he'd do all right."

"Yes," said Kaufmann hollowly. "I think he would."

"So what do you say? I've saved you from the monstrous threat of a Roditis in your bosom! That's a relief, eh, Mark? Isn't it? You look a bit uncertain."

The initial shock was wearing off. Kaufmann had begun to see past his amazement at Santoliquido's coup to the deeper implications. Paul would return to life, yes, as shrewd and as energetic as ever, and with the extra benefit of residing in the body of a young man. That posed something of a threat to Mark's own status as head of the Kaufmann clan.

But no Kaufmann could really accept the reborn Paul as a true Kaufmann. The family would draw upon his reserve of experience and wisdom, but could never accord him full status. At best he'd be a secondary focus of power.

I can handle him, Mark thought. After all, what Santoliquido doesn't know is that I'll have Paul's persona myself. That'll enable me to cope, in case it comes to a show- down between Paul and me. And I should be able to count on Paul's support in the struggle against Roditis.

Kaufmann envisioned the possibility of a three-cornered rivalry: himself, the new Paul, and Roditis. But in such a conflict he would invariably emerge on top, since he'd be Mark-plus-Paul, and thus at least one notch ahead of Paul alone, and two notches ahead of Roditis.

He said, "Yes. Very clever of you, Frank. I approve. Have you broken the news to Roditis yet?"

"No. I thought I'd wait another day or two, until the transplant has actually been carried out. I'd prefer to present it to him as a *fait accompli*."

"That's probably best," said Kaufmann. He chuckled. "I imagine Roditis is going to be surprised."

Chapter 12

Charles Noyes said, "You won't like this, John. Elena says that they've decided not to give Paul Kaufmann to you. They've got some dummy body that a dybbuk was removed from, and they're putting the persona in that."

He waited fearfully for Roditis to react.

They were in the midwestern office of Roditis Securities at Evansville, Indiana, on the top floor of a tower overlooking the river. From the broad windows it was possible to see deep into Kentucky. Noyes had flown, to Evansville that afternoon, after lunch with Elena. This was too important to convey to Roditis by phone.

Roditis seemed strangely calm. He walked past Noyes to the window and peered out into the blaze of light that was the city across the river. Then, turning slowly, he went to the Anton Kozak sonic sculpture that dominated one wall of his office and carefully recalibrated its pitch so that it produced a gentle hum at about fifty cycles. A horizontal component in the sculpture began to oscillate at such frequency that it blurred and became barely visible.

Quietly Roditis said, "Did she learn this from Santoliquido?"

"Yes. She spent much of last night with him, and he told her. According to Elena, Santoliquido is quite proud of what he's arranged, because it thwarts both you and Mark in one stroke."

"What did Mark want done with the persona?"

"Either to be given to him or simply kept in cold storage. Since it obviously couldn't be given to him, Mark preferred that it go to nobody at all. Santoliquido's manipulated things so that neither one of you gets what he wanted, and yet neither one of you has any recourse from the decision."

Roditis, still icily calm, fondled the shining rim of the sonic sculpture. Noyes could not understand his employer's coolness. The man should be raving and shouting. Was Roditis drugged in some way? Up to the eyebrows in pills? System flooded with a chemosterilant to damp down any response?

"Does Kaufmann know of the decision?" Roditis asked.

"Yes," Noyes said. "Santoliquido phoned and told him about it two days ago."

"How did he take it?"

"Angrily. Very angrily. But then he gave his agreement. He had no real choice."

"And when is this transplant supposed to take place?"

Noyes shifted his weight uncertainly from leg to leg. "It was done this afternoon."

"Paul Kaufmann's walking around in a body without a controlling mind?"

Noyes nodded.

"Kaufmann's a dybbuk, then. Without even having to struggle for it."

"Yes."

"Dybbuks are illegal."

"Not this one," said Noyes. "Santoliquido apparently found some sort of legal loophole. Don't you see, this was approved on the highest level, meaning Santoliquido. Therefore, by definition, it can't be illegal. Paul Kaufmann's back in the world, and he's got full command of a body."

"Whose body was it?"

"An Englishman named Martin St. John. One of the younger sons of some lord. He was pushed out of the body by a Frenchman who had earlier murdered a girl at a ski resort, then was killed himself and picked up by St. John as a persona. They tracked him down, erased him after getting a confession under mindpick, and Santoliquido had the bright idea of putting old Kaufmann into the empty body."

"Very clever of him."

"You aren't upset by all this, John?"

"Not at all. I was expecting it, in a way. You can choose not to believe this, but I foresaw some such arrangement down to the actual details. I was braced for it. And I also have a plan of action ready to meet the situation."

"I knew you would, John. What do you have in mind?"

Roditis smiled. "Where is this St. John body now, do you know?"

"Probably still in New York. That's where the transplant was performed. I doubt that he'll do any traveling until he's achieved physical coordination in the new body."

"Good. Go to New York. Find St. John, Charles. Find him and kill him."

"You want me to discorporate—"

"That's right. Kill him. Destroy the St. John body."

Noyes sat down abruptly. His head whiled. Within, James Kravchenko gave a mighty leap, battering against Noyes' defenses. Noyes shivered at the persona assailed him. it was a moment before he could reassert his control over Kravchenko, and another moment before he was able to meet Roditis' level gaze.

"I can't do that, John!" Noyes gasped.

"Yes, you can, and you will. Damn it, do you think I'm going to let a dummy walk off with that persona? Look: Santoliquido doesn't have an infinite supply of empty bodies sitting around ready for Paul Kaufmann to go dybbuk in. Discorporate St. John and you're actually tossing Paul back into the soul bank, right? The master recording is still there, ready to be used again if something happens to the old man's current carnate embodiment. Okay. Remove St. John. I reapply for the Kaufmann persona, which is again available. Only this time I put more pressure on Santo than before. I don't waltz around so diplomatically. I threaten a little. I pound the table. I make it clear to him that I won't tolerate a second trick of that sort. He'll have to give in. I'll get my way at last."

"But I have to commit a discorporation," Noyes said in a weak voice. "What if I'm caught? What if I bungle it?"

"You won't be caught, and you won't bungle it. Don't worry, Charles. I'll arrange everything. As soon as you've done it, we'll whisk you back out here and have you blanked for the hours of the discorporation. We'll fill in false memories, an alibi that nobody can challenge. You'll be beyond the reach of mindpicking. Do you really think I'd allow my oldest and closest friend to run any real risks?"

"Still, can't you hire some thug—program a robot—"

"I need someone I can trust. There's only one person in the world I can rely on for this, Charles. You've been with me on every stage of the operation."

"But

"You'll do it, Charles." Roditis came over, standing above Noyes' chair, and put his hands on Noyes' shoulders just alongside the clavicles. His thick, powerful fingers dug sharply into the flesh. His eyes, compelling, almost hypnotic, sought for Noyes' and locked on them. Noyes knew he was being coerced, but he had never been able to resist Roditis' pressures before, and he doubted that he would succeed this time.

Earnestly Roditis said, "Do you have moral objections?"

"Well, in a way.

"Look at it this way. You aren't actually taking life. The real Martin St. John was discorporated long ago. The only intelligent thing in that body is the persona of Paul Kaufmann, which has no right to be there. Kaufmann's had one life already, one body. That's all he's entitled to on an autonomous basis. Now he's supposed to be riding—as a passenger, as a persona. You dispose of the St. John body and Kaufmann reverts to his proper status, minus the illegal nonsense Santoliquido has invented out of cowardice. You'll actually be performing a pro-social act, Charles. You'll be canceling out an anomaly. Do you follow that?"

"I think so. I—"

"You can't kill something that's already dead. Both Martin St. John and Paul Kaufmann are already dead: one because his persona ejected him, one because his natural span was over. What you'll be doing is disposing of some superfluous protoplasm. Nothing else. You'll do it for me, Charles. I know you will."

"How will I do it?"

Roditis straightened up, went to his desk, ran his fingers over the protruding green studs of a safety cache. The cache door sprang open and he thrust his hand inside, pulling out a lemon-colored box less than an inch in diameter. Roditis popped the box onto his palm and stuck his hand under Noyes' nose. A touch of his finger and the box fissioned along its vertical axis to reveal a minute capsule containing a few drops of some turquoise fluid.

"This," said Roditis, "is cyclophosphamide-8. It's an alkylating agent that has the effect of breaking down the body's fail-safe system for tolerating its on chemical components. Let a little of this get inside a man and he rejects his own organs, the way he'd reject an organ graft from another person without proper chemical preparation."

"Some kind of carniphage?" Noyes asked uncertainly.

"Not exactly, but close enough. Your true carniphage causes the cells of the body to destroy themselves through autolysis, through enzyme release. This stuff has the effect of turning the body into a conglomeration of alien components that can't function homeostatically any more. Gland secretions become poisons; organ coordination ceases; antigens are poured forth to attack the very tissues they ought to be defending. The loveliness of it all is that nothing the medics can do can possibly save the patient The more they meddle, the more quickly the rate of destruction accelerates. Death comes in less than an hour usually."

"Carniphage is quicker," Noyes pointed out.

"But carniphage is too obvious. When a man turns to a puddle of slime inside of fifteen minutes, it's a clear case of carniphage dosing. But with cyclophosphamide-8, the cause of death remains in doubt. It's an ambiguous finish."

"How is the drug administered?"

"In the fine old Borgia fashion. Conceal the box in your palm, like so. Offer your victim a glass of water. Pass your hand over it, squeeze the muscles together. The box opens, the capsule drops in. It dissolves in a microsecond. The turquoise color is lost upon contact with any other fluid. No taste. No odor. It's that simple." Roditis closed the lemon-colored box. He presented it gravely to Noyes. "Get aboard the next flight to New York and find Martin St. John. I've never needed your help more, Charlie-lad."

Dazed, Noyes shortly found himself high above Indiana, eastward bound. One of Roditis' secretaries had booked the flight for him; he himself seemed incapable of taking any positive action at the moment. He carried the capsule of poison in his lefthand breast pocket. In his righthand breast pocket there nestled, as always, the flask of carniphage with which he proposed to end his own miserable life just as soon as he found the courage to do it

This would be an excellent moment, Noyes told himself morosely.

He did not want to be a catspaw for John Roditis any longer. He was tired of rushing around compromising himself for the sake of fulfilling the little entrepreneur's ambitions. Committing murder now. True, true, Roditis had produced a pack of sophistries to persuade him that slipping cyclophosphamide-8 into Martin St. John's drinking water was not murder in any valid sense, and so persuasive was Roditis' glibness that Noyes had been nearly taken in. Nearly. Yet he knew that the quaestors would take a harder line with him if he were caught before Roditis could blank the crime from his mind. They'd accuse him of deliberate discorporation, and there was no more serious crime. He'd be erased. A small loss, maybe, to the universe and even to himself; but nevertheless humiliating. A man should destroy himself, not allow others to destroy him.

Gulp the carniphage now, he thought. You'll make a mess in the plane, and the stewardess will throw up, but at least you'll die an honest death.

His hand stole toward his righthand breast pocket.

—Go on, Kravchenko urged. Why don't you do it and get it over with? I'm so sick of being stuck in your lousy head, Noyes, you can't possibly imagine!

The hand halted short of its goal.

Some lingering Puritan sense of obligation assailed him. To kill himself now would be cowardly; he'd be running out on Roditis' assignment. He had no right to do that. Roditis trusted him; Roditis relied on him. And Roditis had given him employment and a purpose in the world for many years past. Sure, Roditis was overbearing, tyrannical, self-centered, and all the rest. Sure, Roditis had bullied him into compromise after compromise, until at the end he was even crashing parties on the man's behalf and sleeping with strange women to win a nugget of useful information. Nevertheless, those were the conditions of his employment. He had accepted them. He could not spurn them now. He owed it to Roditis to carry out this final assignment, this meaningless discorporation, this destruction of a body already dead and tenanted by a dead man's ghost. After that, if he wished, he could swallow his carniphage at last, with even more justification than now. Running out on unfinished business was surely not in the Noyes tradition.

Noyes realized that he had just made use of his New England heritage to justify an act of murder.

So be it, he told himself. So be it

The decelerating rockets whined. They were landing in New York. Kravchenko, mocking as always, set up a clamor of derision as Noyes moved his hand away from the carniphage. But Kravchenko, Noyes knew, could not have followed the complex inner processes of decision-making. The persona was simply trying to keep him off balance and unsettled. It was not really in Kravchenko's interest to goad him into actually drinking the carniphage; merely to get him so rattled that he'd be vulnerable to the sudden swift strike of a counter-erasure, the violent ejection by a triumphant dybbuk.

He wondered how he was going to find Martin St. John.

He could not simply look him up in the master directory. St. John was an Englishman and wouldn't be listed here. Of course, Santoliquido would know where St. John was staying. But Noyes wanted to avoid tipping his hand to Santoliquido. It was too obvious that Roditis had an interest in getting Paul Kaufmann out of his present carnate form, and if Roditis' known confederate Noyes were suddenly to begin making inquiries about St. John, any chance Noyes might have of gaining access to St. John would disappear.

Noyes decided to ask Elena.

Elena seemed to know everything about everyone. She was at the center of the nexus, tentacles reaching toward Mark Kaufmann on the one hand, toward Santoliquido on the other, toward Noyes on the third. And she still had a tentacle or two left to extend in Roditis' direction. She'd be a likely source of information.

She had a small apartment registered in her on name in New Jersey. Noyes scarcely expected to find her there, but it was the logical place to begin. He called from the airport and was surprised to find her answering.

Her privacy code appeared on the screen. Noyes identified himself. The screen cleared, and Elena came into view. She was nude, but the scanner cut her off at the breasts, and in any case the tiny screen in the booth did not give him much of a view.

"I've just come hack from a visit to Roditis," he said. "In Indiana."

"You told him about—"

"St. John? Yes."

"He must have been furious!"

"Actually, he was quite cool about it," Noyes said. "He seemed to be expecting some sort of fast shuffle of that kind, and he was braced. Listen, Elena, how soon can I get to see you?"

"Why not right now?"

"You're free this evening?"

"Very much so. Would you like to take me to Jubilisle again?"

"No," he said. "I'd just like a quiet visit. There are— some questions I'd like to ask."

"Questions, questions, questions! Very well. Come to my apartment. When should I expect you?"

"How about an hour from now?"

"That will do." She tapped out the hopter program for reaching her house, fingers moving swiftly over the data keys. An instant later the program card came chuttering out of the data slot in Noyes' telephone booth. He seized it and blew her a kiss. Grabbing his one suitcase, he rushed up the ramp and stepped into a traveler's-aid station, where he underwent a vibrator bath while his clothes were being pressed and refurbished. Freed of the grime of his journey from Indiana, Noyes proceeded toward the hopter zone, pausing on the way for a short snack. He chartered a hopter and slipped Elena's house program into the receptor slot. The vehicle took off, found itself hung up momentarily in a delay pattern over the crowded airport, then discovered an exit vector and made its way toward New Jersey.

He arrived at Elena's place a little after nine that evening.

Noyes had never been there before. His previous meetings with Elena had taken place at his apartment. He did not know what to expect: a place of palatial luxury, perhaps, or some steamy, overdecorated temple of amour. But in reality the apartment was nothing more than a pied-à-terre, as simple and austere as his own little suite. Despite Elena's known predilections for opulence, she did not seem to require it here, perhaps because it served only as a way station for her on those rare nights when she was not sleeping out. Greeting him in diaphanous, swirling pink robes that did very little to hide the exaggerated voluptuousness of her body. Elena seemed like some overblown tropical blossom blooming in a humble northern meadow.

They embraced tentatively and distantly. Elena evidently was ready for any kind of overtures he cared to make, but Noyes was too tense, too bound up in his own situation, to do more than go through a kind of ritualistic contact.

They broke away. She offered drinks. He settled into a chair; she chose a divan. Her robes parted to reveal tawny thighs. Noyes wondered if, as a matter of strategy, he should respond to her wanton unvoiced invitation. Or was she only teasing him? He was well aware that in all their relationships she regarded him only as a surrogate for other men. Sexually, she reached through him to make love to Jim Kravchenko. And when she passed secret information to him about the doings of Mark Kaufmann or Santoliquido, it was in the hope of winning favor with Roditis.

He said, "I need your help, Elena. I'm trying to find Martin St. John."

Her eyebrows rose. Her full lips drew apart. "Roditis is after him so soon?"

Noyes made an effort to conceal his reaction. "I'd simply like to talk to the man."

"About what?"

"Does it matter?"

"It might," she said.

Fidgeting, Noyes improvised. "All right. Roditis is interested in working out a deal with Paul Kaufmann. As long as old Kaufmann's back in circulation and Roditis can't have the persona himself, he'd like to come to an understanding with him. You see, Roditis is worried that Paul and Mark will form a family alliance to crush him. So he'd like to drive a wedge between them as rapidly as possible. Does that make sense to you?"

"A great deal of sense."

"So I've been sent here to make contact with Kaufmann/St. John. Only I don't know where to find him."

"And you think I do?"

"If anyone does, you do. Certainly Santoliquido's aware of St. John's location, and probably Mark as well. You're close to both of them. So—"

"You're right," said Elena. "I do know."

"Will you tell me?"

She stirred idly. Her robes opened, probably not by accident, and for a brief dazzling moment her entire body was bare to him. Noyes let his eyes rest on the huge globes of her breasts. She had mounted a fusion node in the great valley between them, and its tireless sparkle lulled him. Just as casually, Elena covered herself.

Softly she said, "Perhaps I might tell you. But there would be a price, Charles."

"Name it. Any amount."

She laughed. "Not money. A favor."

"What?" he asked uneasily.

"You carry the persona of a man who once meant a great deal to me," Elena said. "You stand between me and that man, Charles. If I lead you to Martin St. John, you will step aside and make that man available to me. Yes? I can take you to St. John tonight."

"You mean I should have Kravchenko erased and let his persona be given to someone else?"

"Not exactly," she replied. "I mean that you should allow him to take you over. So that I may enjoy him directly in your body."

Noyes was thrown into such turmoil that Kravchenko nearly was able to eject him then and there. He struggled for control. Never had he experienced so direct a blow to his ego. Calmly, casually, Elena had invited him to commit suicide for her convenience! His lips worked incoherently. At length he said, "You have no right to ask that of me. It's insane to think that I'd do any such thing!"

"Is it? Why do you carry that flask of carniphage, then?"

"Well—"

"Your suicidal tendencies are well-known. Very well, Charles: here's your moment. Be of some use. Restore Jim Kravchenko to the world he loves, and remove yourself from the world you hate. While at the same time fulfilling your obligations to Roditis by speaking with St. John. Yes? It is perfect, you see."

In a stunned silence Noyes contemplated the symmetry of Elena's proposal. True enough, he had already contracted with himself to swallow the carniphage once he had done this last deed for Roditis. Elena seemed to recognize, somehow, that he had declared himself superfluous. In the long run, what difference did it make which exit he chose? To drink the carniphage would be a petty way of revenging himself on Kravchenko for many slights, but in short order Kravchenko's persona would be in a new body, and what then of his revenge? This way, at least, he could graciously step aside and deliver up his body to Kravchenko, not for Kravchenko's sake but for Elena's.

But yet it was so damned humiliating—to have a woman suggest that he voluntarily let his own persona go dybbuk. Did she really think he was as worthless as that? Yes. Yes, she did. He scowled. Perhaps, he thought, it was time for him to junk his old-line ideals and try a little craftiness. He could always promise to do as Elena wished, and change his mind afterward. The important thing now was to get at St. John.

He said heavily, "You ask a stiff price."

"I know. But there's logic to it. Isn't there?"

"Yes. Yes." He paced about, clenching his fists. "All right," he said. "Damn you, yes! Have your Kravchenko!"

"A deal, then?"

"A deal. Where is Martin St. John?"

"He was taken to Mark Kaufmann's Manhattan apartment."

Noyes gasped. "I should have known it. But I can't see him

there, Elena! I can't walk right into Mark's own house and—"

"Mark went to California yesterday on business," said Elena. "He won't be back until tomorrow. His daughter's still in Europe. There's no one in his apartment but St. John and the servants looking after him. I'll take you there now."

"Let's go," he said.

She shed her robes with no trace of modesty while he watched, and selected light sprayon garments. They went out. The hopter journey to Manhattan was swift. Noyes felt as though trapped in a dream, with every event converging on a predestined climax with incredible rapidity and ease.

At the door of Kaufmann's apartment, Elena presented her thumb. The door did not open. She explained, "I don't have instant-access privileges. The scanner reports that I'm here, and checks to see if there's any order to bar me. In the absence of a specific order, I can come in."

"Why all the precaution?"

"Mark sometimes has other women with him," she said simply, as the door opened.

Noyes had never been in Mark Kaufmann's home before. It was elegant and spacious, with wings of rooms stretching to the sides and straight ahead. A blank-faced, snub-headed robot appeared. Elena said, "We're here to visit Mr. St. John."

The robot ushered them into a bedroom of huge size, dark, decked with brocaded draperies rising from projectors at the baseboards along the floor. Tones of green, cerise, and violet played across the ceiling. Sitting propped up in bed was a weary-looking, blue-eyed young man with light yellow hair, sallow skin, a rounded nose, a weak chin. Noyes paused at the doorway.

He realized, numbed, that he was in the presence of Paul Kaufmann.

There was an electric moment of confrontation. The unprepossessing figure in the bed seemed to take on strength and intensity as though it were flowing to him from some inner reserve. The eyes brightened; the head rose; the chin jutted. Above the bed was mounted a solido portrait of Paul Kaufmann in late middle age, an imperious eagle of a man. Despite the total difference in physical appearance, the man in the bed suddenly had that same imperious look.

"Yes?" he said. "Who are you?" The voice was cracked and unfocused; Paul Kaufmann, only hours into his borrowed body, had not yet mastered it.

"My name is Charles Noyes. I believe you already know Elena Volterra."

"Noyes? Noyes of Roditis Securities?"

"That's right," Noyes said. "You know me?"

"It was my business to know the Roditis organization, yes. Well, what are you doing here? How did you get in? Roditis men don't belong here."

"I brought him," said Elena. "He asked to see you, and I owed him a favor."

"Take him away," Kaufmann/St. John snapped. He waved his hand in what was meant as a gesture of dismissal; but his coordination was still poor, and his arm flapped in an awkward overswing that brought it slapping against the headboard.

Elena looked stymied. She did not move.

"Away," came the petulant command. "Out of here. *Out of here!* I must rest. I've been through a great deal. If you knew what it was like to die, to awaken, to enter a strange body ..." His words trickled away into incoherence. The Kaufmann dybbuk seemed exhausted by the effort of speaking. The brilliance and intensity vanished from the eyes as though a switch had been thrown; he was resting, regaining his powers.

Elena said doubtfully, "If he doesn't want to see you—"

"He'll give me five minutes," Noyes told her. "Look, wait outside for me, yes? I won't be with him long."

She nodded and left the room.

Noyes did not pretend to himself that Elena would fail to comprehend what he was about to do. But he doubted that she would expose him. He closed the door carefully behind her.

Kaufmann/St. John looked harsh and arrogant again. "I order you to leave!"

Approaching the bed, Noyes said quietly, "Just a few minutes. I want to talk. Do you find it very confusing, coming back to the world? You expected to have to fight through to dybbuk, didn't you? Not to have a body handed to you like this. You know, there was quite a dispute over who was going to be your carnate. Roditis was very anxious to get you. But Santoliquido flimflammed him by finding this empty body. Don't you agree it might have been more interesting to wake up in Roditis' skull?"

As he spoke, Noyes steadily drew nearer the bed.

Paul Kaufmann glowered at him. The flaccid muscles of his new face strained with the effort to rise and hurl the intruder from his room. But he could not do it.

"If you don't leave here at once—"

"Can't we discuss things peacefully?" Noyes asked. His long fingers enfolded the container of the cyclophosphamide-8 capsule. "Here Have a drink of water. Let me tell you about a deal Roditis has in mind. A great profit opportunity."

He picked up a drinking glass in his left hand, filled it halfway with water, and began to bring the concealed capsule toward it. But it was no use. Those strange washed-out blue eyes moved twitchingly, taking in everything. Noyes realized he could not bring off the sleight-of-hand successfully. Kaufmann/St. John would guess what he was trying to do and would put up a fight, clumsily, perhaps, but effectively enough to spill the irreplaceable poison or to get the robot servitors into the room.

Noyes could not afford to be subtle.

He leaned toward the man in the bed. In a low voice he said. "You'll be better off in a different carnate form."

"What do you—"

As the lips parted, Noyes shot his hand forward, applied pressure to the lemon-colored box to open it, and sent the deadly capsule into his victim's mouth. At the same time he pressed two forked fingers of his other hand against Kaufmann/St. John's Adam's apple. The man gulped. The capsule went down.

There was scathing fury in the blue eyes.

Kaufmann/St. John flailed impotently at Noyes with weak, badly coordinated arms. His hands wobbled as if about to fly from their wrists. But the face was a study in malevolence; all the full vitality of Paul Kaufmann was harnessed and hurled forth in a crescendo of frustrated rage and vindictive hostility. Clusters of muscles churned and spasmed beneath the surface of his cheeks. Exposed to that blast of hatred, Noyes recoiled, singed by the fire of this incredible old man.

But then, within the minute, the discorporation began.

Noyes watched only the beginning of it. Backing away from the bed, he saw the fire go out, saw the look of puzzlement and anguish appear. Strange internal events were commencing. The floodgates of the ductless glands had opened all at once, pouring forth an impossible mixture of secretions that mingled and reacted violently. The synchrony of heart and lungs was destroyed. The brain itself scorned the messages of its sensory perceptors. Instant by instant, the body of Martin St. John proceeded toward self-destruction.

Noyes fled.

Elena caught hold of him in the corridor outside. "Where are you going? What happened?"

"Get a doctor," Noyes burst out. "He's sick—some kind of stroke, I don't know—"

"What did you do to him?"

"We were just talking. He got angry. And then—"

A wild, screeching groan came from the bedroom, a sound ripped from tortured and disintegrating vocal cords. Elena went in. She emerged only moments later, looking appalled.

"You gave him a poison!" she cried.

"No. I don't know what happened. While I was with him, suddenly—"

"Don't lie. Roditis sent you here to kill him. And you told me you just wanted to talk to him!"

"Elena—"

With savage fury she pulled at him, tugging him out of the apartment. She seemed almost berserk with fear and shock. But in the fresh air she calmed; she had had a moment to digest the event, and her control had returned.

"Now we go to my place," she said. "You tricked me once tonight, Charles, but not again. Now you keep your bargain."

Noyes was close to collapse. Drenched in sweat, trembling, terrified, he let her shepherd him across to her little apartment in New Jersey. He tumbled wearily onto a couch. Elena stood over him, eyes bright, features rigid with malevolence.

"Now, Mr. Discorporator," she said, "you've done Roditis' filthy work and made me an accomplice. You owe me something for that. Out of that body now!"

"No," Noyes said feebly.

"No? *No!* We have a deal! Come, now. Shall I give you a drink? To make it easier? No trickery, Charles!"

Noyes felt Kravchenko hammering vehemently at the fabric of his mind, making a savage attempt to go dybbuk. Desperately Noyes resisted. I won't do it, he told himself. This is one bargain I won't keep. They can't make me destroy myself this way. I've got to get out of here, back to Roditis to get blanked, fast.

—You miserable cheater, Charles. You filthy pig!

It was Kravchenko. Noyes was stunned to realize that he had spoken nothing aloud. Kravchenko had tapped right into his flow of interior monolog! That meant the persona had taken a deeper hold than ever before on him, and was now in direct contact with his mind.

"Let's go, Charles," Elena said. "Out!"

"No. No, please—"

She seized him by the shoulders and shook him in a wild fury. He tried to push her away, but she was too strong for him; and now he could feel Kravchenko ripping at his brain, uprooting neural connections like saplings, drilling his way through the centers of control. Already it seemed to Noyes that whole sectors of his brain were cut off, that he was being thrust aside, pushed into a single lobe, isolated, undermined—

Ejected.

"No!" he cried. "The deal's off! I never meant to—"

"—but now I've changed his mind for him," Kravchenko finished.

Elena rose in triumph. "Jim? Jim, that's you, yes?"

"Yes. Me. God, it's good to be free!" Kravchenko stretched lavishly. He took a few steps, stumbled, recovered. "The coordination takes a little while to come back, I guess. But to have a body again! To feel! To breathe!"

"He's really gone?" she asked.

"I've rammed him down far out of sight. Nothing left of him but a few shreds, and I'll hunt those down and pull them out. Free, Elena! After all those years penned up in that sniveling hulk of a man!" He reached for her. His fingers clutched at the taut cones of her breasts, missed aim, got her shoulders instead; with an effort he drew his arms downward.

Softly he said, "I've got some other reflexes to test, Elena!"

He found that coordination returned more swiftly than he expected, although not altogether at a satisfactory level. It would take some time, he decided. Time and practice.

As dawn came Elena said, "Now we head for Indiana."

"What for?"

"So that Roditis can blank you, stupid! As far as the world knows, you're Charles Noyes, right? And Charles Noyes has discorporated Martin St. John. The memory of that must be wiped from your mind. Come. Come."

Kravchenko nodded. "You're right. I'll have to go to Roditis—

bluff it through, let him blank me on the killing. Then I'll quit him and we'll go off together, eh?"

"Yes!"

"But why are you going to Indiana?" he asked.

Elena gave him a slow, simmering smile. "Do you think I'm going to be apart from you even for an hour, now that I have you again?"

Chapter 13

"Dead?" Mark Kaufmann asked. "How could he possibly be dead? The St. John body was in good health. I saw it myself before I went to San Francisco."

The medic shook his head. "There was a total breakdown of autoimmunity. A civil war inside him, so to speak. No hope whatever of saving him."

—Murder, Paul's persona said.

But it did not take any great shrewdness to see that. Mark said, "Can such a thing happen naturally?"

"Most unlikely. You realize, Mr. Kaufmann, that it's statistically possible for such a thing to occur, but—"

"Not very probable?"

"No. Not at all."

"What was it, then? Carniphage?"

"These are not the effects of a carniphage," said the medic. "However, the poisoner today has an extremely wide choice of drugs. I've been running a data check, comparing effects with possible causes, and this is what I've come up with."

He handed Kaufmann a data sheet. It was headed:

CYCLOPHOSPHAMIDE-8

Mark scanned it hastily. "Is this drug easily available?"

"I'd say it costs roughly a million dollars fissionable an ounce," the medic replied. "The lethal dose is perhaps a hundredth of an ounce, though."

"Expensive, but not prohibitive. Rare?"

"It can be had. The sources are difficult to reach, but they exist. With enough money—"

"Yes, with enough money," Mark said. "Have you found any

traces of this—this cyclophosphamide in the body?"

"It leaves no traces. It metabolizes completely in use, and the only indication it leaves is in its effect."

"In other words, proof of use has to be empirical, deduced from the ruin it makes out of the victim?"

"Essentially, yes," said the medic smoothly. "The quaestorate is now conducting a second autopsy, and naturally will be making every effort to determine the actual cause of death. But I venture to predict that the ultimate verdict will be the same as mine: poisoning by cyclophosphamide-8."

"All right. Thank you. Go."

—You need to tighten your security net, Paul told him. A murder committed in your own apartment is shameful.

"There are finite limits to security," Mark said. He moved about the apartment, scuffing at the carpet. This incident left him tense and baffled and angry. He did not mind at all that someone had discorporated Martin St. John. the dybbuk Paul Kaufmann, so speedily after the transplant. But it offended him that St. John could be discorporated right here, of all places. And he was troubled by the possibility that suspicion of the discorporation might come to rest on him.

It was poor business. If the quaestorate hatched the idea that he was in any way connected with the murder, he'd be hauled down on a mindpick warrant, and not all the money in the universe could buy him out of that. Naturally, the mindpick would show that he had no complicity in the discorporation of Martin St. John, since in fact he had not been involved at all.

But at the same time the mindpick would reveal the illegal presence in his mind of the persona of Paul Kaufmann.

This had to be the work of Roditis, Mark thought. To take advantage of his absence by sneaking an agent in here to kill St. John, thereby opening him to mindpick and disgrace—no, no, Roditis could have no inkling of what he had been up to in San Francisco, and it was a mistake to attribute to the man more deviousness than he actually possessed—unless, that is, Roditis had his hooks into the lamasery too, and had instantly received word that Mark had come there to undergo a *sub rosa* persona transplant...

Exhausted by the intricacy of his own hypotheses, Mark sank down on a couch to collect himself.

—Fool, you're panicking over this.

"Let me think, Paul. Please."

—Think all you like. But think fast! An hour from now you may be under arrest.

"No, there's more time than that. The quaestorate hasn't finished the autopsy. And then they'll have to move through channels, deciding if they dare to arrest me, swearing out the warrant, arranging the mindpick. I've got at least twenty-four hours."

Paul did not reply. His head aching, Mark attempted to reconstruct the sequence of events.

He had seen Donahy Tuesday afternoon. That same day Santoliquido had called to announce his intention of transplanting Paul's persona into the vacated St. John body. On Wednesday, Mark had inspected the St. John body, then had flown to San Francisco. Also on Wednesday, Donahy had abstracted last year's persona recording of Paul Kaufmann from the archives. Wednesday night, in San Francisco, Donahy had transplanted the persona into Mark. Mark had remained out there on Thursday, resting and adapting to the powerful new persona. Meanwhile, in New York on Thursday, the most recent Paul Kaufmann persona had been transplanted into the St. John body, and St. John had been taken to Mark's apartment for recuperation. Sometime late Thursday night St. John had been murdered.

Now it was Friday afternoon, and Mark, back from San Francisco, found himself in deep trouble.

Just when everything had been going so well, too. He and Paul had adjusted to one another remarkably smoothly. There had been none of the tests of strength, none of the jockeying and probing that might have been anticipated when strong-willed old uncle entered strong-willed nephew's mind. Paul had been delighted at getting a new carnate trip, fascinated by the shady way Mark had obtained his persona, and absolutely overjoyed to learn that a second and later version of himself was also going to be at large in dybbuk form. He showed no resentment of the fact that the provision in his will barring transplant to a member of his family had been circumvented, possibly because that codicil had been added after this particular persona had been recorded. Recognizing Roditis as the real family enemy, Paul was willing to aid his nephew in every way, while at the same time helping to isolate and immobilize the dybbuk-Paul whom Santoliquido had spawned. Of course, Mark was prepared for conflict with his uncle sooner or later, possibly even a sneaky attempt to go dybbuk at his expense. But for now, at least, their mutual adaptation was splendid, and Mark reveled at having the crusty, indomitable old brigand finally safe in his mind.

Then, to fly home and walk into this—

Well, there were certain obvious first steps to take. The most obvious of all was to check last night's scanner records and see who had been in his apartment. He had a pretty good idea. There weren't many people who had even conditional access, and the only one with full access, Risa, was still in Europe, so far as he knew.

The scanner file gave him the quick answer.

Elena had been here. She had applied for admission just before eleven last night, and the robots had let her in. Mark saw her on the tape, and there was nothing unusual about her expression, as there might have been if she had come to commit a discorporation.

But who was this who had come in with her? This tall, blond fellow with the taut, edgy look in his eyes?

Noyes? Charles Noyes?

Noyes of Roditis Securities?

Elena had brought him *here*?

—There's your killer, Paul said. He *must* be.

"Not so fast," Mark muttered. "Noyes is Roditis' man, sure, but Roditis doesn't do foolish things. If he wanted to kill St. John, he wouldn't send someone like Noyes here to do the job. It's too transparent."

—What do you know about Noyes? I recall that he's not too stable.

"No, not very."

—Then perhaps Roditis picked a bungler. Run the tape a little further.

Mark moved it along. The figures of Elena and Noyes appeared at the door again some ten minutes later. Noyes looked more tense than ever, almost close to collapse. And Elena, now, gave every impression of hysteria. Obviously something significant had happened in those ten minutes—such as the murder of Martin St. John. The two figures were exchanging hurried conversation at the door. Mark could not read their lips, nor was there any audio on the scanner tape, but he knew that a simple computer analysis of lip patterns would tell him what they were saying. He watched Noyes hurry from the apartment. Then Elena disappeared from the door. About twenty minutes later she left looking calmer. That concluded the Thursday night record. The file of outgoing calls showed none until one in the morning, when a robot had noticed St. John dead and had summoned the quaestors.

"That's it, then." Mark said. "She let him in, and he killed St. John."

—There's no proof. It's all circumstantial, Mark. Where's the weapon? Where are the witnesses? St. John might have been killed by someone else before Noyes ever got here, for all your records show. A blowdart through a window, maybe.

"It's enough to authorize a mindpick, Paul. And a mindpick will show Noyes' guilt. I've got to get him picked before anyone thinks of mindpicking me, or they'll find you."

—You might try talking to Elena, Paul suggested.

But Elena did not answer when he called her apartment. Curiously, she had not even left a forwarding number. Mark buzzed her inner number, thinking that perhaps she had posted a forwarding number for limited distribution to close friends, but that drew a blank too. Where was she? She never went anywhere without notifying him first. And she surely knew that he was due back in New York sometime today.

He phoned Santoliquido next.

As usual, it was a slow, bothersome job to get through to him. When Santoliquido appeared, his quizzical expression showed that he had heard the news.

"Where have you been, Mark?"

"Away on business since late Wednesday. And when I got back-St. John—"

"I know. The quaestors notified me."

"What is this all about Frank?"

"I haven't any idea. But of course I have my suspicions."

"Such as?"

"Never mind," said Santoliquido. "They're unfounded at present. The important thing is that your uncle is discorporate again, and we have to start the whole process from the beginning."

Mark felt a secret pleasure at the knowledge that his uncle was far from discorporate. He heard the old man's silent, complacent chuckle within him.

To Santoliquido he said, "Do you expect Roditis to reapply?"

"Why shouldn't he? The persona's available again."

"And you've run out of ways to avoid giving it to him."

Santoliquido nodded. "For the moment at least"

"Listen to me, Frank, I want one last favor. Stall him off. If only for a few days. I can't explain now, but I've got reason to think you'll be wasting everyone's time if you give Paul to Roditis now.

Will you wait at least until the report of the quaestors is issued?"

"I'll do that, yes," Santoliquido agreed.

"Good." Mark paused a moment. Then, in a carefully more relaxed tone, he said, "You haven't seen Elena lately, have you?"

With the same deliberate casualness Santoliquido replied, "Lately? Well, let's see ... I had lunch with her yesterday. Is that lately enough?"

"I meant today."

"No. The last I saw of her was one in the afternoon yesterday. You've phoned her apartment?"

"Of course," Mark said. "I suppose she's taken a little trip. I imagine I'll be hearing from her soon."

Roditis said, "So it's all done, and you're back here, and no one's the wiser, Charles. Was that so bad?"

Kravchenko attempted to keep his facial muscles fixed in the bland, idiotic expression of benignity that he imagined Charles Noyes customarily to have worn. He was on edge, here in Roditis' Indiana headquarters, for this was the first test of his dybbukhood. If he failed to fool Roditis, he'd be on the scrapheap by nightfall.

He said carefully, "Well, John, I don't deny I was uneasy about it But it went off more smoothly than I dared hope.

"And now we'll get you blanked, and splice in a set of phony memories for last night, and you'll be safe."

"Yes, John."

"Want to take a little workout first? Get yourself back into shape?"

"I think we'd better tend to the blanking first," said Kravchenko. "I've got a few things on my mind that I'm better off without."

Roditis nodded. "Right. Come with me."

Kravchenko followed the stocky little financier through the maze of the building. He did not much like the idea of submitting to a blanking; he hated to surrender consciousness, hated to go under the machine. But so long as he still carried around

memories of the discorporation of Martin St. John, he ran serious risks. Noyes, whom he pretended to be, might well be under
suspicion of that discorporation. It they picked him up, ran a
routine mindpick on him, and found the evidence, all would be
up not only for Noyes—whose personae would be destroyed because of his crime—but for Kravchenko as well, since the routine mindpick would be followed by a deep pick that would reveal who was actually running the Noyes body. Kravchenko
thought he could conceal his dybbuk status if the pick merely
went scraping around looking for a specific event, the
discorporation episode. But he was finished for good if they sank
the pick beyond the surface. His only hope of avoiding that was
to blank out everything having to do with last night. Which Roditis
now proposed to do.

Technicians were readying the blanking apparatus.

Kravchenko studied it warily. A blanking was something like
getting a persona transplant-in reverse. Instead of having taped
information poured into your receptive brain, you yielded information. Instead of being doped with mnemonic drugs to damp
out memory decay, they washed your mind with a selective
memory suppressant, carefully measured to obliterate a certain
chronological segment of the memory bank Kravchenko dis-
trusted all this fiddling with the brain. Yet he admitted the ne-
cessity of it.

"Will you lie down here?" a technician said.

Kravchenko waited. They gave him injections. They strapped
electrodes to his skull. They took EEG readings of Noyes" brain
waves. Silently they bustled about while Roditis hovered som-
berly in the background.

"Ready, now," someone said.

A helmet was lowered over his head.

"Don't worry about a thing. Charles," came Roditis' confident
voice. "We'll clean you up in no time."

"*Now*," said a technician.

Kravchenko went tense, imagining that switches were being thrown and contacts made. He could see nothing. His drugged mind grew foggy. Abruptly he heard what sounded like a colossal explosion, and in the same instant a burst of intolerably bright lightning shot through his brain. He felt as though his skull had split apart

Chaos enfolded him.

He was swept away by a terrible tide—down, down, down-out of control-helpless-and with his last conscious thought he asked himself how this could be happening, when a blanking was supposed to be such a trivial thing. Then he was swallowed up in darkness.

This was her moment, Elena thought. Jim was downstairs undergoing his blanking; afterwards, he'd be resting for a few hours. Now was her chance to add Roditis to her collection.

She hadn't felt like telling Jim that one of her motives in accompanying him to Evansville was to seduce John Roditis. Newly returned to corporate status by her scheming, Kravchenko would not understand that he was not going to be the only man in her life. She loved him passionately; but she wanted Roditis. Two hours ago, when she and Kravchenko had arrived here, Elena had met Roditis for the first time. They had exchanged perhaps ten words; Roditis had hardly seemed to take notice of her. He was too preoccupied with the maneuvers surrounding the St John discorporation, as was only natural. But she had taken notice of him. That muscular, powerful body held promise of physical delight; and the strength of the man was unmistakable. To Elena, a connoisseur of strong men, Roditis seemed an ideal mixture of raw power and intuitive intelligence. Santoliquido and Mark Kaufmann and the others had palled on her; Kravchenko, now that he was back, offered many pleasures, but he was shallow, a floater, a playboy; new adventures beckoned to her. With Roditis.

She said, "I've always been curious about you. It's strange we never had occasion to meet before."

"I don't move in your high-society circles." Roditis seemed distant even bored.

"You really should, you know. We aren't such ogres. A man of your vigor, your enterprise—you'd inject some new vitality into our group." Surreptitiously she moved closer to him. Elena regretted that she was not dressed for her purpose; she had flown to Evansville in workaday travel clothes, and there had been no chance to change into something more clinging, something more revealing. In this drab garb she felt as though locked into armor. Yet it was a handicap she felt she could overcome.

Roditis said, "I object to snobbery, Miss Volterra. I am a wealthy man, yes, but no playboy. My values are not those of your set. I have work to do every day."

"You ought to let yourself enjoy the benefits of your work," she purred. She stood beside him now, at his desk, examining the sonic sculpture. "How beautiful," she said. As she reached forward to caress the piece the soft hill of her breast pressed into Roditis' elbow. It was hardly a subtle gesture, but she did not regard Roditis as a subtle man.

He moved smoothly away, breaking the contact.

Elena nibbled her lip. She threw him a coquettish glance; she asked him about the sculpture, found that it had been made by one of his personae, praised it extravagantly; she adopted a posture so sensual it might almost have been self-parody. Roditis seemed unmoved. What's the matter with the man, she wondered?

Her approach became even more direct. She flattered him; she told him how thrilled she was to have met him at last; she cornered him behind his own desk and filled his ears with praise. She could not have made it more obvious if she had stripped and sprawled out spread-legged on the carpet. And Roditis grew more brusque, more withdrawn, as she fought to reach him.

It was a dismal moment. Elena sensed that she was being refused, which had never happened to her before, and she could not imagine why. From what she knew of Roditis he was unmarried, heterosexual, promiscuous. Why, then—?

To hell with it, Elena told herself.

She thrust herself into his arms.

Her breasts crushed up against him. Panting, eager, she hunted for his lips, while her hands clawed the muscular ridges of his back. By now she was so angry that she felt only the counterfeit of desire; but she came on in seemingly uncontrollable passion, determined to sweep Roditis off his feet. He would have her on the floor, she resolved. A wild bestial coupling. She'd show him her abilities, and afterwards he'd need less coaxing.

His hands went to her breasts. Not to caress, though, but to shove. He pushed her back, disengaged himself, adjusted his clothing. He looked ruffled; his eyes were steely. In a frosty voice he said, "This is no pleasure palace, Miss Volterra. This is a workingman's office. I'm not in the mood for a wrestling match now."

She cursed him eloquently in Italian. Then, inspired, she went on to roast him in Greek; but not even that got a rise out of him. Incredulously she stared as he summoned a robosecretary and instructed it to show Miss Volterra to her lodgings.

"Dog!" she cried. "Eunuch!"

Roditis glowered, slammed fist into palm, and switched up the vents to get the reek of her perfume out of the room. Damn her! He could hardly believe what had happened—the coarseness of her, the grossness of her assault. He had known from the very first naturally, why she was here, hitchhiking along with Noyes to get an introduction to him. All that ogling and rump-wiggling when she had first showed up had not failed to get through to him. And now, in his office, the winks, the ever broader hints, the breast nuzzling against his arm, finally the desperate lunge and clutch—he had not expected the famed Elena Volterra to be quite so blunt.

Unless, he thought she regarded him as the sort of man who was lured with such tactics.

The episode had jangled his nerves. She was a handsome woman, yes, well up to advance word; no doubt it would have been an interesting hour or two in bed for him. But Roditis had enough handsome women to keep him busy for centuries. This was one he would not touch, though she had the beauty of Helen of Troy. He was unwilling to push Mark Kaufmann too far. He was about to get his uncle's persona; he would not try to take his woman too. Once the elder Kaufmann was safe in Roditis' brain, he planned to strike a truce with Mark; and it would be much harder to arrange that if Elena Volterra were in the picture too.

Of course, Roditis conceded, he had just made an undying enemy out of Elena. Hell hath no fury, etc. That could have its strategic uses too, though. What was Elena, anyway? A bed-hopper, a gossip, a seeker of vicarious power, an animated bundle of desires and greedy ambitions, a fleshy construct of breasts and buttocks and thighs and loins. Mark Kaufmann, who controlled real power, had not been able to harm him; what damage could Elena do?

She might succeed only in forging a Roditis-Kaufmann alliance. If she screamed loudly enough to Mark about the "insult" visited upon her, it might just give Mark the idea that John Roditis didn't mean to grab everything within his reach. And that could be the beginning of the Kaufmann-Roditis *détente* that Roditis saw as the key to major power expansion.

So let her do her wont, Roditis thought.

There's no way the slut can hurt me. None!

Noyes, crouching in darkness, was amazed to find light lancing through. Sudden brightness from above told him that the lid which had been crushing down on him was cracking. He stirred; he tested his strength and found that he could lift the lid.

What was happening? Why was Kravchenko losing control?

For an uncertain and perhaps infinite span of time Noyes had lain huddled in a corner of his own mind, Kravchenko's prisoner. No sensory inputs had reached him here. He was wholly cut off; and he had assumed that eventually Kravchenko would bear down and finish the job of destroying him. First came ejection from motor control, and then loss of the voluntary brain centers, and finally the ripping away of all contacts, so that the dybbuk would be alone in the body they had formerly shared. Bleakly Noyes had awaited his fate. He could not comprehend the turn of events; but quite plainly Kravchenko's grasp had slipped.

Noyes burst from confinement and flooded back into every lobe of his brain.

He encountered Kravchenko. The persona seemed dazed and helpless, lost in a fog. It was an easy matter for Noyes to recapture motor and sensory power from him.

He let his eyelids flutter open and took stock. He found himself lying on a laboratory table, with apparatus strapped to his skull and chest, and technicians bustling about him. "He's coming out of it," one of them said. Noyes thought at first that he was in a soul bank, but then he recognized his surroundings: this was Roditis' place in Indiana. What had they been doing to his body at the moment of his unexpected return to control, though?

A technician said, "You look a little shaken up, Mr. Noyes. Everything all right?"

"I—well, more or less," he said. He sat up. It was not difficult for him to operate his body, and that was encouraging; it told him that relatively little time had passed since Kravchenko had thrust him out. Tentatively he formed a theory that this was only the day after St. John's discorporation. According to the plan, he was supposed to have returned to Evansville to have all knowledge of the crime blanked. Presumably that was what had been taking place in this laboratory.

But if I've been blanked, Noyes wondered, how is it that I still remember the discorporation?

He realized that he would have to move warily until he could draw some clues from those about him. Something very strange had taken place, and he had to be careful not to tip his hand.

Roditis entered the room, scowling, tense. He brightened as he saw Noyes, though, and said, "Well, Charles, how did it go?"

"F-fine," Noyes said. "My ears are ringing just a little, maybe."

"They say you sometimes have a hangover after something like that." Roditis dismissed the technicians with an impatient wave of one hand. His face grew serious once more. In a low voice he said, "Have you heard the news, Charles? Martin St. John was discorporated last night in New York!"

So this was a test of how well he had been blanked.

Noyes said, "St. John? St. John? I'm not sure I place the name."

"An Englishman. The persona of Paul Kaufmann had been transplanted to him. You remember, don't your

"I'm afraid I'm a little hazy about all that. Discorporated, you say? Do the quaestors have any clues?"

"I doubt it," Roditis replied. "The poor quaestors are always three jumps behind the criminals. It's so hard to enforce the law properly when a murderer can have all sense of guilt blotted from his mind, By the way, Charles, where'd you spend the night?"

He was caught off guard. Desperately improvising he said, "If you have to know, John, I was with a woman. I'll give you the details if you wish, but a gentleman really doesn't—"

Roditis chuckled. "No, a gentleman doesn't. But she's a hot one, isn't she? Elena, I mean." He slapped Noyes heartily on the back. "She's waiting here in town. I'd like you to escort her back to New York right away, yes, Charles?"

"Whatever you say?"

"And now, if you'll excuse me, it's exercise time."

Roditis went out. Noyes, relieved, paced around the room as he drew together the strands of the mystery. He had discorporated St. John, and then Elena and Kravchenko had teamed up to push him out of his mind. Noyes shuddered at the recollection. Afterwards, the dybbuk-Kravchenko and Elena had flown out here, with Kravchenko obviously masquerading as Noyes. That was how it must have been, Noyes decided. And, naturally, Roditis had wanted to blank the crime from Noyes' mind.

But the blanking had gone awry.

Noyes thought he understood why. A blanking was a simple thing, in its way, but only if no unknown factors fouled up the settings of the machine. Doubtless they had calibrated their dials for the brainwaves of Charles Noyes —and then had tried to blank the Noyes brain, unaware that they were really working on the mind of Jim Kravchenko. The clashing of Noyes' brain waves with Kravchenko's consciousness had driven the dybbuk into shock, permitting Noyes to resume control. But Noyes had not been blanked after all, since he had been cut off, beyond the reach of the instruments.

So I am a murderer and still unblanked, Noyes thought and I have won out over my own dybbuk, and Roditis is sending me back to New York with Elena. What do I do now? May all the Buddhas help me, what do I do now?

Mark Kaufmann spent much of Friday afternoon patiently tracking down leads in the hope of solving the double mystery of St. John's discorporation and Elena's disappearance. Through various channels he was able to gain access to a great deal of information normally available only to the investigators of the quaestorate. The world was full of scanners, monitors, and other data-recording devices that took down impartial, impersonal accounts of the comings and goings of individuals, and with luck and influence one could tap this ocean of data for one's own needs. Not all the information received was immediately relevant, but Kaufmann sifted it searching out the patterns. He had a better-than-normal faculty for finding patterns in seemingly random data. And now he had the advantage of his uncle's judicious, practiced eye to aid him in his examination.

He knew by now that Noyes had come in from Evansville and had made contact with Elena some hours before the discorporation of Martin St. John. Now both of them had vanished, but this was not a world in which anyone could stay vanished for long. Keying in to the data bats of the transport terminals, Kaufmann succeeded in learning that Noyes had flown to Evansville at one that afternoon. Closer examination of the passenger list of that flight showed that Elena had been with him.

—Has she been keeping company with Roditis in the past?

"No, never," Mark told his uncle's persona. "They haven't even met."

—Sure?

"Positive. Noyes must have set this up for her."

He puzzled over the *quid pro quo*. He knew that Elena had developed a fascination for Roditis and was yearning to meet him. Very well. She had taken Noyes to the apartment where Martin St. John was being kept. St. John had met a mysterious death. Now Noyes had taken her to Evansville, and, presumably, to an assignation with Roditis.

It looked very much like a sellout

—Put tracers on Elena right away, Paul advised. Get men busy in Evansville. Pick her up and bring her back here for questioning before she does any more damage.

"I'm already doing so," said Mark.

It took him a few minutes to arrange for the surveillance, not only of Elena, but of Noyes as well. Whenever they left Roditis, they'd be watched and followed, and at the proper moment they'd be taken into custody. Elena had never done anything overtly treacherous before, but Mark knew her capabilities. He visualized a conspiracy involving Noyes, Roditis, Elena, and perhaps even Santoliquido, by which Paul's persona was speedily liberated from the hapless St. John body, and just as speedily reincorporated into John Roditis on second application.

The phone chimed.

He switched it on and found that Risa was calling—not from Europe, surprisingly, but from the New York airport.

"You said you were coming back next week," he told her.

"It's a woman's privilege to change her mind. I got bored over there. And I missed you. There's a hopter waiting, and I'll be home in a hurry."

"Wonderful, Risa."

She looked at him strangely. "Mark? Is there anything wrong?"

"Why?"

"You're very drawn. You've got a peculiar expression on your face."

"It's been a hectic day, love. Too hectic for me even to begin explaining now. I'll fill everything in when you're here."

They broke contact. Mark felt pleased at Risa's arrival. In this time of crisis, with unexpected things happening much too swiftly, it would be good to have her around. A man had to depend on family at a time like this. Paul within him... Risa beside him...

He smiled. It was a tacit admission that Risa had crossed the borderline from childhood to womanhood these past few weeks. You didn't think of a child as a potential ally. But she had shown him her true strength, first in the matter of obtaining a persona for herself, then by her sleuthing to find Tandy's killer. He would cease to delude himself into thinking she was a child, now. She was a woman, a Kaufmann woman, and he wanted her with him.

She reached the apartment more quickly than he expected. Her European adventures seemed to have sobered and matured her; or was it the presence of an extra mind within her own? She was the same slim, boyish-bodied girl who had left so suddenly for Stockholm not long before, but the cast of her features was different now, the set of her lips, the glow of her eyes.

Paul was astonished.

—This is Risa? he asked, as she entered. Your little girl? Mark, how long was I in storage?

"You haven't seen her for over a year, your time," Mark told his uncle quietly. "It's been a big year for her."

—She's impressive. She has the right bearing. There's no doubt she's a Kaufmann, is there?

Moving gracefully, almost sinuously, in a style she must certainly have learned from Tandy Cushing, Risa crossed the room to her father, embraced him, brushed his lips with hers. Then she stepped back and eyed him searchingly.

"You've changed," she said.

"I was just about to say that to you."

"I know *I've* changed, Mark. I have Tandy with me now. But you—you're different tool"

"In what way?"

"I'm not sure," she said. "Your eyes—your whole way of standing—"

"I told you, Risa, it's been a frightful day. I'm tired."

She shook her head. "It's not fatigue I see. Fatigue subtracts. You've got something extra. You're standing taller. You could almost be Uncle Paul, you know, except that the face and hair are wrong. But you hold yourself the way he did."

Mark smiled feebly. "The Kaufmann genes win out."

"I'm serious. Mark, have you had some sort of persona transplant since I went overseas?"

"Sure," he said. "I bribed Santoliquido and he gave me Uncle Paul." Better to make a joke about it, he thought, and destroy the possibility that she'll sniff out the truth.

"Really, Mark. You *did* get a transplant, didn't you? Maybe not Uncle Paul, but it's someone new. I'm sure of it."

"Sorry, sweet. I don't mean to shake your faith in your own womanly intuition, but it just isn't so. What you think you see in me is the nervous reaction of a bone-tired man." The phone chimed. "Excuse me, will you?"

As he turned away from her, Mark passed a mirror and peered into its oval depths. Yes, he thought. She's right. There is a change. I didn't notice it, but she, who was away—

The effect was an odd one: as though an overlay of Paul's features had been placed on his own. There was a tension about his facial muscles, perhaps resulting from some new disposition of his features. Mark felt a twinge of distress. If Paul had infiltrated him to this extent so fast, was an attempt at going dybbuk lying just ahead? Paul was, above all else, sly. This present mood of benign cooperation might simply be Paul's way of setting him up for the kill.

And, also, he wasn't happy about the accuracy of Risa's guess. She was a smart girl, of course, but was it so obvious that he had taken possession of Paul's persona? If she saw it, would others? He was ruined unless he maintained the secret.

He picked up the telephone on the fifth chime.

"Yes?"

"Miss Volterra is on her way back to New York," a flat, mechanical voice reported. "She left Evansville twenty minutes ago."

"Is she being tracked?"

"Yes, sir."

"And Noyes?"

"He's with her. They seem to have had a quarrel. He looks upset. And she's the angriest-looking woman I've ever seen."

Chapter 14

Risa went to her apartment a floor above her fathers, unpacked, changed, and returned to the lower apartment. She had never seen Mark in such a state before. Usually, no matter how severe the crisis might be, he remained at the center of the storm, calm, self-possessed. Something must be very seriously wrong now.

His appearance puzzled her too. A man of forty didn't alter his whole facial makeup between one week and the next, not unless something of impact had occurred, like taking on a new persona. He denied that he had. Why, then, did he have this new gleam in his eyes, that feral radiance that she associated with Uncle Paul? Jokingly he had told her of bribing Santoliquido and getting Paul's persona. Well, Santoliquido was beyond reach of bribery, no doubt, but such things could be arranged in other ways. Risa was aware of her father's tactics, more so, possibly, than he realized; she had seen him many times bluntly admit some outrageous act simply to make it look inconceivable that he had committed it.

The more she mulled it, the more convinced she was that he had somehow obtained the illegal transplant. Only that could account for the alteration in his bearing. Risa knew quite well that a transplant could bring about such changes; she had seen it in herself since Tandy had come to her. Her look was softer, now, more feminine; she had shed the chip-on-the-shoulder tomboyishness in favor of a more seductive approach, and she credited that to Tandy.

In her father's apartment Risa listened in astonishment to the story of the discorporation of Martin St. John.

"You helped to solve Santoliquido's problem for him, you know," Mark told her. His hand tapped his knee in a gesture uncomfortably reminiscent of the old man's. "By hunting down that dybbuk, you handed Santo an empty body at just the right time, and he dumped Paul into it."

"Couldn't you have stopped him?"

"I didn't really want to, Risa. Short of keeping Paul in cold storage forever, I had to let him go to someone. I figured it was better that he go to St. John than to Roditis."

"Agreed. But the discorporation—"

"It happened last night. As I reconstruct it, Roditis sent his flunky Noyes to Elena. Elena not only told him where St. John was being kept, but brought him here. Noyes gave St. John a tricky poison. This morning, he and Elena flew out to one of Roditis' headquarters. Now they're on their way back."

"I never trusted that bitch, Mark."

He laughed. "I know. I wrote it off to your monstrous Electra complex."

"Which is genuine. But not so monstrous that it distorts every judgment I make. Elena's worthless, and I've been trying to get you to see it all along. But at least she hasn't done you any real harm. You don't lose anything by St. John's discorporation."

"I do," he said, "if Roditis reapplies for Uncle Paul and gets him."

"But if he's part of this discorporation conspiracy, he'll be sent to erasure himself!"

"If anything can be proven."

"You seem to have reconstructed everything," Risa said.

He nodded. "To my own satisfaction. Not necessarily to that of the quaestorate. I've got to get Elena to admit she cooperated in the murder. That'll allow the quaestors to demand a mindpick of Noyes. If Noyes is picked, he'll incriminate Roditis, and we'll have won—maybe. But it's a tricky road."

"If I were Roditis," Risa said carefully, "I'd get hold of both Elena and Noyes and give their minds a good blanking. That'll cut the line of incrimination before it reaches him."

"I suspect he's done just that. They spent the morning with

him in Indiana, and now they're on their way back— most likely with their minds swept clean of last night's fun." He clenched his fists and struck an attitude of anger and determination, incredibly Paul-like. "No matter what happens, Roditis won't get Paul! Maybe he's won this round, maybe he's lost everything— but the persona won't go to him. Somehow. Somehow."

Risa was startled by the depths of her father's agitation. She couldn't see why he was so troubled over this discorporation, annoying and infuriating though it was. His reaction seemed all out of keeping with the event. Yes, Elena had betrayed him. Yes, Roditis had managed to make Uncle Paul available again, just when it seemed the troublesome persona was locked away in St. John for keeps. But that simply meant that the status was back to what it had been a few days ago. Why this frenzy of tension? He was so worked up that he had taken her fully into his confidence, something he had never done before. Risa was flattered by that. It wasn't so long ago—only at the beach party—that he had coolly told her to run along and play, that these things did not concern her. The change in him was so dramatic that it was suspicious.

Why was he worried?

Was he afraid that the investigation of the St. John murder would turn on him? That he might be mindpicked by the quaestors? That they might discover something he wished very much to hide—like the presence in his mind of an illegal Paul Kaufmann persona?

Everything seemed to be coming back to that, Risa observed.

Her father excused himself to take another call. Risa wandered about the apartment, assessing the intricacies of the situation. It seemed imperative to discard the notion that her father was in possession of Uncle Paul's persona. The persona had gone to the empty Martin St. John, hadn't it? Then it couldn't simultaneously have been imprinted on Mark. They took strict precautions against a double transplant of that sort, Risa thought. Sealed the master recording away in a special vault, or something, until it was needed again, if ever it was. In this case, since St. John had been so quickly discorporated, the master would be needed again. But ordinarily, the Paul Kaufmann persona would be passed along as a secondary within its next carnate possessor's persona, and so there'd be no call for reverting to the old master.

Yet that recording of Paul Kaufmann would still exist in the files, yes? And what about all the earlier recordings of him? Surely they weren't thrown away.

Risa began to see vast scope for chicanery within the supposedly foolproof regulations of the Scheffing Institute. She began to see how plausible it was that her father might have obtained a bootlegged transplant of Uncle Paul.

—Go easy, Tandy warned her. You're getting all tied up in this thing.

Risa tried to slip her leash of sudden tensions. She noticed a green-bound volume lying on a table and picked it up idly. It was the *Bardo Thödol* she discovered with some surprise. The Tibetan Book of the Dead, the cult book of the new religion that was sweeping eastward from California. She hadn't known her father owned one. This copy looked brand-new. Risa touched the activator stud and flipped through the book, wondering how people could get so enmeshed in the silly stuff merely because rebirth had become a practicality. To dig up an obscure branch of decadent Buddhism, with absolutely no relevance to the Scheffing process, and to devote time and energy and money to its study—

"From the Eastern Realm of Pre-eminent Happiness," she read, "the Buddha Vajra-Sattva, the Divine Father- Mother, with the attendant deities, will come to shine upon thee. From the Southern Realm endowed with Glory, the Buddha Ratna-Sambhava, the Divine Father-Mother, with the attendant deities, will come to shine upon thee. From the Happy Western Realm of Heaped-up Lotuses, the Buddha Amitabha, the Divine Father-Mother, along with the attendant deities, will come to shine upon thee.

From the Northern Realm of Perfected Good Deeds, the Buddha Amogha-Siddhi, the Divine Father-Mother, along with the attendants will come, amidst a halo of rainbow light, to shine upon thee at this very moment."

Her father returned to the room. Risa held out the book and said, "Mark, what's this?"

"I visited the big lamasery in San Francisco when I was on the Coast. They gave it to me as a souvenir." He shrugged the book aside. "They've picked up Elena and Noyes at the airport. Elena claims she was on her way to see me anyway. She'll be here any minute."

"And Noyes?"

"He's being brought along separately, and not so willingly. I want to keep him apart from Elena until I've heard her story. I've arranged for him to be held upstairs in your apartment for a little while. All right?"

"I suppose. But where am I going to stay?"

"Right here with me," Mark said. "I'll need your assistance." He tossed her a recording cube. "Get every word of the conversation onto this, and make sure Elena doesn't see you doing it. Also, get ready to jump her if she tries to attack. I'll have her scanned for concealed weapons before she's brought in, but she'll still have her fingernails."

Risa felt a tremor of delight at receiving these responsibilities from her father. She said, "Do you really think you'll learn anything from Elena or Noyes, now that they've been out where Roditis could blank them?"

"I can't say. I doubt that he'd be foolish enough to let them get away with their memories intact. But big men sometimes slip up in the details." A signal flashed at the door. "Elena's here."

He had her sent in—without any of the guards who had picked her up and accompanied her here. Risa was taken aback by the fury in her eyes; Elena seemed to be bubbling with wrath. She was dressed in what was for her a plain, even dowdy costume, and she strode into the room with a vigor far removed from her usual languid saunter.

"Mark! Oh, Mark, I've got so much to tell you!" she burst out.

"I imagine you have," Mark said. He shot a glance at Risa, who had quietly switched on the recording cube. Risa nodded.

Elena looked at her too. "In private," she said.

"You can speak in front of Risa. She's already aware of what's happened. At least, she knows as much about it as I do. But you must know a lot more."

Color came to Elena's cheeks. She looked clearly uncomfortable about Risa's presence. There was an exchange of glares.

Mark said, "I want to know what took place in this apartment on Thursday, Elena."

Elena paced the room in barely suppressed rage. "For most of the day, I have no idea. Martin St. John was here, in the guest bedroom, watched over by a squad of robots."

"Yes. Then?"

"Charles Noyes came to me. He said he had important business to discuss with St. John. He begged me and begged me until I agreed to bring him here."

"That was a grave mistake, Elena."

"I know, Mark. But I brought him. We went into St. John's bedroom together."

"You saw St. John? What condition was he in?"

"Alive," said Elena. "Fatigued, but doing well. Your uncle was working hard to get control over the body. Noyes asked me to leave him alone with St. John for a few minutes. I did. Very shortly Noyes came out of the room. St. John was screaming. He was having peculiar convulsions. Noyes left the apartment, and soon St. John was dead."

"Would you say he was murdered by Noyes?"

"That's reasonable to assume," Elena admitted.

"How did Noyes explain what had happened?"

"He said St. John had had a kind of stroke."

"Did you notify the quaestorate?" Mark asked.

Elena shook her head. "I stayed here for a while after Noyes had left. Then I went home. I notified no one."

"Not even me."

"Not even you, Mark."

"You helped Noyes discorporate St. John, then," Mark said.

"No." Elena's nostrils flared in anger. "I had no idea he would do such a thing! I swear it, Mark! I was wrong to let him in here, to allow him to be alone with St. John, but I never suspected he meant to murder him!"

"Perhaps," said Mark. "But in any case your actions are strange. First you let a known agent of Roditis into my house and give him carte blanche to murder my guest. Then you rush off without calling the authorities. And the following morning you fly away to see Roditis himself. You spent a couple of hours in Evansville today, didn't you? Didn't you, Elena?"

"Yes," she said hoarsely. "But I was never working for Roditis. I had no part in this murder, except through stupidity in giving Noyes access. I'll take a mindpick to prove it. Let the quaestors pick all they want."

"I will," he assured her.

"If Roditis had obtained any help in discorporating St. John, don't you think he would have blanked me while I was in Evansville?"

Kaufmann conceded the point. Clearly Elena hadn't been blanked, which meant that Roditis had no knowledge of her status as an accessory. "But what were you doing there, then?"

"You won't like the answer, Mark."

"Tell me anyway."

"Not in front of your daughter."

"Risa can hear it."

"What I have to say is—not complimentary to you," Elena said. "You would prefer not to have anyone but yourself hear it."

"I'll take my chances."

"Well, then," Elena said, "I went to Evansville to make love with Roditis. I've desired him for months. This was my opportunity. You were away. Noyes was with me, and he was flying to Evansville, and I asked him to take me along. While Noyes was being blanked by Roditis' men, I went to Roditis and—"

"Noyes was blanked?" Kaufmann said leadenly.

"Of course. Roditis knew that he'd probably be traced to St. John. Noyes had to be blanked so that the trail wouldn't lead back to Roditis. So I went to Roditis. He would not have anything to do with me. He refused me!" She was flushed, agitated, her breasts heaving wildly. "I went close to him, and he pushed me, like this—away. So it was all for nothing. I humiliated myself to him and he pushed me."

There was a lengthy silence in the room. Risa feared that Elena might hear the throbbing of the recording cube, so silent did everything become. But Elena stood transfixed, hearing nothing but the thunder of her own indignation.

—She was turned down, Tandy said. No wonder she's so mad now! She's willing to tell your father anything, just to get even with Roditis.

Risa agreed. She could not help feel a pang of pity for Elena in this moment of her defeat. To be spurned by Roditis, to have to come back here and reveal not only her promiscuity but her rejection—how that must sting!

Mark said finally, "Noyes was definitely blanked, eh? You're sure of that."

"Positive. He will be of no use to you as a witness. I am the only one who can testify," Elena said.

Mark shook his head. "You didn't see the crime. We've already got evidence that you and Noyes were at the apartment at the time of the discorporation, but the best we could hope for from that would be to get a mindpick on Noyes. Which will come up blank. We couldn't possibly get any court to grant a mindpick of Roditis on your suspicions alone. We're stopped, Elena."

"No! No! Fight, Mark! We all know Roditis was behind this murder! Put your best lawyers to work!"

Mark smiled coolly. "You'd love to see Roditis ruined, wouldn't you, Elena? But only because he turned you down. If he had slept with you, you'd be selling me out right and left, wouldn't you?"

"Don't deal in ifs, Mark. I've told you the truth. You're free to hate me, free to throw me aside, but don't preach to me. All right?"

"All right, Elena. Will you go into that bedroom and wait there? I want to talk to Noyes now."

"He's here?"

"They're holding him upstairs. Please stay out of sight while I'm questioning him."

"You will get nothing from him. Nothing!"

"Please," Mark said.

Elena entered the bedroom and closed the door.

Risa's eyes met her father's. Mark looked wearier than ever, but that strange Paul-like effect was even more pronounced. He appeared to be drawing on an inner reservoir of will.

He picked up the phone and asked to have Charles Noyes brought in.

Noyes edged into the room like a beast brought to bay by hounds. The strain was getting fearful. All the way back from Evansville he had pretended to Elena that he was Kravchenko, to keep her from turning on him again. And meanwhile Kravchenko had recovered from his shock and was awake again, fighting more strongly than ever to gain control, now that he had had a night's taste of freedom.

Kravchenko hammered at Noyes' forehead. Noyes' clothing was pasted to his skin by the sweat of fear. His knees were watery. His eyes moved in quick birdlike flickers, nervously, warily. He knew he was caught, knew that all was over. Elena, in her fury with Roditis, was determined to spill everything. And he, unblanked, was caught in the middle, his mind full of unwanted knowledge that was sure to come out.

Guilty of willful discorporation. Sentenced to erasure.

Not so bad, perhaps. Peace at last. No more turns of the wheel of karma. Oblivion, nirvana. At-one-ment.

Mark Kaufmann confronted him. The financier showed evidences of strain. His face was different, Noyes noticed immediately. Well, no doubt mine is, too. We've all been living on this anvil so long, taking blow after blow.

And there on the couch the daughter sat. Risa, the sexy little minx. She also looked different, older, shrewder, more predatory. They'll devour me alive. Elena's told them everything. I've been betrayed by all of them. Why is she doing this? Did Roditis turn her down? Why couldn't he have bedded her? Why would he choose to antagonize her this way? Didn't he see that by scorning her, he was inviting her to tell the story? I should have let him know that it was through Elena that I had gained access to St. John. But he hustled me off to be blanked while Kravchenko was still running me, and obviously Kravchenko didn't tell him. And afterward there was no way I could, because I wasn't supposed to know anything about the discorporation any more.

Kaufmann said, "I believe you've been in this apartment before, Mr. Noyes."

"Well—"

"Recently. Last night, in fact. Isn't that so?"

"Who gave you that idea?" Noyes said with his last shred of bravado.

"You came here late last evening in the company of Miss Elena Volterra," Kaufmann said. "At your insistence she admitted you to the bedroom of Martin St. John. There, alone with him, you introduced a small but lethal quantity of a drug known as cyclophosphamide-8 into his metabolism, causing a speedy but horrible discorpor—"

"*No!*" Noyes screamed. "I didn't do it! It isn't so!"

"We have mindpick evidence against you."

"You don't! You're bluffing!"

Kaufmann said, "We have conclusive mindpick evidence of your guilt, Noyes. Enough to persuade the quaestorate to conduct a mindpick examination of your own memory bank, after which they'll certainly recommend erasure. Of course, if you agree to testify voluntarily, and explain on whose behalf it was that you committed this foul crime, you may receive better treatment from the law."

Noyes shook. Elena had told him everything, then. As he had expected her to do. He was trapped.

—Might as well make a clean breast of it, Kravchenko advised.

"We're prepared to recommend every leniency," said Kaufmann in a soothing voice. "We understand that you were not acting as a free agent when you committed the discorporation of Martin St. John. If you'll aid us in convicting the motivating force behind this crime—"

Of course, thought Noyes. That's what you're after, to nail Roditis! It figures. You don't care about me any more than anyone else does.

He swayed. Waves of disorientation swept his brain. The world was spinning, the center did not hold, everything was shattering. Six Mark Kaufmanns faced him. Six Risas. His eyes would not focus. It seemed to him he heard Kravchenko's vicious laughter, rising in volume, becoming a howl of triumph.

The flask of carniphage in Noyes' breast pocket seemed to blaze against his skin.

Take it, he told himself. You've threatened to do it for so long— just self-dramatization, isn't it? But now, this is the right moment. Pull it out, gulp it down. They've got you anyway. He talks of leniency, but he's lying. You'll be erased after you've been mindpicked. But at least you can save Roditis. There's no solid evidence against him. Roditis is a bastard, but you owe him your loyalty, you always have, and if you drink the carniphage before

Kaufmann gets anything out of you it'll take Roditis off the hook.

—You're a bigger fool than I think you are if you can worry about Roditis at a time like this, Kravchenko burst in.

Once again the persona had tapped his thoughts. The last time that had happened, it had signaled imminent ejection.

—Cook Roditis' goose for him, Kravchenko urged. Tell Kaufmann everything you know. Why not? You don't owe anything to Roditis except credit for wrecking you.

"No," said Noyes. "I won't."

"You won't what?" asked Mark Kaufmann.

"I think he's talking to his persona," Risa said. "Look at his face! He's cracking up!"

Noyes made a heavy gargling sound. It was beginning again: Kravchenko rising from captivity, uncoiling, filling his mind, grasping the levers of control.

"Stop it!" Noyes shrieked. "Let me alone! I won't let you—get out of there—"

He was silent.

Kravchenko said coolly, "If you don't mind, Kaufmann, we'll call this inquisition to a halt right now. I'd like to consult my lawyer. And I'll answer the questions put to me by the quaestors, not by you. Is it understood?'"

"It's a different voice," said Kaufmann. "A different persona. Calmer—the eyes—"

"Will you excuse me, please?" Kravchenko asked. "You've brought me here by abduction, and I intend to make you pay for it, but this kangaroo court is hereby adjourned. Don't try to prevent me from leaving."

He walked gracefully toward the door.

Risa burst from her seat. "*Dybbuk!*" she yelled. "Don't you see, the persona's gone dybbuk right in front of us!"

The bedroom door opened. Elena appeared, pale, extending a quivering hand. She looked altogether confused. "Jim?" she said. "Noyes? Which are you? What's happening?"

"Quiet Elena!" Kravchenko said.

In that moment Charles Noyes launched a desperate and instantly successful counterattack. Erupting from the corner of his own mind in which Kravchenko had penned him, Noyes sped through the neural wreckage within his skull, taking Kravchenko off guard. They grappled. Kravchenko, not as thoroughly in control as he had believed, was thrown from command, hurled down only moments after his brief triumph.

Noyes sagged to the floor and crouched there.

"Listen to me," he said, shaping the words with terrible effort. "This is Noyes again. Noyes. See, the right voice? He didn't quite reach dybbuk. A good try, that's all. Listen. Are you recording this, Kaufmann?"

"Every word."

"Good. I've been an idiot. I've let everyone use me. But no more. My mind's my own. Last night—Roditis sent me here. John Roditis of Roditis Securities. With orders to kill St. John. So that he could reapply for the Paul Kaufmann persona. I gave St. John a drug—cyclo— cyclophosphamide-8. I confess this of my own—free—will."

He could not sustain even the crouching position any longer. Now he lay on his left side, half his body limp.

"I repeat: I killed St. John at Roditis' orders. Mindpick Roditis and you'll see it's so. Two favors, please. Don't let Kravchenko have another carnate trip. You saw—he almost went dybbuk. *Did* go dybbuk, for a minute. And also—for me—no more trips either. Just sleep. I want to get off the wheel."

I ought to utter a mantra now, Noyes thought. Go out with a flourish. *Om mani padme hum.* But why bother?

His hand went into his breast pocket.

He felt Kravchenko fighting him, furiously trying to seize their shared body again. But Noyes held him off. His coordination was almost destroyed, yet he was able to get his hands on the beloved flask of carniphage, fondled so often, so sensually, his constant companion, his dearest friend.

He brought it to his mouth. He bit down.

The flask shattered and its contents spurted down his throat.

Mark Kaufmann stared in shock at the writhing, deliquescing thing on the carpet.

"Carniphage," he said thickly. "Risa—Elena—don't look!"

Elena had fled. But Risa was watching the process of decay with somber fascination. Kaufmann did not try to cover her eyes.

Surely Noyes must be dead. The inward rot was nearing the surface; his body was chaos. Yet still it moved, jerking and twitching as it traveled its one-way road to destruction.

Risa said, "Why did he confess? He was trying to be defiant at first."

"He was showing everyone. Roditis. Kravchenko. Right at the end, he finally found a little strength."

The limbs were flowing into shapelessness. The motions of the body were ceasing.

"Will that confession be any good?" Risa asked.

Mark nodded slowly. "The voiceprints will show that it was really Noyes speaking. The recording will show that he was nearly ejected by a dybbuk, fought back, blurted his story, and killed himself. It'll be good enough to convince the quaestors that Roditis should be mindpicked."

"And then?"

"They'll erase him," Kaufmann said. He felt little triumph, somehow. He took one more look at the ghastliness on the floor, and then went to put in a call to the quaestors.

Chapter 15

It was July now. A season of stifling weather had set in, beyond the capacity of the weather controllers to handle, and many people had fled to cooler climes. Risa remained in New York. The trial of John Roditis had just ended, and now there was a great deal for her to do.

Roditis had been found guilty, of course. Noyes' recorded testimony had induced the quaestorate to seek a mindpick against him, and the motion had been granted. Roditis' lawyers had undertaken a delaying action based on the ancient constitutional principle of freedom from self-incrimination; but the legality of the mindpick was firmly established, and Roditis was put to the test. His complicity in the deliberate discorporation of Martin St. John was undeniable after that.

The defense tactics shifted. Now the lawyers asserted that, while Roditis and Noyes had undoubtedly conspired to destroy the St. John body, there was no injured party, since St. John was not his own body's tenant. The only occupant of the body, the persona of Paul Kaufmann, was legally dead and therefore not capable of suffering discorporation.

It was a fine point, and gave the jurists of the quaestorate considerable exercise. It caused a good deal of embarrassment for Francesco Santoliquido, too, since he was responsible for creating the anomaly of the deliberate dybbuk. In the end, the decision went against Roditis, but the charge was reduced from murder to antisocial actions of the first degree. Which, when Roditis was found guilty, resulted in these sentences:

• Forfeiture of citizenship and Civic privileges.

• Mandatory destruction of any recorded Roditis personae on file with the Scheffing Institute.

• Erasure of all present personae carried by Roditis, and their return to the soul bank for redistribution to others.

• Five years of corrective therapy, including, if needed, a total reorientation of personality to remove aggressive impulses.

"He's finished now," Mark Kaufmann said to his daughter as the verdicts were announced. "He'll come out of the therapy a broken man—polite, amiable, lacking in purpose and direction. A pleasant nobody. A nothing. A shell."

"It seems like such a waste," said Risa. "All that drive—all that energy thrown away—"

"He was too dangerous to remain as he was, Risa. He had a greatness, I'll admit, but his ambitions weren't tempered by the moral sense. He was without a governor."

"And you? And Uncle Paul?"

Kaufmann looked at her sharply. "We have our family traditions. We have our sense of what is honorable. Roditis was a wild beast. Now he'll be tamed. There's no comparison between a Roditis and one of us, Risa. None."

Risa had private reservations about that. She had no wish to anger her father; but it seemed to her that the real difference between the shattered, defeated Roditis and the triumphant Mark Kaufmann was more a matter of luck and diplomacy than of breeding and honor. Roditis had overreached himself, and Mark had destroyed him. But Mark's methods, though they stopped short at murder, had hardly been gentle.

Roditis disappeared behind the fortress walls of Belle Isle Sanatorium for corrective therapy. No one would ever again see the old John Roditis in public, that man seething with vitality and shrewdness. When Roditis emerged, several years hence, he would still be a wealthy man, but he would be an aimless, smiling ruin, cheerfully acquiescing in the decisions of the court-appointed trustees who managed his financial empire.

A great waste of dynamism, Risa decided.

Perhaps, she thought, such a squandering might be in some way avoided.

On the hottest day of that July heat wave, soon after the sentencing of John Roditis, Risa brought her hopter down in the employee lot of the Scheffing Institute building. She parked it deftly and crossed the sweltering strip of ferroconcrete in a hurry. It was three in the afternoon the first shift of technicians was about to leave.

Within the building Risa picked up the first telephone she came to and requested to speak to a certain employee. Moments later, his face appeared on the screen.

He looked baffled.

"Hello, Leonards. Remember me?"

He was young, pale, good-looking, pinch lines forming between his eyebrows. He moistened his lips. "M-Miss Kaufmann?"

"That's right, Leonards. Go to the head of the class."

He forced an uneasy smile. "Is there something wrong? Can I be of service?"

"No, there's nothing wrong, and yes, you can be of service. You're finished working for the day, aren't you?"

"Good. My hopter's parked in Employee Lot D. Meet me there right away and we'll take a little trip."

"But—"

"I'll be waiting, Leonards!"

He did not disappoint her. He did not dare.

Looking mystified, he entered the hopter, taking his seat beside her as she indicated. The little craft lifted and headed north. Risa said, "You did an excellent job with my transplant, Leonards. Tandy and I are very happy together."

"That's good, Miss Kaufmann. Perhaps you could tell me—"

"Where we're heading? Of course. We're going uptown. To my apartment."

He scarcely seemed to believe any of this was happening to him. His posture was rigid; he looked straight ahead, never venturing a glance in her direction. He was terrified of her.

She brought the hopter in for a smooth landing at her home

lot. Minutes later, they entered her apartment.

"Take a good look around," she told him. "It's nice, isn't it? Ever been in a place like this before?"

"N-no, Miss Kaufmann."

"Call me Risa. Why are you so frightened, Leonards? You're a big, handsome young fellow, aren't you? A skilled technician, a man with a bright future? Are you married?"

"Yes, Miss Kaufmann."

"Children?"

"One child. We're going to have another after my next increment comes through."

"Fine, Leonards. I'm sure you're a wonderful family man. And I'm glad to know you're so virile." She put her hand to her shoulder, touched a stud. Her light summer clothing fell away in a rustling swirl. She stood before him incandescently nude, and, he gaped at the sudden sight.

He backed away from her, shielding his eyes.

"Come here, Leonards," she said in a husky voice Tandy Cashing had taught her how to use. "You're not really afraid. You want me, don't you? Admit it. I'm yours for the taking. The experience of a lifetime. A Kaufmann in your arms. Why run away?"

"Please—I don't understand—"

She swept up against him. She took his hand and put it to her small breasts. Her own hand traveled expertly over his body. Leonards gasped. Leonards moaned. Leonards shook his head and tried to push her away, but the attempt was not a success.

"I want you, Leonards! What's your first name?"

"Harry."

"Harry! Harry! Harry! Love me, Harry!"

She tugged at him and they toppled to the floor. Her lithe body entwined itself with his. Urgently she awakened his desires and banished his timidity.

"Harry," she whispered. "*Harry!*"

He made a sound that was half a protest, half an acceptance.

And then, with sudden desperate willingness, he pulled her against him.

He was not very good, Risa concluded. But he was appealingly earnest.

When it was over, she slipped away from him and got nimbly to her feet. He lay still, rumpled and glassy-eyed.

"You've just committed an act of rape," Risa told him. "Your helpless victim was a girl of the highest social position, less than seventeen years old. You'll get your mind blotted out for a crime like that."

Leonards came to a sitting position, and the color drained from his face a moment, then returned in a crimson rush. "What are you saying?"

"I'm explaining to you the nature of the trouble you're in. Forcibly entering my hopter while I was visiting the Scheffing Institute, compelling me to bring you here, disrobing me, inducing me through superior strength to submit to sexual violation—oh, it's bad, Leonards, it's very bad!"

"I feel like I'm in a dream," he whispered.

"It's real enough. I'll have the quaestors here any minute."

"Why are you doing this?"

She crouched before him, her face close to his. "Would you like to avoid going to trial? Would you like me to forgive you for your audacity in perpetrating this hideous rape?"

"What do you want from me?"

"A favor," she said harshly. "A small favor, and I'll forget all about what happened here today, and leave you with your memories of pleasure."

"What kind of favor?"

"You'll have to break the rules of the Scheffing Institute," she said. "But that's a much smaller crime than raping a girl my age, and if you're smart and lucky you'll get away with it. There's a certain persona I want, Leonards. Get it for me from the files, just borrow it for a little while tomorrow. And transplant it to me. That's all I ask. I'll come to the tower, and you'll handle the transplant, and we'll call it quits. But we'll have to move swiftly, because this particular persona recording is due to be destroyed very soon. All right, Leonards? Do we have a deal?"

"Everything's settled, then," Mark Kaufmann said. "My uncle's persona remains in storage indefinitely."

"Yes," said Santoliquido. "Which is to say, at least another year or two."

"Long enough for some of the voltage to bleed out of the dynamo, at any rate. He'll be less formidable coming back then. If he comes back at all."

Santoliquido shrugged. "I'll hold him in storage until a qualified recipient appears, Mark. And with Roditis permanently disqualified, it might be a long, long time. You don't need to worry about that."

"Fine. See you at my party on Saturday?"

"Of course," said Santoliquido. "I'll reach Dominica about noon, I suppose. It'll be a novelty, going south to the tropics to find cooler weather. My best to Elena, yes?"

"Of course."

Kaufmann broke the contact. He smiled, leaned back, touched the tips of his fingers together. All was well at last. Roditis was neutralized, entirely out of the scene. Santoliquido, who had come out of this affair very poorly indeed, was helpless before his wishes. There would be no extra Uncle Paul at liberty to interfere now. Elena, a chastened woman, had settled into something very much like fidelity. Risa, taking on new depth and maturity day by day, had ripened into a fitting Kaufmann heiress, ready to assume new responsibilities in the family empire. And he himself was home free with his uncle's potent persona well integrated into his awareness, unknown to the rest of the world.

"How do you like that, you old fox? I've handled things pretty well, haven't I, eh?"

—You've done well for yourself, Paul replied. But don't get over-confident. Smugness was Roditis' undoing.

"Don't worry about me," Mark replied. "I try to calculate all the angles. And with you in there helping me, we shouldn't miss very many of them."

—There's always the unpredictable. Be on guard for it.

"Mark?" It was Risa's voice, outside. "I'm here, Mark."

"Come in," he said.

She entered his office. In her sketchy summer wrap she looked crisp and cool, and she carried herself with a no-nonsense self-possession that he admired greatly. Here was the one person in the world who mattered most to him; and also the one person to whom he might be vulnerable. He had an idea that Risa suspected what he had done with Paul's persona. She knew Paul's mannerisms, and of course she knew his own, and she seemed conscious that a fusion had taken place. But after the first day she had ceased to betray any suspicions. Mark had no way of telling what was going on behind the smooth mask of his daughter's face. Somehow, though, he felt certain that she knew the truth.

"I'm here for a business discussion," Risa announced.

"What kind of business?"

"Preliminary business, really. I'd like to get some idea of the family assets. What we have where, in whose name, what slice of equity in each."

Kaufmann nodded. "It's time we went over all that anyway, I suppose. I mean to bring you much more closely into our activities. To groom you for the time when you're running the show. The world of business genuinely interests you, eh, Risa?"

"You know it does. And now that Roditis is through, we can begin to make a new move, Mark. I'd like to close in on that Latin American electrical empire of his. I've been thinking, we could undercut the Roditis trustees by a takeover of the company that makes the transmission pylons, and then—"

"Do you have a cold, Risa?"

"Why?"

"Your voice sounds odd. Deeper. Hoarser."

She shook her head. "That's just Tandy's influence, I guess. She must have had a very lush contralto, and she's trying to pitch my voice down there too. You know how it is, the way a persona influences the host in little ways, certain mannerisms—"

"Yes," Kaufmann said. "I know."

"Very well, then. If we can get a grasp on the pylon company, we'll have Roditis Securities caught between Scylla and Charybdis, and—"

"Between who and whom?"

"Scylla and Charybdis," she repeated impatiently. "The monster and the whirlpool. Book Twelve of *The Odyssey*. By Homer."

"Yes. I know. I didn't realize you were a student of Homer, Risa."

"Every civilized person should have a deep knowledge of Homer," she said. "Has there ever been a greater poet? A man with a more vivid imagination? There are lessons we can learn from him even today." Risa laughed self-consciously. "Back to the transmission pylons, though. Here's what I have in mind—"

Mark Kaufmann watched his daughter construct an elaborate holding-company scheme with quick scrawled stokes of stylus against pad. But he paid little attention to her financial theories just now. A sudden implausible notion sent a chill of disbelief through him.

Homer? Holding companies? Transmission pylons?

A deeper voice?

No, he thought. No, it isn't possible. She wouldn't—she couldn't—

From somewhere far away, Paul Kaufmann's persona delivered a silent booming laugh.

—There's always the unpredictable, Mark,

Quietly Mark agreed. He peered closely at Risa, seeking for

signs, for proof, for confirmation of this strange and frightening fantasy of his. If it were true, a new, invincible force had entered their family, and all plans must be reconsidered. But it *could not* be true. It could not be true. It could not be true.

"There we are," Risa finished. She shoved the pad toward her father. "What do you say, Mark? How does the plan look to you?"

"I'll have to think about it," he said warily. "But it's worth considering. If we can use Roditis' own way of thinking to cut chunks out of his holdings, why not?"

Risa grinned. She pointed to the somber, brooding portrait of Uncle Paul hanging behind her father's desk. "I think *he'd* go for the idea. I think the old buccaneer would be very amused by it. Perhaps a little proud of me. Perhaps even a little jealous."

"He is," Mark Kaufmann said, and looked beyond his window to see the sky suddenly grow dark with the fury of a summer storm.